THE
EX
I BURIED

BOOKS BY NATALI SIMMONDS

While My Baby Sleeps
My Daughter's Revenge

THE EX I BURIED

NATALI SIMMONDS

bookouture

Published by Bookouture in 2025

An imprint of Storyfire Ltd.
Carmelite House
50 Victoria Embankment
London EC4Y 0DZ

www.bookouture.com

The authorised representative in the EEA is Hachette Ireland
8 Castlecourt Centre
Dublin 15 D15 XTP3
Ireland
(email: info@hbgi.ie)

Copyright © Natali Simmonds, 2025

Natali Simmonds has asserted her right to be identified as the author of this work.

All rights reserved. No part of this publication may be reproduced, stored in any retrieval system, or transmitted, in any form or by any means, electronic, mechanical, photocopying, recording or otherwise, without the prior written permission of the publishers.

ISBN: 978-1-80550-271-5
eBook ISBN: 978-1-80550-270-8

This book is a work of fiction. Names, characters, businesses, organizations, places and events other than those clearly in the public domain, are either the product of the author's imagination or are used fictitiously. Any resemblance to actual persons, living or dead, events or locales is entirely coincidental.

To Linda

ONE
21 DECEMBER

I left Cragstone ten years ago and vowed never to return. Yet here I am again, back in my hometown, attending my ex-boyfriend's funeral.

I'm glad it's raining. Good weather shouldn't be wasted on the dead. It's only a light drizzle yet I keep my large umbrella open, thankful to have something to hide behind. I tilt it so it shields my face as I head up the high street towards St Anne's church, its black spire cutting through the misty air like a dagger. I don't want to see anyone I used to know back then. I don't want to answer their questions or witness that look they'll give me that's not quite pity and not quite scorn. I shiver, pulling my coat tighter around my throat. It's always colder here than in London, with a sea wind that worms its way beneath your collar and bites at your fingertips. I should have worn comfortable shoes, but instead I chose appearance over practicality, needing anyone who sees me to recognise I'm not the eighteen-year-old Eva Walsh they used to know. I'm an adult now. I've made it. I got out and I'm not staying here for long.

The pavement is slippery with ice, forcing me to slow down and walk with precision. A white Christmas has been forecast for four days' time. I've never been to a funeral this close to Christmas Day. What a selfish time to die.

A sob escapes my throat and I clamp a gloved hand over my mouth, leaning against the wall of the church until the stone's cold seeps through my smart woollen coat and my breaths become smoother, less ragged, not as painful. I loved Jacob so much. Coming back to Cragstone was a mistake. I never stopped thinking about him but being away from here made it so much easier to turn memories opaque. He's gone for good now and I already miss him like we never spent a day apart.

Jacob was a year older than me. He turned thirty a few months back, his accident happened three weeks ago, I found out by text yesterday and the funeral starts in five minutes. I take a deep breath and tell myself I only have to stay for the service, then I can go back to my hotel room, rest and catch the train back to London tomorrow afternoon. Nothing good ever comes from revisiting your past.

I tilt my umbrella up and squint through the misty rain at everyone in black congregating outside the church. There are lots of people my age, a few I recognise from school, and some older people, friends of the family I presume. A woman with straight hair dyed black is having a cigarette and talking to a man. I know them both – Bianca Clarke and Harry Hilborn. Bianca used to be a peroxide blonde with lips outlined in dark pencil. The class bully. Harry, meanwhile, with his freckly skin and whiny voice, spent all of his time in the library staring at me through the window. Neither of them was close to Jacob growing up, and they certainly weren't chummy with one another. I guess in a town this small everyone ends up being friends eventually.

I scan the rest of the drawn, wintry faces as one by one they enter the church. I can't see Jacob's sister, Charlie, or his mother. They're the ones who I should be paying my respects to today, yet they're the ones I'm trying to avoid.

I wait until the last person has gone inside before I fold up my umbrella, leave it by the door and slip inside the church, where I choose one of the back pews. I know St Anne's well. This is the same seat my mother and I took every Sunday when I was a child. We weren't a religious family, but she said she liked the quiet.

'Listen to what the priest has to say about being the kind of girl people will like,' she'd whisper while sucking on Polo mints. They did nothing to hide the smell of gin on her breath. 'It's too late for me, but you might turn out OK.'

She'd always be asleep by the second hymn, and I'd keep my eyes down as if in prayer, not because I was talking to God but because I didn't want to see who was looking at us. Not that it made a difference – I could still feel the heat from everyone's judgement like a brand on my skin. Even now I keep my gaze trained straight ahead, fixed on the giant gilded cross hanging precariously over the nativity scene, a reminder of what is to come for the baby in the manger. Beside it is a glossy mahogany coffin with a giant photo of Jacob on top. The coffin is covered in wreaths, festive Christmas firs and white roses. I bite down on my bottom lip to stop another sob from escaping. Who chose those flowers? Jacob hated cut flowers.

'I don't get why people destroy something beautiful then put it in a vase for a week to watch it slowly die,' he'd say. Instead of picking me flowers, he'd find me interesting pebbles on the beach. Sometimes he'd draw pictures on them or write love notes on the larger ones with permanent marker then tell me, 'Stones last longer than flowers, Eva.'

And he was right. I still have Jacob's pebbles. He would have hated lying in a box covered in pretty dying things.

The swell of the organ has the congregation standing and I get to my feet, smoothing down my fitted shift dress and clearing my throat even though I have no intention of singing. I should have worn something less flashy. Everyone else has chosen appropriate outfits for this bleak weather – trousers and anoraks – not a Ralph Lauren dress and heels. I should have known better than to draw attention to myself. The hymn is 'All Things Bright and Beautiful'. Jacob didn't like that song either.

'I prefer an open casket, myself,' the old lady beside me says. 'Nice to see the face.'

I turn to my right. It's Mrs Allen, the school librarian. She still looks the same as she did when we were kids. Even the glasses haven't changed. Some people are old forever.

'But, of course, the way poor Jacob died they can't have an open casket,' she adds. 'I can't imagine there's much of him in that coffin.'

I swallow down the pain in my throat and nod along to her words, doing my best not to imagine what the police found at the bottom of the cliff. I wonder how much of my ex-boyfriend remained in the twisted metal of the car's carcass, what they found on the jagged rocks, all those pretty pebbles like the ones he used to give me coated in his blood then instantly washed clean by the raging waves.

'Oh. Is that you, Eva Walsh?' Mrs Allen says, tugging on my damp coat sleeve. 'It is! You're Vanessa's girl. Oh my Lord, I didn't expect to see you here. Not after...'

She lets go of my coat and falls silent as the song finishes and the priest talks about Jacob and his family and the struggles of loss.

'The Lord keeps the best for Himself.'

'He will be forever in our hearts.'

'Taken too soon and now watching over us.'

Empty words. Tired, Hallmark card phrases that do nothing to fill the yawning chasm making my stomach ache. I keep my eyes closed like I used to as a child in church, blinking back tears, counting the minutes until they take Jacob away forever and I can leave Cragstone for the final time.

I was a few months from turning nineteen when I first left

this place. I felt so grown up back then, so sure I was doing the right thing, but I was still a child. A scared, lost child with no father, a dead mother and a loving boyfriend who would eventually leave her. Now he's gone forever too. The final thread tying me to this place has finally snapped.

The priest has stopped talking and people are standing again. Everyone turns towards the door, each sniff and mumble amplified in the cold echo of the church. The service is over. Mrs Allen leaves the pew from the other direction without so much as a goodbye. I keep my head down as the mourners shuffle past, the back pews first, then the middle, then the front like on an aeroplane.

I did it. I got away with it. I managed to return to Cragstone and say goodbye to the last vestiges of my past without any drama.

'*You?!*' someone shouts.

I snap my head up. A woman is stumbling up the aisle, her tear-stained face red and twisted with hate. She's pointing at me, her black hat tilting to one side as she runs in my direction. I scramble to leave the pew but I'm too late, she's blocking my exit.

'How dare you show your face around here, Eva Walsh?' she screams. Her hands reach out for me, fingers like talons grasping at my face and pulling at my hair. 'You killed my son!'

TWO

My head is pushed down as I fight off the woman's clawed hands, sharp fingers twisting in my hair, tugging harder the more people try to pull her off me. All I can see are shoes. My attacker's are black court shoes, with flesh-coloured tights baggy and sagging at her thin ankles, and beside hers there are high-heeled leather boots under flared trousers, and now there's a pair of men's Oxfords followed by the smell of cedarwood and black pepper. I know that scent.

'Iris!' the man is shouting. 'That's enough!'

'Mum! Please,' a woman cries. 'You're hurting her!'

Fingers are untwined from my hair as someone adjusts my coat and I right myself, my head held as high as I dare.

I can't see at first, my eyes cloudy, stinging from the mascara running down my face. I push back my hair and blink three times and there's Jacob's sister, Charlie, looking at me like *I'm* the monster, curiosity and fear weaving like shadows over her pale face. A heavy hand lands on my shoulder. It belongs to Michael, Jacob's father. It was his aftershave I recognised. Anyone watching would interpret his gesture as a sign of comfort, but I know he's pinning me down, stopping me from running away again, forcing me to face this moment.

'Are you OK?' he asks.

I sniff and nod and smooth down my dress. Michael's hand remains on my shoulder, heavy and firm. *You're not going anywhere*, his hold on me says.

Charlie is talking in hushed tones to the woman who attacked me, the priest hovering by the altar. I imagine he sees grief play out in myriad ways in his church, beneath the vaulted roof adorned with scenes of suffering and forgiveness. It takes me a moment to realise that Charlie is talking to her mother. The woman who just accused me of killing her son. But this woman looks nothing like the Iris Donnelly I used to know.

Iris owned Cragstone's premier estate agents. She sold the historical country manors dotted around the surrounding fields, and the large mansions perched on the clifftops, and the cottages with beach views, oversold to rich Londoners so they'd have somewhere pretty to stay during the three sunny weeks of the year. Back then Iris appeared in the local paper all the time, at award shows and gala dinners and charity events. She was bubbly, blonde and brilliant – big hair, big boobs, big smile. She was the epitome of old-school glamour and every woman in town envied her wardrobe and confidence. That was the Iris I knew. This haggard woman before me with short grey hair and puckered lips is not the same Iris.

'I'm sorry for your loss,' I mutter to no one in particular, shrugging Michael's hand off my shoulder and turning towards the door.

'Wait!'

Charlie is running up the aisle behind me, her heels ringing out against the flagstones like gunshots. She looks different too. Her long hair, once so golden it used to look like the sun was always setting behind her, has been cut into a neat bob. No dangly earrings or plum-coloured lipstick for her anymore. My former best friend is just another grown-up in a dark suit looking tired and full of sorrow. Of course she does. She just lost her only sibling.

'Are you hurt?' she asks, scanning my face for any damage. 'I'm so sorry she did that to you.'

'Charlie,' I say with a sigh, attempting to inject so many feelings into one word. *I'm sorry your brother is dead. I'm sorry your mother is suffering. I'm sorry I never spoke to you again after I left this horrid little town.*

'Thank you for coming. I was hoping you'd be here,' she says in a quieter voice.

I'm surprised she's surprised to see me. She was the one who texted me about her brother's death and I confirmed I'd be at the funeral. Did she think I'd let her down? Am I still a liar to her like I am to everyone else in this town?

'Why did your mum say that?' I ask. 'Why would she think I had anything to do with Jacob's accident?'

I glance over Charlie's shoulder. Iris has gone but Charlie's father, Michael, is still there with an elegant woman to his right and two boys standing in front of him. They look around seven and nine years old. That must be his shiny new family and the reason why his first family crumbled to ash.

I don't realise I'm shaking until Charlie places her hand in mine. I want to pull away but instead I leave it there, cold and limp.

'Why did your mum attack me?' I ask again.

Charlie looks down and shakes her head slowly. 'I'm so sorry. It's the grief. She's not been herself lately. Dad left and then you left and then Jacob...'

Now *Charlie* is blaming me? I left Cragstone ten years ago. How long does it take for a family to fall apart? My hand is still in hers, but I can't bring myself to squeeze it back. I had no choice about leaving Cragstone and Charlie never stopped me.

Her father is still behind her, looking over at us, his arms around both boys as if keeping them away from his former fractured family. Protecting them from cutting themselves on the broken pieces of his mistakes. Did the boys know their older brother? Jacob wasn't speaking to his father by the time I left, but Michael is here, mourning his son. Ten years is a long time. Surely amends were made.

Handsome Michael hasn't changed a bit. He was the only man in this town who could match Iris with looks, charm and income. While Iris attended galas, Michael ran marathons, both of them young, vivacious parents with successful businesses, making life look easy. Perhaps life got *too* easy for him and that's why he left his two children and perfect wife to start again. Men like Jacob's father always win, coming away from the wreckage of their old lives not only unscathed but victorious. I wish the same could be said for me.

Michael is still looking in my direction, but I won't meet his eye.

'I have to go,' I say, giving Charlie a fleeting hug before marching quickly out of the church. If these shoes would allow it, I'd be running. It's still drizzling outside but I don't stop to collect my umbrella. I walk as fast as I can without twisting my ankle, past people milling around the entrance to the church, talking quietly, their murmurs accompanied by furtive glances. As I hurry past, I pick up remnants of conversations that I'm certain are about me.

'I can't believe she had the cheek to show her face again.'

'Did you hear what Iris said? I don't blame her.'

'Poor Jacob. It was never going to end well.'

I keep walking, the rain running into my eyes and mud splashing up my tights. I don't want to slow down to put on my gloves and I can't walk as fast with my hands in my coat pockets, so I keep my fists clenched by my side, the biting wind slowly turning them into balls of ice.

Cragstone has one main road full of the usual high street

chain stores interspersed with bougie artisanal bakers, florists and craft shops so the out-of-towners can justify the extortionate prices of their summer residences. Every building is old and made of sandstone, so in the daylight the high street looks like a row of sandcastles and at night the shops and houses glow. Tonight, the street twinkles invitingly, enticing the last of the Christmas shoppers with sash windows sprayed with fake snow and sparkly displays of nutcracker men and gingerbread houses.

Even though the town fills up at Christmas and in the summer months, Cragstone only has one hotel. The Black Lion is a converted seventeenth-century pub with five bedrooms upstairs and a dozen pretty little cabins in its garden, set back off the main road with woodland views and the sea in the distance. I didn't want to stay the night in a cabin, a glorified shed set apart from the main building with nothing but cold wind and fields surrounding me, but the receptionist said that at this time of year there's little choice. At least it has hot water and WiFi. All I want right now is a shower and an early night before catching the train out of here tomorrow and getting back to my real life. Or what's left of it.

I keep my head down as I stomp up the main street, hair whipping around my face and sticking to my glossy lipstick. I thought I had it all until a month ago, but just like every one of my lives, that one collapsed too. Now my life is frozen in no man's land: behind me a past I don't want to revisit and before me an empty space where a future used to be. No matter how hard I try I can't make anything stick.

A collection of snapshots flickers through my mind. The first day I met Mario in my office, unaware of who he was. Mario Florentino, eldest son of my boss, Bruno Florentino, famous for his garish furniture stores full of overpriced candles and vases. I'd not been working there long; I was so proud of my new job as an interiors buyer for such a famous, opulent brand. I wasn't paid much but I was told I had a lot of potential. The moment I saw Mario I was imagining how his thick, wavy hair would feel between my fingers, marvelling at the cut of his suit and how perfectly his belt matched his shiny leather shoes. I still blush at the memory of my thinking he was there for a job interview. He thought it was funny and took me for a drink that night, much to the chagrin of every woman in the office who, unbeknownst to me, had had their eyes on him for years. The first time he kissed me I kept it to myself; the second time we kissed the whole office saw, and I felt the envious stares of all my colleagues like a million darts aimed at my back. It wasn't long before I became Mario's girlfriend, then I was living with him, then we were engaged all in the space of under a year.

The quickest way to alienate yourself from work colleagues is to get engaged to the boss's son. Everyone treated me differently after that; all they ever said to me was how lucky I was to be marrying into the prestigious Italian Florentino family and how I'd never have to work again. They pressed their dreams into my hands without once asking me what my own were. My dream hasn't changed since I was a kid... money and prestige don't matter to me, all I've ever wanted is a family where I belong. But that's all gone now. Mario gave me a taste of how beautiful my future could have been, then snatched it away again with his betrayal. I should have known better than to think I would ever be a true Florentino. No matter how kind and hospitable a man's family may be, they are connected to one another by blood and you're not. You can't infiltrate that. I already learned that lesson with Jacob. When he left me, I lost them all.

I shake my head and blink away the tears gathering on my lower lashes. How many exes can I mourn in one day?

I turn right off the high street and down a winding lane, my legs aching and hair matted from the wind. It's not even four o'clock but at this time of year afternoon quickly turns to night. The mist has started to grow thicker and heavier too, like a blanket smothering every sight and sound. I know The Black Lion is at the end of this narrow road somewhere, but all I can see before me is a foggy tunnel with no end.

Out of the gloom I spot the hotel's Christmas lights twinkling up ahead like a rainbow beacon. I speed up but I can hear something; someone else is lost in the mist. I stop and listen, trying to work out which direction the footsteps are coming from. Someone is behind me. I speed up and so do they. A quick glance over my shoulder only shows me a shadow, a dark shape against the white fog. Whoever it is they're bigger than me... and they're running.

'Wait!' they call out.

A hand reaches out and grasps my coat, pulling me backwards and making me stumble on my high heels. I rub my eyes, pushing my wet hair away from my face and squinting into the darkness until I finally recognise the person looming over me.

'What the hell do *you* want?' I hiss.

THREE

Michael steps backwards.

'Sorry. I didn't mean to startle you,' he says, holding his hands up in surrender. He's out of breath, his skin glistening in the moonlight from either sweat or the light rain. 'I just wanted to check you were OK.'

'Oh, so *now* you're worried about me?' I shout. 'Ten years after ruining my life you're finally checking I'm OK?'

He rubs his face, and my stomach lurches at how familiar his features are, how strange it feels to be an adult standing before him and not a teenage girl in need of his help. He looks younger than his fifty-five years, but perhaps he didn't come away as unscathed as I first thought. Even in this faint light I can see every ounce of pain etched on his skin, the loss of his son hanging heavy behind his dark eyes now fixed on mine, pleading to be heard.

'Jacob's dead,' he says, his voice cracking. 'My boy is dead.'

I step forward and he falls against me, leaning into my embrace, heaving heavy sobs on to my shoulder. It used to be me crying into the crook of his neck, my tears soaking his shirt collar after work.

I used to envy Charlie for having a father. On the days my mother would pass out on the sofa, leaving me to heat up frozen fish fingers in the microwave and help her up the stairs to bed, on those days I'd fantasise about a man appearing on my doorstep claiming to be my dad. In my mind this man would be strong like Michael, and smell clean and expensive, and he'd fix my mother and take me away from Cragstone. It never happened. It was Charlie and Jacob's family who saved me. But Michael is no longer that formidable hero; now he's the one crying on my shoulder.

'Sorry,' he says, straightening up and taking a deep breath. 'That was selfish of me. I've been trying to hold it in for weeks. You know, stay strong for the family, but seeing you after all this time... God, Jacob loved you so much.'

I look away, anywhere but at this broken man's face. In the photo on his coffin Jacob had his father's sharp jaw and kind eyes, and his mother's hesitant smile and thick hair. He had been cute at nineteen, but I had no idea he'd gone on to be so ridiculously handsome. I wish I'd got to know the adult version of him. I know he loved me once, but did that love last? Maybe he continued to love me in the same way I continued to love him. Secretly, silently, a warm pebble left out in the sun then tucked away inside my pocket. I flinch at the stabbing pain in my chest. I can't think about that anymore. It's all too late.

'I only found out he died yesterday,' I say.

Michael takes another shuddering breath, his nose and eyes red. 'Oh, you poor child. You must still be in shock. I'm surprised you came back.'

'Charlie invited me.'

His brow creases in confusion but he doesn't ask me any questions. 'The wake is at The Swan. Join us.'

I shake my head even though it's one of the nicer pubs in town.

'Please,' he continues. 'Charlie would like to talk to you, and we could all do with a stiff drink.'

'What about Iris?' I ask. I can't face Jacob's mother right now.

'She's gone home.'

'Why did she say those awful things to me?'

'I don't know. I haven't seen her in a long time. She's been... She's not well, Eva. Don't pay her any attention. Come on, the pub is just around the corner.'

'I know where it is,' I say sullenly. 'But I'm not walking in with you. You know how people talk.'

He gives a light laugh and, although none of this is funny, I smile back at him. Michael has been a lot of things to me over the years – a father figure, a hero, a disappointment – but now he's just a grieving man who's lost his son. What he did ten years ago ruined my life and forced me to leave Cragstone, but perhaps today will seal shut the pain I've been carrying all this time.

The Swan is a small pub, and everyone in it is here for the wake. The landlord has made a half-hearted attempt at Christmas decorations with tinsel framing the mirror behind the bar and some baubles in a vase. The air is thick with the scent of yeast and impending snow, the huddles of warm bodies making the windows steam up. I stand at the threshold of the pub, looking at all the faces that once meant something to me.

'Are you in or are you out, love?' an elderly man says to me. 'You're letting in the cold air.'

I shut the door, even though Michael is a few steps behind me, and shuffle my way through the crowd. I'm instantly sweating beneath my woollen coat but it's too busy in here to easily take it off. Someone calls out my name before I reach the bar. There's a table full of people in the corner and they're waving over at me. I suppress a groan. They already look tipsy. I spot Charlie with them and push my way through the throng until I'm standing before the table of five people my own age. I recognise most of them, even though I've not seen any of them since we were teenagers.

'Eva!' a man shouts out. 'It's so good to see you. Come. Take a seat,' he says, patting the space on the bench beside him.

I look at Charlie first, needing her permission. She gives me a small smile, so I join them at the crowded table already covered in empty glasses, plates of cold sausage rolls and curling egg sandwiches. There's a pile of winter coats forming a mountain against one of the benches. I take mine off, add it to the others and sit down.

The man beside me is Harry, the old classmate I'd seen outside the church earlier. The other three are introduced and, although we all went to school together, I instantly forget their names. One is a woman I vaguely remember from the year below and the other two are brothers, I think. It doesn't matter. I'll never see any of them again.

'My, my, Eva Walsh,' Harry says, shaking his head from side to side. He still has the same nasally voice and plummy accent that's not from around here. 'What a blast from the past. If only Jacob was here to see you looking so lovely.'

A silence falls across the table as Harry realises his faux pas, then everyone bursts into nervous laughter. Everyone but me and Charlie.

'Sorry, sorry,' he says, waving his hands in the air and downing the dregs of his Guinness. 'Funerals make me... I wasn't thinking. Sorry, goodness. It's all so awful,' he says, reaching across the table and patting Charlie's hand.

She looks at me, and although it's been seventeen years since we first met on our first day of secondary school, and we haven't been friends since we were eighteen years old, I know exactly what she's thinking, and it makes both of our lips twitch in unison. We thought Harry was a tedious swot when we were teenagers, an insufferable try-hard who never knew when to shut up, and clearly nothing has changed.

'So, tell us all about the Big Smoke!' he says, turning to me, his face beaming with fake jollity.

Oh God. I should have got a drink first. As if by magic a vodka and Coke appears before me. I look up. It's Michael. He hands his daughter a drink too and kisses her cheek before walking back to his family at the bar. The table falls silent, and everyone looks down at their empty glasses. Why did he have to come over?

'London is great,' I say to Harry, injecting as much enthusiasm into my voice as I can.

'I like your handbag,' the woman whose name I can't remember says, pointing at my bag. She has a sharp fringe cut too short, which coupled with her round cheeks and dyed orange hair makes her look like a surprised pumpkin.

'My fiancé bought it for me,' I reply, without thinking.

The table falls silent again and I realise that was possibly the worst thing I could have said. I know what they're all thinking: *Look at that Eva Walsh, coming back here in her designer dress fresh from the big city, bragging about her fiancé weeks after her ex-boyfriend tragically died.*

But wasn't that what I wanted? For them to know that I'm no longer the girl I used to be? I can't tell them the truth, that Mario and I are no longer together – that would be embarrassing. I can't tell them how I moved in with him and we set a date for the wedding, but he chose to sleep with my assistant the day we were meant to be visiting wedding venues. How a month ago I walked away from my man, my home and a great job, and I'm staying in my friend Amanda's spare room, wondering whether my savings will run out before I get an interview for any of the jobs I've applied for. I can't tell them any of that. Instead, I let them think that the sad girl from school with the alcoholic mother has her life together because she was the only one brave enough to leave this god-awful town. I'd prefer them to hate me for that than for what they believe happened all those years ago.

'Did I just see Eva fucking Walsh walk into the pub with Jacob's *dad*?'

I dig my nails into the palm of my hand. The dark-haired woman I saw Harry talking to outside the church is standing behind Charlie, putting her packet of Marlboro Gold back in her handbag. Charlie swings around and glares at her.

'Shit, sorry, Charlie. Didn't see you there.' She looks up and meets my eye. 'Holy shitballs, so I wasn't imagining things. I pop out for a quick ciggie, and I miss all the drama. Hello, Eva.'

Bianca Clarke was the meanest girl in school and judging by her opening line she hasn't changed. Harry is laughing nervously beside me while the others talk amongst themselves. I take a long swig of my drink, but it does nothing to quell the bubbling anger rising in my chest. We're at Jacob's wake, following Jacob's funeral, following Jacob's death, yet the only person to mention Jacob is Harry with his tasteless joke. Why is no one talking about my ex-boyfriend? Why doesn't anyone except his sister look upset that he's dead? Do they all think I had something to do with his death too...?

Bianca squeezes in beside Charlie so she's sitting directly in front of me. She picks up my drink and takes a sniff.

'Is there vodka in there?' she asks, raising an eyebrow. 'Wow, top shelf already. Like mother, like daughter.'

I snatch my glass back and don't answer, using every last drop of willpower not to throw the remnants of my drink in her face. But Bianca never was one for letting sleeping dogs lie. She places her elbows on the sticky table and rests her chin in her hands.

'So, tell me everything, city girl. How's the capital treating you?'

How pathetic that everyone in Cragstone thinks London is so exotic.

'Great,' I answer.

'Why are you here, then?'

'Because my ex-boyfriend died,' I say, deadpan, looking her right in the eye. These idiots may have all stayed the same since we were children, but I haven't. She no longer scares me.

Bianca pulls a fake sad face and searches the table for a glass that still has something in it, knocking back what's left of somebody else's white wine.

'Leave it, Bianca. Today has been hard enough,' Charlie says quietly, but Bianca isn't listening. She's pointing her finger at me. I notice all her nails are acrylic, decorated in festive reds and greens.

'You've got some nerve coming back, that's all I'm saying.'

I take another gulp of my drink. I came here to say my final goodbyes to a boy I've loved since I was a child. That's all. My plan was to slip in quietly, pay my respects, then leave the next morning. My plan wasn't to find myself at a crowded table in a damp pub being shouted at by drunk classmates who hate me. I want to get up, but I'm wedged in – Harry to my right and the woman with the orange hair now pushed up to my left. When did she move seats?

'What was I meant to do?' I hiss at Bianca. 'Ignore the fact Jacob is dead?'

'How did you even find out?' she shoots back, like she's won a point at a game I don't want to play.

'Charlie texted me yesterday and asked me to come.'

'No, I didn't,' Charlie says, her voice more confused than angry.

Bianca guffaws.

Why is Charlie saying that? She *did* text me. I can't believe she'd gang up on me too.

'See?' Bianca says, folding her arms and looking around the

table triumphantly. 'Once a liar, always a liar. What's the matter, Eva, not enough excitement for you in London so you had to come back here and stir things up again? Why don't you leave the Donnellys alone? Didn't you cause enough drama last time?'

I jump up so fast I knock the table with my knee, sending glasses crashing to the floor so loudly the pub falls silent. Charlie looks away, tears rolling down her cheeks. Bianca has the audacity to laugh.

'Oh no! Eva is going to run away again.'

Out of the corner of my eye I see Michael whisper something to his wife and march over, unaware that he's about to make everything worse. He ignores the warning look I give him and silently ushers me and a crying Charlie away to the corner of the pub, but not before I hear Bianca shout out, 'There's no smoke without fire, Eva. We all know what I saw all those years ago, and we all know it's your fault Jacob is dead!'

FOUR

'We're OK, Dad. Just go. I'm fine,' Charlie says, pushing her father away. He looks at me and I nod. His wife and children have their coats on already, standing by the pub door. I don't blame them for wanting to get out of this place. Michael gives me a sorry smile. Somehow, I know this is his final goodbye and that I'll never see him again. It hurts more than I thought it would.

Charlie has found us a little nook in the corner, away from the noise and the people, hidden behind a pile of empty drinks crates.

'When are they ever going to stop with all their bloody gossiping?' she says with a sigh, glancing over at our old school friends, who are laughing at the table as if nothing happened. 'I thought everything would be different after all these years. I should have known people around here never change.'

'Aren't they your friends?' I ask, wishing I'd brought my drink with me. Bianca has probably finished it already.

Charlie shakes her head. 'I haven't seen any of them since I left for university. I don't come back often.'

Doesn't come back often? But she was so close to her family

– it makes no sense. I let her words sink in, imagining Jacob's big, warm, raucous, happy house empty of family. Empty of love. I swallow down the ache of impending tears and place a hand on her arm.

'Where do you live now?' I ask.

'France.' She gives a light laugh at the shocked look on my face. 'Dad's new wife, Amelie, inherited her mother's house in the Loire Valley, which they go to in the holidays. I spent a few months there while I was studying, met a local guy and moved nearby. Leon and I are married now, and we have a little boy. Henri. With an "I".' She takes out her phone and shows me photos of a man with kind eyes, and a cute little toddler hugging a Border collie outside a house with sunflowers growing against the wall. It's all very idyllic. The boy looks like the baby photos I've seen of Jacob, and it makes my chest swell.

I'm relieved Charlie got out of this town, although the fact her husband and son aren't here with her isn't lost on me. Why would she not bring them to her brother's funeral? Did the Donnellys completely fall apart after I left?

'I guess your French A levels came in handy after all,' I say instead of asking the million questions buzzing around my head.

'*Oui.*'

Her face turns serious, and I know what she's thinking. She's thinking about the promise we made to one another as kids that when we finished our A levels we'd interrail across Europe and stop in Paris and see the *Mona Lisa*. I wonder if she's been. I haven't. Going without her would have felt like a second betrayal.

It must be nice to have a husband and a child and a cute house with a pretty garden.

'I'm glad all your dreams came true,' I say, realising right away what a ridiculous thing that is to say on the day of her brother's funeral. I lean closer, our knees touching beneath the small round table. 'Tell me about Jacob,' I say quietly. 'What happened?'

All I know about Jacob's death is what Charlie wrote in her text to me yesterday morning:

Hi Eva, it's Charlotte Donnelly. I'm sorry to be the one to tell you, but Jacob is dead. His funeral is tomorrow at 2.30pm at St Anne's, Cragstone. I hope you can make it.

Why did she tell Bianca she never sent me the text? I'm not going to mention it again. Grief can affect your memory and all of this is stressful enough.

When I received Charlie's text I ran straight to the toilet, vomited then burst into tears. I told my friend, Amanda, that I had to go back to Cragstone, booked a train ticket then googled what had happened, all in the space of five minutes. I only managed to find one reference to Jacob's death online, an article in the *Cragstone Chronicle* stating that a local thirty-year-old man, Jacob Donnelly, had accidentally driven off a local cliff and died. Drink driving was suspected. Nobody else was involved. They hadn't even featured a photo of my ex-boyfriend, just a pretty, scenic image of the craggy cliffs, a nearby beauty spot where wildflowers grow in the spring and the waves become deadly in the winter. I know those cliffs: they're right next to the beach Jacob and I used to go to. That's where he'd find me pebbles and we'd buy ice creams from a café near the steps that led down to the beach. Residents have been complaining for years that it needs better barriers as the edge of the cliff is too close to the main road. Maybe now they'll do something about it.

Charlie strokes the image of her boy on the screen before taking a deep breath and putting her phone back in her bag.

'Everything turned to shit after you left,' she says so quietly

I have to lean in closer to hear. 'Jacob never went to university in the end.'

My old best friend may as well be speaking another language. What does she mean Jacob never went to university? Jacob is, *was*, the smartest person I knew. He got a scholarship to a boarding school two hours away in Wales, then achieved five top-grade A levels when most people are proud to get three. He had his pick of any university in the world. I didn't get to know him properly until I was seventeen and he was eighteen, even though I'd mooned over photos of him since I'd befriended his sister in year seven, eager to catch a glimpse of him during the holidays. I never did.

When he finally graduated from boarding school, Jacob Donnelly returned home a hero. That brilliant boy was more than just my best friend's older brother; he may as well have been famous. All the townsfolk spoke about him as if he were a celebrity, telling one another about the times they'd seen him doing something clever or cool or interesting, speculating about what his future would be like. Cragstone's prodigal son. That summer my crush turned into real love and that's when everything changed for me. Jacob made the impossible feel possible.

'He didn't make it to Oxford?' I ask.

'He never made it to *any* university,' Charlie says.

What? Studying medicine meant everything to Jacob; he had big plans and dreams. He was meant to leave for Oxford University a year before Charlie and I graduated, but he deferred for a year. He told his mother he wanted to focus on his charity work and save up some money, and she was more than happy to have him around a little longer, but the truth was he stayed for me. There's no way he would have given up on his studies after I left.

'What happened?'

'He got sick,' Charlie says.

'Sick?'

She rubs her face, her mascara already smudged beneath both eyes and her hair hanging limp. I'm exhausting her. I should ask someone else about Jacob.

'He was never officially diagnosed with anything. He said he was ill, and Mum said he was ill, but Dad and I never believed it.' She tucks a stray hair behind her ear, her gaze fixed on the tabletop, where she plays with a drop of water. 'Whatever. What does it matter now anyway? Jacob messed up his life and now he's dead. Happy?'

'Happy? Why the hell would I be *happy*?' I cry.

Charlie's head snaps up. Her face has grown red and mottled but she doesn't answer. I don't understand why she's being like this. Why would I be glad my ex-boyfriend didn't reach his potential? I didn't even know he'd been unwell. I don't understand why everyone is so angry with me.

Charlie sighs, harder this time through her nose like a little blonde dragon. 'I'm going home.'

I'm being too intense. I've pushed her too far.

'Want me to walk you back?' I ask. 'Does your mum still live in your old house?'

She shakes her head as she returns to where we were sitting, back to the fabric mountain of coats. Is that a no to walking her back or to where Iris lives now? I follow her and find my coat too, realising that everyone who was at the table with us before has left. They aren't the only ones. The pub is beginning to empty and through the misted-up windows I can see it's already pitch-black outside.

'My mother is still at the same house but I'm not staying with her,' Charlie says, wrapping a giant scarf around her neck three times. 'I said I'd meet Dad and Amelie at the Chinese restaurant down the road. I'm staying with them tonight. They live in Fiveacres.'

I don't know the town of Fiveacres well, but I do know it's pretty and affluent and at least a thirty-minute drive away. I wait for my dinner invitation, but she stays silent. Which is probably for the best.

'Dad's taking me to the airport tomorrow morning,' she says.

'Oh,' I reply. 'You're not seeing your mum before you go?'

She shakes her head.

'I was hoping we'd have a chance to catch up more,' I add.

She stays silent and buttons up her coat. As we step outside, the night pulls at the shadows of her face, and I have to remind myself this isn't a school reunion. This woman has just lost her brother. Jacob, my Jacob, belonged to her first. I blink back tears; it feels almost selfish to be crying when I've spent the last ten years trying to eradicate Cragstone and everyone in it from my mind.

'Bye, Eva,' she says, turning my name into a sigh.

I go to hug her tentatively and she draws me into a tight embrace.

'I've missed you,' she says into my shoulder.

'I've missed you too. So much.'

I let the tears fall freely now, the sharp wind making them burn against my cheek.

'Let's swap numbers.' She pulls away and rummages through her handbag. 'We should talk properly. You know, when things are less... raw.'

'Well, you already have my number, so I have yours too now,' I say. 'Call or message me any time.'

'What?'

I show her my phone and the text she sent yesterday telling me about the funeral.

'I told you, I didn't send you that,' she says, scowling as she squints at my screen. She clicks on the message. 'That's a UK number. Mine is French. It starts with 0033.'

'But it says, "Hi Eva, it's Charlotte."'

'When have I ever used my full name? I didn't send it.'

My heart starts to race as I read the message again. Why would someone pretend to be Charlie to get me here?

'Who did, then?' I ask.

She shrugs. 'Call it.'

I tap on the green call button and put it on speakerphone. It goes straight to an automated answerphone. I hang up.

'Don't worry about it. It's probably some sick joke Bianca thought up,' Charlie says.

No. Bianca looked genuinely surprised, and angry, to see me. Charlie is the only one who would want me here, she must have sent it.

'I don't understand. Who invited me?' I push. 'Tell me the truth!'

'I don't know, but it wasn't me,' she shouts back, tears streaming down her face. 'I knew this would happen. I knew this awful town would destroy us all one by one. I should never have come back.'

And with that, she's gone. Up the street, around the corner, lost to the mist and the night.

FIVE

I sit on the low wall outside the pub, not caring that it's wet or that it's leaving a mossy green mark on my expensive woollen coat. My entire body is trembling, and I want to cry, but I'm too numb to do anything but stare into the distance. The strange text, everything Charlie told me about Jacob, people accusing me of his death. So many questions flit in and out of my mind like house flies, but as soon as I try to make one land it zooms off again.

I take my phone out of my bag and read the text again. I don't understand what anyone would gain by pretending to be Charlie and inviting me to Jacob's funeral. I go to check my work emails, remember I no longer have a job and swallow down more tears. Today has been beyond exhausting. I scroll through my social media accounts out of habit, an attempt to numb my brain. No messages. I unfollowed my ex-fiancé on all social media and blocked his telephone number after I caught him cheating on me; he denied it but I saw the emails between him and my assistant on his phone. There are three missed calls from Amanda. I call her back and she answers on the first ring.

'How did it go?' she asks breathlessly. 'You said the service was in the afternoon, so I figured it was safe to call this evening but you didn't answer.'

Amanda and I have been friends since university, although we've become less close the older we've got. Her dorm room was next to mine and by the end of the first week she knew everything there was to know about my life. Poor thing had to listen to me talk about Jacob non-stop after we broke up. That was a messy year. We became flatmates, then she moved in with her boyfriend, then they broke up and she moved back in with me, then I moved in with Mario, then we broke up, and now Amanda and I are flatmates again. I'm not entirely sure she likes having me back but she's all I have in London. I can't believe I turn thirty next year and after all this time I've gotten nowhere.

'Sorry,' I say. 'My phone was on silent. It's been hell. I wish I'd never come back.'

'Were all your old classmates there? Did you see Jacob's sister? Want to talk about it?'

'Not really.' My throat aches from all the tears I've been trying not to cry. 'I'll tell you about it tomorrow. Can I still spend Christmas Day with you and your mum?'

'*Of course.* I'm heading there now so get here whenever you want. It won't be very exciting, but you're welcome to join us.'

I was meant to spend Christmas at Mario's parents' villa in Lake Garda. He'd planned an elaborate trip to Limone until he remembered I hate the smell of lemons, so he reorganised everything and got us tickets to a masked New Year's Eve party in Verona instead. My future was all set, and it was going to be full and decadent. But more than anything I was finally going to have a family to call my own. That's all gone now.

'So... Mario called me today,' Amanda says as though reading my mind. 'He's pissed off you blocked his number.'

I puff out my cheeks and let out a long sigh. 'I told you to block him too.'

'I did. He called from his work phone. He really wants to

see you, Eva. I know he's the bad guy in all of this but he's very convincing when he says he never cheated.'

'Too convincing,' I reply, knowing full well how charming he can be. 'Amanda, I don't have the head space to deal with him and his excuses right now.'

'I know. Of course. Sorry. I wouldn't have mentioned it except he said he has a box of your belongings. Random things from your childhood, apparently. Notebooks and a necklace.'

He must be talking about my old diaries and a few other things I kept when I left Cragstone, like the stones Jacob gave me and my mother's jewellery.

'Tell him to throw it away.'

'You don't mean that,' she says. 'I'll tell him to bring the box to the flat after Christmas.'

I make a non-committal huffing sound.

'Are you still wearing your engagement ring?' she asks.

'No. I left it at yours. I'm going to sell it.'

My friend knows how good I am at getting messed around by men. Everyone I've ever dated has chased me then dumped me. She says it's because deep down I've never been fully committed to any of them as I never truly got over Jacob. She may be right. For years Amanda told me to get back in touch with my ex. Once she even threatened to hack into my Facebook and message him pretending to be me. She didn't, of course, but I never found the courage to seek closure. I guess Jacob dying did that for me.

'Did you tell Mario where I am?' I ask.

'Of course not!'

Mario also knows about Jacob and was instantly jealous of him. I never understood how a man as handsome and successful as Mario could be jealous of a boy I dated when I was eighteen, someone I'd had nothing to do with ever since. Maybe Amanda was right and how I felt about my ex was evident to everyone, boyfriends included. When I talked to Mario about his jealousy, he insisted it was only because he wished *he'd* been my first love. I said I wished he had been too, but I was lying. I've dated plenty of men between my first love and my last, but none of them made me feel as safe, secure and at peace as Jacob did… before it all turned bad. Not even the man I planned to spend the rest of my life with. I often wonder whether Jacob and I would have married one another had all that drama not unfolded, or if I'd had the guts to get back in touch with him. I wrote all of this down in my journals, hoping it would help me process my emotions, but it made no difference.

'Oh no!' I cry, a terrible thought popping into my head. 'What if Mario has been reading my old diaries?'

Amanda tells me I'm being silly. Why should he care about my life as an eighteen-year-old in Cragstone and my early years in London? But I feel sick. I don't want him knowing about my past, who I was, what happened. Amanda knows everything about me, but not Mario. How could I have told my charming fiancé, a man who has never had a bad day in his life, about finding my alcoholic mother dead and the chaos that followed? I needed him to believe I was cool, stable and loveable. The problem is I haven't given Mario the opportunity to explain himself and it's driving him mad. If he figures out I'm back in Cragstone, he'll come looking for me, but I don't want to deal with him so soon after saying goodbye to Jacob. It's too much.

'Don't tell Mario where I am,' I say to Amanda. 'I'll talk to him in the new year.'

'I promise. Stay safe and I'll see you tomorrow.'

Stay safe? I try not to laugh. At least that's one thing I can be certain of in this stupid town. Someone stole the charity collection box from the post office once and it made it to the front page of the local paper. Cragstone is boring, not dangerous.

'I'll call from the train tomorrow,' I say.

Amanda blows me a kiss down the phone, and I smile,

thankful that outside of my awful childhood town I made a real friend I can depend on.

I sigh. I shouldn't have shouted at Charlie. I didn't realise how much I'd missed my old best friend until I was hugging her, breathing in the familiar scent of her shampoo.

Charlie was my only real school friend. The only one who didn't laugh when my mother turned up drunk at my school one lunchtime and threw pennies at me through the window because the school had contacted her to say I was always hungry. Seventy-four pence in total, as if that would buy me a sandwich. Charlie was the only friend who thought to give me sanitary towels because she knew my mum spent all her money as soon as she had any, which meant I often had to make my own sanitary protection from the paper hand towels in the school toilets. Charlie would also sneak my dirty uniform in with her own laundry on a Friday night so her parents would wash it, and sometimes she'd even fill up empty bottles for me with shampoo and the fancy strawberry-scented shower gel her mother bought her. I loved that my best friend and I smelled the same.

We didn't even exchange numbers in the end. I'll probably never see her again.

'Pretty girls like you shouldn't be sitting on their own in the dark.'

I look up. A man is standing before me, the hood of his anorak obscuring his face, steam rising from the parcel he's clutching in his hand. I go to get up, but he lowers his hood and I relax again.

'Oh,' I mumble. 'Hello, Harry.'

He stays hovering over me, but I'm too shaken up for a chat, too tired to walk to my hotel and too cold to stay put.

'Mind if I take a seat?' he asks, not waiting for me to reply before perching on the edge of the wall.

I hardly knew Harry at school – he was one of those boys

who was always lurking in the periphery but never in the mix. I'm not sure I ever saw him with any of the other boys.

'Chip?' he asks, thrusting the white paper bag at me. I peer inside at a mountain of pink goo. 'I couldn't decide on mayo or ketchup, so I added both.' He's slurring, his words running into one another. I wonder if the wake had a free bar. I feel like 'free drinks all night' is something Michael would have insisted on.

I take a floppy chip out of the bag Harry is holding and chew on it slowly. It's strange how people get older but still look the same. Harry is wearing a tie that looks like it once belonged to his dad, and his rusty-coloured hair is shorter than it used to be with greying sideburns giving him a more discerning look. Yet the rest of him appears somehow boyish and innocent. His face, although a little more lined, is still covered with a smattering of freckles. Strange to think we're both nearly thirty. He's staring at my fingers, which are now covered in sticky pink sauce. I suck on my thumb, which makes him look away. Charlie used to tease me, saying Harry had a crush on me at school. Maybe he did. I wonder if he still does.

'No ring,' he mutters.

'Pardon?'

He points at my left hand. 'In the pub earlier, you mentioned you had a fiancé, but you're not wearing a ring.'

'It's in my hotel room,' I lie. 'I didn't want to lose it.'

I take another chip and we eat the soggy mess in silence, the warm carbs helping settle my stomach although I need more than chips to stave off the chill that has settled in my bones. I shiver and pull my collar up. I should have packed a scarf. Harry reaches for something inside his coat pocket and hands me a bottle of whisky. Not as large as a normal one, but not minibar-sized either.

'For the cold,' he explains.

I've never noticed how pale his eyes are before, or the way they crease at the edges when he speaks. I nod my thanks and take a swig. It's already half empty, which explains why Harry is so drunk.

'You've made short work of this,' I say, holding up the bottle.

'I hate funerals.'

'No one likes funerals,' I reply.

'True. At least it wasn't a family member.'

It takes him a few seconds to realise what he just said. 'Sorry. About your mum, I mean. I know it was a long time ago but today must have been extra hard for you. First her, then him... I mean, I gave you my condolences at the time, if you remember, but I'm just saying it again because I'm sorry... as in, I'm still sorry she died.'

'It's fine,' I say under my breath. But my mother dying when I was eighteen was not fine. I'm still angry with her.

'Is she buried at St Anne's too?' Harry asks, either too drunk to pick up on my body language or unbothered that I'd like to talk about literally anything but the death of my alcoholic mother on the day of my ex-boyfriend's funeral. Ten years have passed since I found her on the living room carpet, where she'd choked on her own vomit. In London those memories are hidden somewhere in the back of my mind, but in Cragstone my mother is everywhere. And now Jacob is too.

'She was cremated,' I reply.

I can't remember who paid for the service – probably Iris and Michael. The Donnellys were the only ones who were there, with Jacob on one side of me and Charlie on the other. No school friends. No extended family. I was handed her ashes in a little bag, and we scattered them out to sea, even though she didn't like the water. All I cared about was no longer being tethered to her. No gravestone or final resting place that I was obligated to visit and tend to. I'd spent most of my life looking after her and for what? I hadn't been able to save her in the end. I moved in with the Donnellys after that, somehow passing all my A levels and getting accepted at a top London design school. I paid my own way eventually, the sale of my mother's house covering all my expenses and then some. She ended up doing more for me dead than she ever managed to do alive. The irony was not lost on me.

'I gave you a flower the day of your mum's funeral,' Harry tells me.

That's right. He did. I'd forgotten about that. A white carnation. I threw it away at the time, rolling my eyes at Charlie when Harry was out of sight and calling him 'weird'. It was cruel of me, but Harry always gave me the creeps. I didn't like the way he stared at me in class and used every opportunity to talk to me, always needing to borrow a pencil or offering me his sweets. But perhaps he was just another lonely kid who needed a friend, and there I was scared of being kind to him in case it made the mean kids hate me even more. Plus I didn't want Jacob to hear about it. I'd waited so long to make him mine, I wasn't going to let anyone get between us, least of all Harry bloody Hilborn.

All these people who mattered are all gone now. Can you call it the same life when it's made up of missing parts? Yet here is Harry sitting beside me, over a decade later, sharing his dinner. The only person in the entire town worried about how I'm feeling right now. The irony of that isn't lost on me either.

The chips have nearly gone. I take another sip of whisky, my body growing warmer and my head a little lighter.

'I know you split up with Mario,' Harry says after a while. 'That was your fiancé's name, right? Mario Florentino?'

The chips I've just eaten form a congealed stone in my guts, the pink sauce turning rancid in my throat.

'What do you know about my ex?'

'Which ex?' he says. 'Because when it comes to you and secrets, Eva, there are far too many to choose from.'

SIX

The wall Harry and I are sitting on is so cold and damp I can no longer feel my behind. He's staring at me with those clear glass eyes of his, just like he used to at school, enjoying how uncomfortable he's making me.

'Why would you think I'm keeping secrets?' I ask. 'Why do you all keep saying I'm lying?'

'Relax,' Harry says with a high-pitched laugh. 'I was only joking.'

I'm not laughing. 'What do you know about my ex-fiancé?' I ask again.

'It was just something Jacob said about how you got back in touch with him.'

'I didn't! We hadn't spoken in ten years.'

'Well, I needed to know for myself, so I looked you up on Facebook to see if you followed one another.' His head lolls forward as he speaks, taking his time to annunciate each drunken word. 'I couldn't tell because your account is private, but your profile picture isn't, and that's when I saw the photo of you with that ruggedly handsome man. Very dashing. Everyone in the comments was congratulating you and some guy called Mario on your engagement. He was tagged, so I checked his profile out too, and lordy, lordy, Eva.' He jabs my shoulder with his finger. 'You certainly landed on your feet. He has a large following on TikTok, you know, with his "the routine of a successful man" videos. Quite a catch. I guess pretty girls like you always get what they want.'

I ignore the last comment.

'And you told Jacob all of this?'

'Of course. But your profile photo changed a few months later. It was of just you, on your own, and everyone in the comments was calling Mario a piece of shit. So I knew you'd split up. You never accepted my friend request, by the way.'

I can feel the chips curdling in my stomach, acid climbing up my throat. I wash it down with more whisky. I should have trusted my initial instincts about Harry... He's still a creep.

'My break-up with Mario is quite recent. I'm still getting over it,' I say.

'It must have been nice to have Jacob to talk to about it.'

I screw up my face in disbelief. How drunk *is* this idiot? 'I just told you that I haven't spoken to Jacob since I was eighteen!'

Harry raises his thick eyebrows. 'You shouldn't lie, Eva. It's why people around here don't trust you. Your lies broke up the whole Donnelly family, remember? Then, in the pub, you lied about having a fiancé, when you don't anymore, and now you're saying you and Jacob weren't in touch when everyone knows you were.'

'I'm not lying!' My voice is so high I sound hysterical... like I'm lying. 'OK, so I mentioned that my fiancé bought my handbag, which implied I'm still engaged, but that's only because it was easier than telling everyone my life story. Why are you being like this?'

Harry looks down at his muddy shoes, scuffing the tip of his brogues along the icy pavement. His breaths come and go in little puffs like he's smoking.

'It's just hard to know what's real with you sometimes,' he says.

'But why the hell do you need to know so much about my life, Harry? What I do and who I'm with is no one else's business! Especially nobody here.'

Harry's pale eyes widen but I don't care that I'm being rude. I always forget how toxic Cragstone and everyone in it can be. I go to get up, but I stand too quickly, and it sends my head spinning. I sit back down with a thud and close my eyes. I can't keep running. I need answers. Is Harry so drunk he's talking nonsense or is there something I should be worried about? I think back to the funeral and Iris attacking me and saying I killed her son. What do people around here think they know? Maybe it has something to do with whoever sent me that text message.

'Sorry for shouting at you,' I say, taking a deep breath. 'Can I have your number, please?'

Harry looks up and gives me an enormous grin. I pass him my phone and he makes a big show of typing in his details: his mobile number, his landline, his email address. He adds a heart after his name, which I make a mental note to delete later. The number he's given me is not the one that texted me yesterday. That rules Harry out, but it doesn't answer the question of why everyone here hates me and thinks I'm untrustworthy. Maybe if I knew the details of how Jacob died, I might understand why I'm being accused of hiding something. If anyone is going to speak the truth, it's Harry.

'Hey,' I say softly, placing a hand on his arm. I've nearly finished the last of the whisky and my words are also starting to mix into one another. 'Tell me how Jacob died.'

He raises one eyebrow. 'You don't know?'

'All I know is he drove off a cliff while over the limit. But it sounds like some serious stuff was happening building up to the accident. Charlie said he was ill. Was he depressed? Was he struggling with something?'

Harry laughs. A sharp bark of a laugh that takes us both by surprise.

'Jacob was an idiot. Jeez, at the age of nineteen he had it all, everything any man could ever dream of – the perfect girlfriend, big house, top grades, the opportunity to go to the best schools – and he threw it all away. Some people would call it self-sabotage, but it was just good, old-fashioned self-indulgence. He was an entitled, privileged rich kid who died because he thought he was invincible.'

My eyes widen but I stay still and silent, scared to move for fear of disrupting Harry's bitter tirade. I thought everyone loved Jacob as much as I did. I thought he was untouchable.

'They say his car spun off the road and down the cliff,' Harry continues. 'It was the middle of the night so no witnesses, then a dog walker saw tyre marks in the grass the next morning and looked over the edge.'

He makes a face of horror, as if looking down at the grisly scene himself. I wonder how many people he's gossiped with about this, revelling in the juicy horror of it all.

'Took the police ages to sift through the wreckage; car was mangled and all the contents of his holdall scattered over the rocks. He'd been drinking whisky. They found the empty bottles.'

He hiccups and holds up his own drink as he says this.

'Where was he going?' I ask.

Harry raises his eyebrows, as if I should already know the answer.

'That road leads to the motorway. London, probably. No one knows for sure, but he was definitely leaving Cragstone for good. The police around here are shit. It took weeks for them to pronounce... to announce... to, you know, confirm he was definitely dead. Did you know Bianca's younger brother, Ryan, is a copper now?' He taps my arm as he says this, to ensure I'm listening. 'You know, the guy that was at the pub with us earlier. That boy couldn't figure out how to do the zip up on his hoodie until he started secondary school, and now he's law enforcement. Give me a break.' Harry laughs again, this time letting out a piggy grunt that makes him laugh harder. 'The famous Jacob Donnelly and his charmed life. Even his death had to be cool and dramatic, like something out of a movie.'

I try not to picture everything Harry is saying to me or what my ex-boyfriend looked like when they pulled his battered body out of the car. Something Harry told me earlier is still tugging at the back of my mind.

'Was Jacob upset that I was engaged?' I ask.

Harry rolls his eyes at me. 'He didn't kill himself, Eva. Don't flatter yourself.'

I swallow down the lump in my throat. 'No, I didn't mean that, it's just that...'

'He wasn't the same guy as the boy you left behind. Believe me, this was just a regular drink driving accident.'

I rub my eyes, no longer caring about my make-up or what I look like. None of this feels real, like I'm watching a terrible soap opera in another language. Jacob was a great driver, and he didn't even like whisky. He used to say it tasted of wet wood.

'But Iris said it was my fault,' I say quietly.

Harry's head drops backwards, like it's getting too heavy for him to carry. 'Iris says a lot of things. Who knows what goes through that woman's head?'

I get up, a shooting pain hitting me straight between the eyes. I'm so exhausted nothing is making sense anymore.

'Well, it was nice to see you again,' I say, brushing the dirt off the back of my coat. Lies come easier now that everyone in this awful town thinks I never tell the truth anyway.

Harry gets to his feet then places both his greasy hands on my shoulders. 'It's been lovely to see you too,' he slurs, struggling to keep his eyes open. He grips tighter as he sways on the spot. 'Shit. I'm really pissed. And I have work tomorrow.' He does another of his high-pitched laughs as I prise his fingers off me. 'You can keep my whisky. When will you be back?'

'Never,' I reply. 'I'm never returning to Cragstone again.'

He gives me a smile, although this one doesn't reach his droopy eyes. He leans forward, his breath smelling of alcohol and cocktail sauce.

'You should never have come back in the first place, Eva Walsh,' he whispers, spittle coating my cheek. 'Plenty of people in the church today were wishing it was *you* in that coffin, you know.'

Did Harry really just say that? He goes to give me a hug, but I step back, causing him to fall forward. He nods slowly like a stag, gives me a sloppy salute and stumbles away muttering to himself. I wait until he melts into the shadows then turn in the opposite direction up the high street towards my hotel.

I shouldn't listen to anything Harry says. He was once a creepy kid with a crush on me and now he's a creepy adult, bitter that he never got to have me.

I'm limping, my feet in agony from my high heels and my toes burning with every step. Why did I think wearing this outfit was a good idea? Why did I care so much what these arseholes thought of me? My entire body shudders as I think back to how Jacob died and his mother launching herself at me at the church. If Jacob was pretending we were still in touch, then it's no wonder everyone thinks I'm keeping secrets. I can't wait to get as far away from this place as I can.

I check the time on my phone. It's gone seven thirty, and the streets are deserted, everything closed except for the pub behind me. The streetlights are so dull in the mist that it may as well be midnight. I hold my coat tighter around me, swigging back the last drop of Harry's whisky before dropping the bottle into the nearest bin.

I'm going to feel like crap in the morning, but I don't care. My train leaves at four twenty-three in the afternoon. I'll ask for a late hotel check-out, have a long lunch somewhere away from the high street and do my best to avoid any of the locals until I can get on my train. I turn into the narrow street that leads to the hotel for the second time this evening, doing my best to walk in a straight line. I want to take my tight shoes off, but the ground is gravel, and the weather has turned so cold it must be close to freezing.

Relief washes over me as I spot the Christmas lights of the hotel twinkling up ahead. I'm nearly there, painful step after painful step, but then something appears in my peripheral vision. A dark form near the tree. It's moving. I quicken my step, but I've drunk too much, and it feels like I'm wading through treacle. I'm wobbling on my heels as I try to speed up, worried about twisting my ankle, focusing on the blurry lights in the distance that don't seem to be getting any closer.

I don't know if the fog has gotten thicker, or the whisky has made my vision hazy, but I'm struggling to make out the shape through the gloom. I look behind me. The shadow is still there. It looks like a man in a hood... and he's staring at me.

'Harry?' I call out, his words circling my mind.

Plenty of people in the church today were wishing it was you in that coffin.

I see the entrance to the hotel and start running, my feet slipping along the frozen gravel. I push the reception door, but it's locked, and the lights are off inside.

'Hello?' I call out, banging on the glass with my fists while taking furtive looks behind me, but all I can see in every direction is white, icy fog. I run to my cabin on the other side of the lawn, my expensive heels sinking into the wet grass as I fish about inside my bag for my keys. I keep dropping them as I try to slot them into the lock with cold, numb fingers. The faint thud of footsteps behind me is getting louder. Nearer.

I finally get the door open and look behind me, but there's no one there. Just trees and bushes and a town full of people who hate me.

I shut the door, lock it and burst into tears.

SEVEN
22 DECEMBER

I hardly slept last night. I kept peering out of the window and checking all the locks, eventually ramming a chair against the door handle. I even took one of the wire hangers out of the wardrobe and fashioned it into a shank-like hook, which I held on to all night, my mind a merry-go-round of men: Mario wanting to meet up with me, Jacob in a box in the ground, Michael's heavy hand on my shoulder, Harry with his rancid breath and ominous words. In the end I resorted to watching a cheesy romcom on Netflix at five in the morning, which temporarily emptied my brain of all the ghosts and shadows until I dropped off to sleep. It's now ten o'clock, the mist has cleared, and in the sharp bright white of winter I feel like someone has taken a chainsaw to my head.

I shower, dress myself in jeans and trainers, and grab my rucksack, making my way to reception. I don't bother with make-up and I'm not going to ask for a late check-out. What's the point? My room is hardly a luxurious sanctuary.

The hotel receptionist is not the same one who checked me in yesterday. I recognise this woman from the pub last night, the one with the pumpkin haircut who remarked on my handbag.

'Oh my God, Eva. You're still here!' she squeals, running around the desk and enveloping me in a large bear hug. Her voice is like a chisel to my hangover.

'Hi...' I look at her name badge. 'Orla. Nice to see you again.'

I focus on my breathing, trying to abate my nausea. I can't decide if the smell of fried bacon wafting from the kitchen is making me feel hungry or sick.

I place my keys on the desk and give Orla a shaky smile.

'I'm checking out,' I say, my voice raspy from last night's whisky and too many tears.

Orla studies my face with concern. 'Oh dear, you don't look well. Sit down, I'll bring you a coffee. I'm on a break in a few minutes so I can join you.'

She motions me towards a sofa beside an open fire and I sink into it, the heat from the flames and the sound of crackling wood instantly making me sleepy.

'Here we are,' she says, putting down a tray with a jug of water, a cafetière and a plate piled high with pastries. 'On the house.' She puts her finger to her lips and raises her shoulder like she's a naughty little girl. 'I snaffled them from the buffet. I won't tell if you don't. I meant to ask you, is your hair naturally wavy or do you curl it in the mornings? I've never had much luck with my hair. You have such a pretty nose, too, and your eyes are really green. I forgot how green they were. Are they contacts?'

I don't have the energy for this level of small talk. I smile and shakily reach for the cafetière.

'All natural,' I reply.

'Amazing. God, you're so pretty, Eva. I can see why the boys were always fighting over you,' she exclaims, falling into the armchair opposite as if we're lifelong friends meeting up for a chat. I don't know what I'm meant to say to that so I keep sipping my coffee. 'Anyway, can you believe it's Christmas in three days?'

'Crazy,' I mutter.

I hate this time of year. Growing up I never had a stocking, or a tree. Sometimes my mother would remember to put up some tinsel and I'd take money out of her purse, buy myself something, wrap it up, then thank her Christmas morning. She'd act all gracious, unaware that it wasn't her who had bought it, then I'd go back to school and pretend that I'd eaten all my favourite foods over the holidays and that I'd been spoiled rotten like all my other classmates. It wasn't until my first Christmas with the Donnellys that I understood what all the fuss was about and why family mattered. But I only got to celebrate with them once before everything was ripped away from me.

'So, any Christmas plans?' Orla asks me.

I stuff an almond croissant into my mouth to buy me some time.

'I'm spending it with friends.'

Last Christmas with Mario was everything; we had a tree and all his family came over to our – well... *his* – house. He lives in North London in a semi-detached that looks humble but is worth seven figures. I have no idea if he has a mortgage, inherited it or his dad bought it for him. We had a magical Christmas, a fun New Year's Eve party, then Mario proposed to me on holiday the following month. Now all I have to look forward to is a day with Amanda and her mother. I know I said I'd go last night but this morning I much prefer the thought of Christmas alone at Amanda's flat, eating M&S party food and watching TV.

'How are you spending Christmas?' I ask Orla.

'Oh, the usual. At home with the family. It's never quiet when you're married to a Clarke and have three kids.'

Three kids? Jesus, she was in the year below me in school. What does that make her? Twenty-seven? Nearly twenty-eight?

'Wow,' I reply because I don't know what else to say.

'I married Steve,' she adds with a giggle, like I'm meant to know who Steve is. Was he one of the men at the table last night? 'Bianca always joins us, of course. And Ryan, although I'm not sure if he's bringing his girlfriend this year. They've been on and off lately.'

Oh. The Clarkes. Right. The policeman is Bianca's younger brother so Steve must be the other one. I'm too hungover for family trees.

'I do love a big, busy Christmas,' Orla continues. 'Jacob was with us one year. You know... when he was dating Bianca. That was a lovely Christmas. Poor Jacob.'

I start choking, the flaky pastry from the croissant lodged in my windpipe. Orla passes me a glass of water.

'Jacob?' I say once I get my breath back. I'm no longer feeling sleepy. 'I didn't know he dated Bianca.'

Orla looks at her watch then behind her as if her boss is going to appear out of nowhere and shout at her for taking too long on her a break, even though we're the only ones in reception.

'Jacob never mentioned it?'

'Why would he? I've not spoken to him in ten years.'

Ten years. Ten years. I sound like a stuck record. Orla looks dubiously at me but leans in anyway, clearly excited to share old news.

'Oh yes, they dated, all right. I thought Jacob and Bianca were an unusual couple too – but it worked. It really did. Jacob completely fell apart after you two broke up. No one saw him for years. He was always ill with stomach pains and headaches and the like. He hardly left the house. He got by doing some kind of working from home job like a call centre or something, I've no idea, although his parents were never strapped for cash, so I guess there was no pressure on him. Then one evening he came to the pub, and we were all there, and we had so much fun. Like the old days, you know?'

No, I don't know. Jacob and I never went to the pub together when we dated. Even once I was eighteen and he was nineteen and we were both old enough to be served alcohol, we preferred walking along the coastline and taking day trips in his car. He hated everyone in Cragstone as much as I did, especially people like Bianca who made my life hell. He wanted to get away from this place even more than I did.

'I think that was the happiest I've ever seen him,' Orla continues. 'So animated. He bought everyone a round of drinks and told us how he'd been accepted to Edinburgh University the following September to study medicine. It was November, so he still had a while to go, but he said he could finally see the light at the end of the tunnel. He got chatting to Bianca, who knows Edinburgh well – her aunt lives there so she visits a lot – and I couldn't believe it when we all went to leave at the end of the night and they were kissing!'

She covers her mouth with glee, but I can't bring myself to join in. I can't fathom why Jacob would dump me a week after I left Cragstone, turn down Oxford University, then a few years later get together with the same girl who bullied me. Did his illness completely change his personality? Or maybe it was just a fling. A drunken mistake that didn't last.

'I'm guessing he never made it to Edinburgh, then,' I say flatly, thinking of what Charlie said and how he never went to any university. By the sounds of it he never left this godforsaken town at all.

Orla shakes her head sadly. 'Their relationship got very serious very fast.'

Oh. So not a fling.

'He had Christmas with us that year and, my goodness, Eva, you should have seen him with my kids,' Orla says, grinning like the Cheshire Cat. 'The boys were still babies then, but they loved him. We all did. Jacob softened Bianca, you know? She idolised him, totally smitten. Of course, she'd been obsessed with him since we were in primary school. You were her biggest competition. Probably why she was a bit mean to you.'

A bit? She once ran off with my school bag and threw it in the duck pond. I had nothing to carry my schoolbooks in for a week after that as I was too scared to tell my mother. I can still hear the laughter in the corridor as I walked around with a tatty old Sainsbury's bag. Charlie gave me one of her old backpacks in the end.

'So why did Jacob and Bianca break up?' I ask, trying to keep my voice steady as if we're gossiping about a stranger and not Jacob. *My* Jacob.

'It was all very strange,' she says. 'By May they told everyone they were moving to Scotland together. Bianca's aunt had found her a job, and they were going to stay at her aunt's house because she was away a lot, so they'd have the place to themselves. Jacob was in such good spirits because he was also in touch with his dad again and they were going to visit Charlie in France together the summer before uni. Then... it all got very weird.'

I pull at the collar of my jumper. I feel hot, nauseas, weak.

'In what way?' I ask.

A man in a grey suit has appeared behind the reception desk and is tapping his wrist at Orla. She makes a face at me and stands up. 'I better go. Mr Andrews doesn't let me take more than fifteen minutes for my break.'

'Wait!' I grab her wrist. 'Tell me more. Please. What happened?'

She looks behind her, leans closer and lowers her voice. 'Jacob got ill again. Really bad this time – he even had a stint in hospital. Then he broke it off with Bianca. He said he was too unwell to leave Cragstone and that he didn't love her anymore. A total U turn.'

Orla heads back to reception and I follow her, waiting for her boss to leave again so she can keep talking.

'How did Bianca take it?' I whisper.

'How do you think?'

A family of four with suitcases trudge in behind me. I really need Orla to tell me everything before she has to serve them.

'Bianca went to Scotland on her own. She was there for a year or so and when she came back, she was angrier than ever. She blamed you, actually. Said it was all because Jacob had never gotten over you. Then, of course, once we heard you'd remained in touch with one another it all made sense. I was surprised to hear you're engaged, actually. I thought Jacob had been on his way to see you when he had the accident.'

My blood runs cold and I grip the reception desk tighter. Harry said the same thing about Jacob coming to see me, and everyone keeps saying Jacob and I were in touch. I don't understand. Has someone been spreading lies about me? Again.

My hands are clammy and so is my brow. I wipe it with my coat sleeve.

'I wasn't in touch with him,' I say quietly. 'I promise I'm not lying.' But Orla isn't listening because the family of four has stepped forward and I'm pushed out of the way. I sit back down on the sofa and attempt to finish my tepid coffee and the last of the croissants, but I'm struggling to swallow them down. With every new piece of news about Jacob I feel sicker and more confused.

I rub at my temples, but no amount of deep breathing is going to clear my head. I drag my backpack over to reception.

'Can you keep a hold of my bag, please?' I say to Orla, who nods in agreement. 'I'll come back for it around four o'clock.'

'You should get some fresh air. Maybe go for a walk on the beach,' she says.

Maybe I will – the coast is only twenty minutes away. I'm heading for the door when Orla calls out to me.

'Wait up!' She's waving a piece of paper in the air as she runs around the reception desk and catches up with me at the exit. 'I nearly forgot to tell you. Jacob's mum called early this morning, but I didn't put the call through because I figured you'd be sleeping. I can see the cabin rooms from here, you see, and your light wasn't on. Anyway, she says she was hoping you could pop over to her house because she... Wait.' She squints at her writing on the page. 'She wants to apologise for her outburst at the church and she has something of Jacob's to give you.'

A wave of nausea washes over me, and I have to hold on to the doorframe to steady myself. Iris is the last person I want to see right now. Flashes of her red, angry face flitter through my mind, her fingers ripping at my hair and her venomous words accusing me of killing her son. I don't want to go anywhere near that woman. Nor can I bear to step back into that house where it all began... and where my life came crashing down.

'I'm not going to see her,' I say.

Orla shows me the note. 'But she has something of Jacob's to give you,' she says quietly. She places a hand on my shoulder and gives it a friendly squeeze. 'You need closure, Eva. It might be good for you.'

I take another deep breath and steady myself. Orla's right. It's time to face my past.

EIGHT

Orla was wrong – the fresh air isn't helping. I feel even worse than before, except now, along with a raging hangover and anxiety about seeing Iris again, I'm also dealing with freezing-cold drizzle and aching feet from yesterday's heels. I rub my eyes, wishing I'd worn make-up. Iris has always been big on appearances.

'If you can't be good, be beautiful,' she used to say to me after I'd visited Charlie. She'd always have parting words to accompany her hugs, sending me back home with a slice of cake or homemade cookies. But that was then, and this is now. I'm sure Iris doesn't see me as a second daughter anymore.

I text Amanda to say I'll be on the four twenty-three train, and she texts me back in capital letters.

MARIO CALLED AGAIN. HE KNOWS YOU'RE IN CRAGSTONE. HE SAYS YOU WERE CHEATING ON HIM WITH JACOB. WTF!

I read it again, then a third time, but it still doesn't make sense. I call Amanda but she doesn't answer.

I lean against a wall and run my fingers through my hair, now damp from the freezing drizzle. How could I be cheating on Mario with Jacob? He's dead! No wonder Mario is so adamant about seeing me if that's what he thinks has been going on. God, I hope he doesn't try to track me down. Mario is not a man who gives up easily. The thought of my ex-fiancé being in Cragstone makes my stomach churn.

I bow my head low against the wind and keep going. My legs take me to Jacob's house automatically, muscle memory, as if I was born to walk these streets. I turn off the high street, slowing down as I pass the bus stop, instantly transported to being thirteen again. This was where Charlie and I would get off the school bus together every afternoon and hang out before she went in one direction to her house, and I went in the other. She knew I never wanted to go home, so we'd sit at the bus stop for hours talking and sharing sweets and she'd pretend we were having fun, even when it was raining. Sometimes she'd invite me back to hers, but I'd make excuses because I couldn't bear it. Her house always smelled of nice things: the lavender from her front garden, freshly made bread and fabric conditioner. Whenever I went there, I never wanted to leave. So I'd avoid going because it hurt less. Sometimes it would be dinner time already when Michael would find us at the bus stop and insist on driving me back home. I'd watch the expression on his face as he'd wait for me to let myself into a dark house, often empty, always cold. I could tell he was never sure if bringing me home was the right thing to do or the worst. I'd make sure I was smiling as I said goodbye, keeping the pretence up until they'd driven off back to the dinner Iris had prepared them while I was left dealing with whatever state my mother was in.

I keep walking, memories assaulting me with every step. The street corner where Jacob first held my hand. The bench where he first told me he loved me. The houses that we trick-or-treated at, Charlie insisting we knock around her area because the treats were better, but I knew it was because she felt safer around her neighbourhood than mine. We all did.

By the time I reach the Donnelly residence my heart is pounding and my mouth is dry again. The house hasn't changed. Even the lavender is still there. I stare up at it the way I first did all those years ago, wondering what you had to do in life to have a home like this one – four bedrooms, detached, a bright red door with a gold knocker shaped like a fox's head, and those French shutters at the windows that don't close but look cute.

I blink back tears as I remember arriving here with my suitcases the day after my mother died. I was eighteen, an adult. I wasn't the responsibility of the state, so Michael and Iris stepped in instead. I don't remember anyone formally asking me to live with them; it was just assumed that I was theirs now. Little did I know that what felt like the beginning of a new, better life was actually the end of all that was good.

I hover by the gate, one hand on the latch, contemplating walking up the path. What will happen if I knock on the door? Will stepping over the threshold this time change my life for the better... or worse? There's only one way to find out.

I knock three times and wait, half hoping Iris is out so I can say I went to see her but no one was home. I'm not so lucky. I can see movement through the frosted glass of the door, hear the latch being drawn and the handle turning.

I don't know who starts crying first, but before I know what's happening Iris has enveloped me in a hug and we're standing on her doorstep rocking back and forth in one another's arms.

'Oh sweetheart,' she keeps saying. 'I'm so glad you came. My poor baby. Come in, come in.'

This is Iris. The real Iris. Not the grieving woman who lashed out at me in the church. I came here full of resolution and fire, ready to have it out with her, but in an instant it has all drained out of me, leaving me limp and empty like a toy without stuffing. She ushers me through the door, and I instinctively take off my shoes as I was trained to do as a child when I'd visit. It's warm inside and it still smells like home.

'I made a cake,' she says, leading me to the kitchen.

It's strange to see Iris so thin and all in black, her back ramrod straight, her lips stretched into a thin line. She motions for me to sit at the kitchen table and switches the kettle on. She used to always be smiling. It was her job to be happy and enthusiastic for rich new home buyers, but I don't think she'll ever smile like that again.

'You must be thirsty. Tea? Coffee?' she's saying as she moves from one cupboard to the next, taking out mugs and a sugar bowl. *That's Jacob's favourite mug*, I think as she picks out a red one with his football team's logo on it. He used to joke I was the only person he'd let drink from that mug. My stomach twists and I have to look away.

'Tea would be lovely,' I say, my own smile feeling more like a grimace. She doesn't ask how I take my tea and deep down I like that this woman, who hasn't been a part of my life for so long, still knows me so well.

'My special chocolate almond torte,' she announces, placing the cake in the centre of the table along with plates and tiny golden forks engraved with tiny flowers. I notice that her fingernails, which used to always be long and painted pillar-box red, are now bitten down to the quick. 'I made the cake fresh today,' she adds. 'You don't even need to bake it. It's like a cheesecake but with a creamy chocolate topping and biscuit base.'

She looks very proud of herself; I can't imagine the strength it must have taken her to be baking the day after her son's funeral. I accept a slice, even though I'm full up from all the pastries I ate half an hour ago, and take a small bite. The torte is creamy and nutty but very sweet. Too sweet for me, but it would be rude to leave it so I keep going while Iris fusses around making our tea.

Nothing has changed in this kitchen, yet everything is different. The cabinets are still rustic pine painted white; the double fridge-freezer with the ice dispenser is still there too. I thought that fridge was the height of luxury when I first saw it, along with the TV in the corner of the room. Such decadence to have ice on demand and more than one TV in your home. The kitchen is spotless, every surface glowing white, the fruit in the fruit bowl so shiny the apples look like they're made of plastic. It looks just like it did when I was a child, except there are no schoolbooks on the table, Jacob's football boots are no longer by the back door, and there's no cat basket below the window. I guess Tiddles is long gone too.

I came here to ask Iris why she screamed such awful things at me in the church. Yet watching her fuss over me in her perfect kitchen I realise this is a woman just about keeping it together. I'm sure she didn't mean it.

'Here you go, my love,' she says, handing me Jacob's football mug.

I wash the last of the torte down with some tea. She's put sugar in it. I've never taken sugar – she knows that. Iris sits on the other side of the table, staring at me, her eyes taking me in. I wonder where she is right now, whether she's looking at me as I am today or remembering who we both were all those years ago.

'How are you?' I ask.

'Some days I want to die.'

I swallow my tea too fast, scorching the back of my throat. I reach across the table and hold her hand, squeezing it tight. 'It will get easier,' I say, thinking of my mother and how sometimes days go by and I haven't thought about her once, a strange mix of guilt and relief washing over me. How long will I have to wait until I can go an entire day without thinking about Jacob?

'He was a good boy,' she says, her voice cracking. 'I know

I'm not an easy woman, Eva, but my boy always looked after me. We looked after one another. He loved me so much.'

She starts to cry, pulling something out of her pocket and using it to wipe her face. It's a tatty red cloth of some kind, frayed around the edges.

'Can I help in any way?' I ask, rubbing the top of her arm.

A surge of anger shoots through me as I realise Charlie is on her way back to France right now when she should be here instead. How could she leave her mother behind the day after she buried her son? Iris has lost enough already.

'My pills,' she says, pointing at a white box on the counter. I pass them to her, and she pops two in her mouth, visibly calming before she even has time to swallow them. 'For the nerves,' she explains. 'I shouldn't be keeping you. You probably have to get back to London soon. I hear you're getting married.'

Gossip moves faster than wildfire in Cragstone. 'Not anymore,' I say. 'We broke up. And my train isn't until this afternoon so I can stay a little longer. If you'd like me to.'

She gives me a shaky smile and it's like I'm staring at a stranger. The bright and bubbly Iris who took me in ten years ago, the woman who fed me, clothed me and held me when I was frightened, was bigger than life. The woman before me is nothing but a discarded husk of a mother.

'Oh, Eva,' she cries, her face crumbling again. 'What am I going to do?'

I get up and hug her, telling her everything is going to be all right and all the other lies we tell those in pain. I didn't have many role models growing up; my mother was my only family, and I wasn't around any other adults. When I looked at Iris, I saw a strong woman with a great job, a job she enjoyed and was good at, but she still loved her home and her family, and her husband adored her. As a kid I was convinced this beautiful woman had it all, and I promised myself that when I grew up, I would be just like Iris Donnelly. I would study interior design and run my own business and marry Jacob and have a big family and live in a big house with a double fridge-freezer. But now look at us, both with empty lives, crying over the same boy. I should have been careful what I wished for.

'Can I help with anything?' I ask again.

She looks around her, as if she's forgotten where she is for a moment. I wonder how strong those pills are.

'You could vacuum, if you want,' she says. 'I have a bad back, you see. I can't get around like I used to. Do you remember where to find the vacuum cleaner?'

Of course I do. I help her into the living room, bringing the tea and cake with me, and sit her in the armchair. She's acting like an old lady, but I know her age. She's fifty-five. The same as Jacob's dad. Handsome, strong, kind Michael with two young children and a wife only ten years older than me. A man so stoic and powerful that he's left the mother of his dead son alone to wither away.

'You should eat something,' I tell her. 'The cake is wonderful.'

'Oh no. I don't eat much nowadays,' she says. 'And dairy doesn't agree with me anymore.'

The living room is even warmer than the kitchen. The sofa has different cushions to the ones she used to have, but the mantel is still covered in the same framed photos from years ago. Iris and Michael on their wedding day, a young Jacob as a baby, Iris and Jacob taken more recently; there are even two of me with her son. My heart leaps at the photo of me and Jacob at my end-of-year prom. How happy we both looked. I notice there are no photos of Charlie or Iris's grandchild.

'Why don't you rest while I clear away the plates and clean up?' I suggest.

She nods, her eyelids drooping. Those pills have worked fast. I take the tea out of her hand and place it on the small table next to the Christmas tree. The lights are twinkling, each tree ornament with its own story, and below them gifts wrapped in two different papers. Some are from Jacob to his mother, the rest from Iris to her son. Gifts Jacob will never get to open. My eyes fill with tears, and I have to bite my bottom lip to stop myself from crying.

I spend the next hour washing up, vacuuming downstairs and mopping the kitchen until the floor is as spotless as the counters. It's not a lot, but I did it as much for Jacob as I did for his mother. He would have hated to see her like this. When I return to the living room, Iris is awake again and flicking through an old photo album. Most of the pictures are of Michael playing with the kids, or Iris holding them as babies, but there are also a lot of me and Jacob together. Some that I've never seen before.

'Remember the day we all went to the beach?' she asks.

I smile and nod. I do. No one knew I was with Jacob then. We'd take every opportunity we could to kiss in the sea and behind the rocks where no one could see us. I was worried about Charlie finding out and hating me, and he was worried about what his mother would say. In the end I managed to disappoint everyone.

'I should get going soon. I don't want to keep you,' I say. My train doesn't leave for a few more hours but I need to get out of here, it's all too much.

Iris's face falls and her chin wobbles. 'Please stay,' she says, grasping my arm tightly. 'Stay until tomorrow. We could have dinner together and talk about the old days. I want to hear what you've been up to.'

My headache is returning and all I can think about is getting away from Cragstone. 'I'd like that, but...'

'Please, Eva. Jacob and I were going to have Christmas together, and now it's just me. I ordered his favourite food to be delivered tomorrow but it's all for nothing because I'm going to be alone the entire week. It would be so nice to have you here just for the night. Go home tomorrow.'

I look at the Christmas tree twinkling in the corner and the photos of me still in their frames. Iris cared about me once. I was like a daughter to her, but that time has passed.

'Please,' she adds. 'I have a package for you. Something Jacob wanted you to have.'

Oh yes. The gift Orla mentioned.

'I can take it now,' I say.

'I'll look for it after dinner. You can head back tomorrow, can't you?'

I supress a sigh. Perhaps Iris can tell me more about Jacob. Maybe whatever he left me holds some clues.

'Yes, OK,' I say, picking up my phone and opening the Trainline app. 'I have an open ticket so I can return whichever day I want. Let me check the timetable. There's only one or two trains a day to London from here so I'll see if there's one in the morning.'

Iris claps her hands with glee. She already looks ten years younger.

NINE

There's a train back to London at 10.23am tomorrow so I agree to dinner and staying the night. It's not until I take the empty mugs and plates back to the kitchen that I check the fridge and cupboards and see there's nothing inside them but a few baking ingredients, mainly dry nuts and sugar. Iris wasn't exaggerating when she said she didn't eat a lot nowadays. Aren't people meant to bring over dishes to the bereaved? Where are all the casseroles and pies? Something gnaws in the pit of my stomach at the thought of Iris not having any friends to look after her. She used to have a bustling social life.

Her groceries are being delivered tomorrow, but that's not going to help us right now.

'Shall I get us a takeaway?' I ask. I'm exhausted and just about standing after my sleepless night. I'm craving pizza, or fish and chips, anything to soak up last night's alcohol. Maybe that will get rid of my headache too.

'Oh, I can't do takeaways,' Iris says, reaching for the blanket and covering her legs. 'I have a delicate stomach. Jacob used to make sure I ate well. He did the online food orders for me because I struggle getting around with my bad back and he was often too poorly to go to the shops. He only chose healthy stuff, though. He'd make the dinners and I'd bake us cakes and cookies.'

'Did Jacob come over a lot, then?' I ask.

Iris laughs. 'He lived here. He never moved out. He wasn't well enough to live alone, you see, and I can't manage by myself. We looked after one another.'

Jacob never left home? But he always had so much ambition and drive.

I crouch down beside Iris. 'I heard Jacob was ill. What was it?'

She waves her hand at me, like she's swatting flies. 'We don't know. The doctors tested him for everything, but they never got to the bottom of it.'

Jacob used to be so sporty, vibrant and energetic. I used to joke that he needed an off switch as he was always on the go. An illness like that must have really affected him to still be living at home at the age of thirty. Iris is waving her hand in my face to get my attention.

'Can you cook, Eva?'

'Pardon? Sorry, yes, I can cook. I'll make us something. Let's go to the supermarket,' I say. 'We can pick some things out together.'

Iris shakes her head and reaches for the remote control, flicking the TV on to a quiz show.

'I can't go out there. I don't want everyone staring at me, the mother of the dead drink driver. Not to mention what everyone will say if they saw *you and me* together. People have long memories in Cragstone. You don't get a second chance around here.'

She's talking about the rumour. The stupid rumour Bianca Clarke started that not only broke up Iris and Michael's marriage but resulted in me being run out of town.

'You know there was no truth in that,' I say, the exact words

I used ten years ago. And just like back then she says nothing. 'It's fine. I'll go to Sainsbury's,' I add. 'It's only down the road and I'll collect my bag from the hotel on the way back. How about I buy a selection of things and you can see what you fancy?'

I check my phone. It's nearly four thirty, so there's plenty of time to shop and cook. My train has already left, so I'm stuck here either way.

Iris doesn't answer, so I grab my coat and handbag and head to the shops. I don't know why it's so important to me that Jacob's mother likes me again after all these years, but it is. It's not until I'm halfway down the road that I realise I forgot to ask for door keys; she'll have to let me in when I get back. I used to have my own set for this house years ago. I still have them somewhere, probably in that box Mario has full of old diaries and my mother's jewellery. I wonder if Iris changed the locks when Michael left. I doubt it.

Iris is right. You don't get a second chance in Cragstone because you can never get away from anyone long enough to reinvent yourself. In order to do that, you have to leave altogether.

The walk to the supermarket only takes ten minutes but in that time I've already had to avoid Mrs Allen, the old school librarian, and a few others I recognise from the wake. Don't people get tired of seeing the same faces day after day?

I'd forgotten how stifling living in a small town can be. Everyone I know in London says they can't wait to move away, raise their family in the safety of suburbia, or retire to the sunshine. But the truth is places like Cragstone may be quiet and pretty, but they're suffocating. In a city you can lose yourself; no one knows your past and, more importantly, no one cares. In London I'm a woman nearing thirty with a great education and a good career, but in this town, I'll always be the scruffy twelve-year-old with the neglectful mother, or the problematic teenager who destroyed an entire family. And Iris? Iris is the once-successful town beauty who will now be forever known as the sad, divorcee loner with the dead son. She knows that's who she is now, and that's why she doesn't want to leave the house. No second chances.

I'm relieved to see the supermarket is empty. I grab a basket and wander down the aisles, contemplating what Iris constitutes as a healthy meal. She said Jacob did all the shopping and liked to cook for her. That doesn't surprise me – he was always kind like that. Smart, handsome, popular, yes, but also kind. Perhaps it was his sense of obligation after his father left that kept him living at home and caring for his mother.

Then again, I don't know… Something tells me there was more to it than that. His illness, not going to uni, the accident – can one person change so much in such little time? I open my jaw a little and wince as it cracks. I didn't realise I was grinding my teeth. Where were Jacob's dad and sister in all of this? Charlie and Michael should have been there for him, for Iris too. This isn't the close-knit family I remember.

I take my time looking at everything on the shelves while checking my shopping list on my phone, choosing bananas, apples, some vegetables, chicken and juice. It's boring food but it's probably best to play it safe. Plus I have to carry it all back, along with my heavy rucksack I have to pick up on my way back, so I can't buy too much. Not that I could afford to anyway.

I close my eyes and try not to think about real life and how mine too has turned to dust. I'm having to start all over again with one dead ex-boyfriend and one angry ex-fiancé. Men have always felt like the solution when maybe they're the problem. But I hate being single. I spent long enough lonely and on my own growing up, desperate to be part of something bigger than just me. I like how it feels to have someone by my side, someone to look after me, an anchor. I want to belong to someone and their family again; I don't want to float away.

The bright white lights of the supermarket are turning my headache into a migraine and I'm clenching my jaw again. I massage down both sides of my face with my thumbs, the pain from my head shooting down to my cheeks and neck and shoulders.

I've spent five minutes searching for wholewheat pasta and I just want to get out of here. I spot a woman at the end of the aisle unpacking a crate of spaghetti. Maybe she can help me.

'Excuse me,' I say. 'Do you know where I can find—'

She turns around and my heart sinks. It's Bianca Clarke. Her hair is tied back in a greasy ponytail and last night's make-up is still smeared around her eyes. She gives me a withering look. How could Jacob have dated her knowing all the awful things she'd said and done to me?

'Oh, I bet you're loving *this*,' she says with a curl of her lip. 'Me stacking shelves while you walk about with your designer handbag. Make you feel good, does it?'

'I didn't know you work here,' I say. 'I was just wondering where I can find the wholewheat pasta.'

Bianca rolls her eyes and goes back to placing packets of spaghetti on the shelves. She looks as rough as I feel.

'What?' she says when she notices I'm still standing there. 'Want to know where the champagne and caviar are, too? You move to London then come back here all high and mighty.'

For crying out loud, I only asked where the wholewheat pasta was. Let her be as mean as she wants, I'm no longer scared of Bianca Clarke; I pity her.

'So... I hear you dated Jacob,' I say. 'Congratulations.'

My comment temporarily wipes the snarl off her face. She narrows her eyes, readying herself for a fight. 'Why are you acting like that's fresh news?' she says. 'I bet he told you years ago. I bet you both had a good laugh about it when he dumped me and left me all alone in Scotland.'

I place my shopping basket on the floor and lean closer to her.

'I don't know how many times I need to tell you, or anyone else for that matter, but I never saw or spoke to Jacob since I left Cragstone. I didn't know he lived at home all this time. I didn't know he was ill. I didn't know he never went to uni. And I didn't know you two went out with one another until I heard about it this morning!'

Bianca's face relaxes and she gives a long sigh.

'You shouldn't have come back,' she says, not for the first time.

'I already told you. I wasn't going to miss Jacob's funeral, was I? I know everything ended badly but the Donnellys were good to me. Why did *you* come back? Why didn't you stay in Scotland?'

She puts the spaghetti she's holding on to the shelf and folds her arms. 'My dad got ill. Then he died. So I stayed.'

'Oh. I'm sorry.' I knew her dad. Vaguely. He seemed nice.

'Yeah, well, when you have family, you have commitments. You wouldn't know about that.' She looks at the basket by my feet. 'Why are you buying all of this food anyway? Aren't you meant to be on a train by now?'

'I'm cooking for Iris.'

Bianca's black-rimmed eyes widen. 'Why the fuck are you in Jacob's house with that evil bitch?'

It's my turn to raise my eyebrows. 'Excuse me?'

'You shouldn't be there.'

'Iris wanted to apologise for that awful thing she said at the church yesterday,' I say. Which is what Iris told Orla she wanted to do, although she hasn't actually apologised yet or explained why she thought I had anything to do with her son's death.

'She was right,' Bianca says, her eyes narrowing. 'You *did* kill Jacob. He thought you two had a chance together, which is why he was on his way to see you the day he died. He'd still be alive if he'd stayed home that night.'

Harry said Jacob was on his way to see me, so did Orla, and now Bianca. It doesn't make sense. Jacob didn't even know where I lived... did he?

'If he was coming to see me, I knew nothing about it,' I cry, my breaths coming thick and fast. It makes no difference how angry or upset I get in this town, no one cares. 'I was never in contact with Jacob. How many times do I have to keep telling you all?'

'For once in your life stop lying, Eva,' she snarls. 'Just do us all a favour and go back to London. Leave the food on Iris Donnelly's doorstep and get the hell away from her. Iris is screwed up and you're about to make everything worse.'

How on earth could anything be worse than this hell?

'The woman is evil,' Bianca continues. 'Jacob would never admit it, but I know it's her who split us up.'

Right. Well, that explains her hatred of Iris. Jacob left Bianca and now she's lashing out at the weakest person she can find. Once a bully, always a bully.

'Iris isn't evil! She's a grieving mother who's lonely and struggling. I'm staying the night then leaving tomorrow. It's no big deal.'

Bianca swings around and grabs me by the arm. I try to move away but her grip tightens.

'Whatever you do, don't stay the night,' she says, accentuating every word. Her face is so close to mine our noses are nearly touching. 'You can't believe a word that psycho says,' she hisses. 'Go! Get the hell out of Cragstone!'

TEN

My arm is still smarting where Bianca grabbed it and my heart is pounding so fast I find myself marching down the road in time to its beat. What a cow. Bianca is a vindictive, evil, unhinged cow!

I was shaking at the tills, checking over my shoulder the entire time, my hands trembling as I placed each item on the conveyor belt. Bianca didn't move; she stayed in the pasta aisle staring at me, as if trying to make me disappear with her eyes alone. I'm halfway down the high street but I'm still buzzing with anger, my aching stomach in knots and my throat tight and sore from the tears I'm forcing down.

Bianca and Jacob broke up five years ago. Maybe longer. How twisted must she be to still hold a grudge against a distraught woman who's just lost her son? I know Iris has changed a lot over the years, but she's not a psycho.

I dry heave and swallow down a mouthful of saliva. Oh God, I'm going to vomit. I really don't want to be sick in the street. Bianca used to make me feel like this all the time in school and it's bringing it all back to me now. She'd shout things at me in the corridor, trip me up as we walked into class, tell everyone I had bad breath and BO because my mother couldn't afford to buy me a toothbrush or deodorant. I'd throw up in the school toilets, even though my stomach would be empty so I couldn't bring anything up but pain and shame. Charlie would tell me to ignore her, that she was just jealous of me, but I never understood that. Jealous of what? I didn't have anything she wanted... not until I had Jacob.

I need to eat something. I rummage inside one of the supermarket bags and pull out a banana, leaning against the wall of a card shop as I peel it. The shop is shut. Half of the shops on the high street are shut already. Is anything ever open around here?

It's five thirty in the afternoon and it's already dark, the pavements shiny from the misty air, some of them gold as they reflect the dim streetlights above me. I attempt to regulate my breathing as I slowly chew on the overripe banana, but my throat is closing up as I'm pushed further back into the memories I've worked so hard to bury. Nothing makes sense anymore. When I arrived yesterday morning, I was so sure of what I was coming back to: a family in mourning, seeing Jacob's old friends and meeting some new ones. I was ready to hear about his life; I imagined he may even have a wife or kids by now. Part of me thought... I don't know. Part of me hoped everyone would have forgotten all that silly drama and Iris and Michael would welcome me back like a long-lost daughter. I expected the town to have moved on, grown up, been happy to see me. Or, better yet, totally forgotten about me. Either option would have been better than whatever the hell this ten-year grudge is. In all the time I've been away, nothing in Cragstone has changed but Jacob's fractured family.

I finish my banana but stay leaning on the wall. My stomach is spasming and my headache is now so acute it's affecting my vision. I should have eaten more than breakfast pastries and Iris's torte after last night's drinking binge.

I walk a little slower this time, the plastic handles of the shopping bags cutting into the palms of my hands. I still need to collect my rucksack from the hotel, but the wind has picked up and my face has turned tight and numb from the biting air. I really don't have the strength to walk the extra ten minutes to the hotel, but what choice do I have?

'Eva.'

I stop. Someone is calling my name, softly like a song. I look over my shoulder, but the street is empty.

I keep going. I never did like walking through Cragstone in the dark. The glowing sandstone buildings on this street are hundreds of years old, memories soaked up and stored in their golden stone walls like a sponge. Local legend has it that the statue in the middle of the square wanders around at night, calling out your name. I shiver. In a town like this, where nothing interesting ever happens, kids have to make up their own horror stories.

'Eva.'

This time I place my bags on the damp pavement, and I turn all the way around in a full circle.

'Hello?' I shout out.

Silence.

The air whistles through the branches of the bare trees lining the streets, the square in the distance an empty black hole. I look to my left at the side street where the hotel is. It's pitch dark down there, and it's beginning to rain. I keep my head down, droplets trickling down the collar of my coat, and pick up my shopping bags. As I step down from the pavement, about to cross the empty road, I see him. A man with his hood raised, his face in shadow. He's standing on the corner of the street leading down to the hotel. Watching me. Waiting.

I think of Michael and the way he chased me back to my hotel. And Harry, with his anorak and barbed comments. And Mario, so desperate to defend himself after his betrayal that he's threatening to track me down while making up lies about my cheating on him first. Or maybe it's not a man. Maybe it's Bianca, come to finish what she started.

Stepping back on to the pavement, I look over my shoulder again, but the hooded figure has gone. I'm wearing trainers and jeans today, so it's easier to hurry than it was in yesterday's heels. I walk as fast as I can, but the rain is getting heavier and soaking through my clothes. I break into a run, my chest aching from the cold, and the bags of food hitting my legs with every stride.

You're being paranoid, I tell myself, each laboured step making it harder to breathe. I need to stop taking the things Bianca and Harry say seriously; they're just getting a sick thrill from scaring me. I slow down, glancing over my shoulder every few seconds. There's no one around. The streets are empty. I'm all alone. My lungs are burning and another stab of pain shoots through my stomach, making me double up and trip over a cracked paving slab. With my hands full of shopping, I stumble and fall to the floor, my knees hitting the hard pavement with such force I cry out in pain.

Three apples roll out of one of the plastic bags and my handbag skitters beneath a hedge. The rain is falling so hard now I can hardly see, my hair plastered to my face, my fingers so frozen from the cold that I'm struggling to pick everything up. I find my purse and keys in the foliage and stuff them back into my muddy bag, tiny leaves sticking to my hands and my jeans already soaked through. Every inch of me hurts and I want to cry, just like I did at school every time Bianca tripped me over.

I push my wet hair away from my face and pick up the bags. I'm not going back to the hotel for my rucksack now; I can collect it tomorrow on the way to the station. I just want to go home. My old home.

. . .

I knock on Iris's door, and she shouts out that she's left the door on the latch. Does she do that often? Leave the door unlocked? I walk inside and I'm instantly greeted by a wave of warmth and the comforting hum of the TV. The house smells of toast and something sweet.

'I was getting worried about you,' Iris calls out.

She's in the same armchair, watching a different game show. She looks like she hasn't moved except for the plate beside her.

'I got hungry so I made toast and jam,' she says. 'Good Lord, look at the state of you!'

Now I'm in the light I can see how wet and dirty I am. My hair is dripping on to her carpet and my teeth are chattering together.

'Is that blood on your knee?' she says, getting to her feet. 'Take off your shoes and filthy clothes and get upstairs into the bathroom. Come on, let me run you a bath.'

I put down the bags of shopping and do as I'm told, peeling off my coat and socks. I feel really dizzy, like I'm going to faint. When Iris answered the door to me a few hours ago, she was walking slowly, complaining of a bad back, but now she's racing past me to the bathroom, almost as if having someone to look after again has given her a new lease of life. I can hear the sound of the bath running, the scent of roses wafting through the air.

'Come along,' she shouts down the stairs. 'We can eat later. You need to get in this bath and scrub the day off you. Did you hurt yourself? I have plasters somewhere.'

I make my way upstairs on shaky legs, my knees stinging from the fall. I can't get the image of the hooded figure out of my head. Whoever it was, I'm sure they were watching me. Perhaps it was the same person I heard following me last night.

I stand before the bathroom mirror like a zombie, silently taking off the rest of my sodden clothes. I'm in nothing but my underpants when Iris walks into the room.

'I see you didn't collect your luggage. That's OK. We can make do for one night.'

I try to cover my chest, but I can't as she hands me a pile of fluffy towels and some pyjamas. She's acting like my being naked in her bathroom is completely normal.

'They're Jacob's,' she says, nodding at the nightclothes. 'But they should fit. Did you say you were feeling poorly?'

I don't know. Did I?

'I have some pills for that.' She chuckles. 'I have pills for everything. Now get in that bath, relax, and then we can get the dinner on. How's that, my love?'

She strokes my wet hair and I lean into her touch. My mother never ran me a bath or stroked my hair. I want to cry again. I nod slowly at everything she says and wait for her to leave. The pyjamas she handed me are red tartan. I recognise them as the ones she bought Jacob the last Christmas we were all together. That was such a long time ago. Why would he still have them?

I hold his old nightclothes up to my face, close my eyes and breathe in deeply. They smell of him. My Jacob. I can't hold it in any longer and I burst into tears.

ELEVEN

I've been in the bath so long my fingers have wrinkled and I'm cold enough to have goosebumps. The long soak has helped though: my headache has gone and my knees don't sting so much anymore. I lean back until I'm fully submerged, my face under the water, the echoing bangs from Iris cooking in the kitchen downstairs reverberating all around me. I need to get everything straight in my head. I need to understand what's going on.

It started with the mysterious text message inviting me to the funeral, then I found out Jacob was ill for the last ten years, never left home and dated my school bully. But why did he tell Harry we were still in touch? And what about Mario's accusations and the man in the hood?

I erupt out of the water, gasping for breath. I shouldn't be here, in Jacob's house, with Jacob's suffering mother. I should have got on the train to London and left this place behind me for good.

'Dinner's ready,' Iris calls up the stairs.

I grip the side of the bath and haul myself out, my legs weak and my heart thundering in my chest. I need to pull myself together. The last forty-eight hours have been hell, and being back here, in Jacob's house after his funeral, is making me jittery. That's all this is. The people of Cragstone love to create drama. Jacob dying and me returning is probably the most exciting thing this place has seen since the thrill of me leaving. Well, I'm not giving these idiots the satisfaction of scaring me. I've done nothing wrong.

I dry myself off and find a plaster in the bathroom cabinet for my knee. The graze is minor; it's not even bleeding anymore. I'm so exhausted that my fingers shake as I do up the buttons of Jacob's pyjamas. I stroke the fabric and close my eyes, remembering the feel of the brushed cotton against my face when I'd sneak into his room at night and lay my head on his chest. How the slow rise and fall of his breathing would lull me back to sleep. I felt so secure in his arms. I really did believe him when he told me everything would be OK.

'Ah, there you are,' Iris says, beaming at me as I enter the kitchen. I'd forgotten what a lovely smile she has. She's changed her black blouse to a pink jumper and put make-up on. There's cerise lipstick on her front tooth but I don't say anything, not when she's made so much effort.

'I feel underdressed,' I say with a forced laugh.

'Nonsense. It's nice to see you in my boy's clothes. I loved those PJs. Remember what a lovely Christmas we all had together that year?'

She places the pasta in the middle of the kitchen table. It's not the dish I'd planned to make, and she hasn't added any sauce, so everything is dry. My stomach still aches, and I've lost my appetite, but I scoop some up and add it to my plate to be polite.

'Eat up. Eat up,' she says with a grin. I look away from her stained teeth and eat a mouthful of overcooked chicken. It's hard to chew and even harder to swallow, but I manage it.

'Oh, Eva! You didn't dry your hair,' she exclaims. 'It's making his pyjamas wet.'

'I... I didn't want to keep you waiting,' I stammer.

She waves me upstairs. 'Off you go. We don't want you catching a chill.'

I leave my uneaten food and return to the bathroom. There's no hairdryer in there and I don't want to go downstairs again to ask. Where did she used to keep it? Charlie had one in her room. I open her door slowly, expecting to see it exactly as it used to be when we were kids. She was a big fan of *Teen Wolf* and *Divergent*, so there were posters of Dylan O'Brien and Theo James all over her walls. But it's not Charlie's bedroom anymore; it looks like the back of a charity shop.

Where her bed once stood there are now mountains of clothes piled high. Most of them I recognise as Iris's old work clothes – smart suits and blazers that would be too big for her now, high heels and high-quality handbags. But it's not all her clothes; some are also Charlie's dating back years, as well as some of Michael's. I pick up one of his shirts and I'm struck by his scent again. Cedarwood and black pepper. His aftershave would permeate the house every morning before I left for my A levels. I started to associate the heady smell with luck, as if his expensive cologne was some kind of magical mist I could carry with me like a protective shield. Now it simply reminds me of the day everyone blamed me for Jacob's parents separating.

Stacked against Charlie's bedroom wall speckled with Blu-Tack stains are boxes marked 'school reports' and 'Michael's socks'. Why did he never return for his things? I shut the door quietly and look in the smaller room that used to be Michael's office. A chill shoots down my spine. Nothing has changed in here: the dark wooden bookshelves piled high with books on history and business, the old computer and printer, a pile of paperwork dated 2015 with a pen on top without its lid, as if he'd only just left his desk.

There's no dust in here, so Iris clearly comes in and cleans the room often. But why keep it untouched for all these years?

'I can't hear the hairdryer,' Iris calls up the stairs. I jump at the sound of her voice and quickly shut the door. 'It's in the bathroom cabinet.'

I find the hairdryer buried deep beneath some towels and dry my hair, but by the time I join Iris in the kitchen she's cleared the table and my dinner has gone.

'I'm sorry I took so long,' I say.

Iris looks sad. 'I threw the dinner away. I could see you didn't like it. I'm a terrible cook.'

'No, you're not!' I say as my stomach lets out a loud rumble. We both pretend not to hear it.

A tear runs down Iris's cheek. She rubs at her eyes, adding pink eyeshadow to her red cheeks.

'I try so hard but I never get it right,' she sobs. 'I was the perfect wife to Michael and he still left me. I was a great mother to Charlotte, and she hates me. And my boy. My boy I loved the hardest of all and he had to go and get himself killed. Why does everyone leave me, Eva? Why?'

She's leaning against the kitchen wall beside me, her head buried in her arms. I rub her back.

'Cup of tea?'

She looks up, her eyes bloodshot and her cheeks mottled and puffy. 'Would you like more of my torte?' she asks.

I really don't need any more sugar today – I'd prefer a sandwich and an early night to be honest – but I nod my head and it cheers her up.

'Jacob always liked my cakes,' she says, giving me a watery smile. 'At least that's something I got right. I baked all the time. He always had some of my cookies with milk before bed. Even as a grown man he'd watch my game shows with me as we dunked our biscuits in our hot drinks.'

She starts to cry again so I fill the kettle and take the dessert out of the fridge.

I clear up and make us drinks. Iris is happy now we have tea and cake and insists we take it back into the living room, where she switches on the TV. It's a game show. I think she only watches the game show channel.

'I've seen this one before,' she says, pointing at the screen. 'He wins a car. He's very clever, this man. He knows all about ancient Egypt.'

'Are you not having any?' I ask, pointing at the uneaten slice of torte I cut for her.

She shakes her head. 'I had some pasta while you were upstairs. I'm not hungry.'

Wait. What about the gift from Jacob she wanted to give to me? Perhaps she found it while I was gone.

'Did you find my present?' I ask. Iris looks at me blankly.

'The thing Jacob left for me.'

She waves her hand through the air. 'I'll look for it properly in the morning. It's too much for me right now. Can't you see how upset I am?'

'Sorry,' I say, trying to think of something else we can talk about that might calm her down. 'So, do you still work as an estate agent?'

She shrugs like a bored child.

'I sold the business a long time ago. It paid off the mortgage and there's still enough to live on until my pension starts. My son worked hard too. He was so good to me, making sure I never went without after his father left.'

'What did Jacob do for a living?' I ask.

It's so strange to have such a forced conversation with Iris when I was like a second daughter to her growing up. When I'd visit her house, she'd ask me what I'd been up, how I was doing at school, what my dreams and ambitions were. She was genuinely interested in me and my future, telling me I could do anything I set my mind to.

She doesn't ask me any questions this time and she doesn't answer my question either, so I change the subject.

'I heard Charlie has a little boy,' I say, smiling encouragingly. 'Henri. He looks a bit like Jacob when he was little. And she married a Frenchman. I saw a photo, he seems nice.'

Iris purses her lips. 'I wasn't invited to the wedding, you know. I found out about it from Vicky next door whose son has Charlotte on Facebook. They had a jazz band and one of those caramel-covered cream puff towers instead of a proper cake. A croc-something-or-other. Crock of shit, if you ask me. Despicable. I would have made her a fruit cake for her wedding if she'd asked, a proper English one which she could have kept for her firstborn's christening. That's Donnelly tradition. But not Charlotte. I didn't even know she'd met a man. Her father was there, though. Vicky said she could see him in the background of the photos with that harlot of a wife and their devil children. I saw them at the funeral too, don't think I didn't. The cheek of them, turning up like that. I also noticed my grandson wasn't at his uncle's funeral. God forbid he gets to meet his grandmother the day her only son is put in the ground.'

Oh no. I thought talking about Charlie was safe territory, but I was clearly wrong. Iris starts crying again. I put my arm around her, and this time she leans into me.

'Do you like my cake?' she asks though her tears.

I nod and accept the slice she hasn't touched, even though the last one I ate was so sweet it's brought my headache back.

'I'm not feeling great,' I tell her after eating a couple of mouthfuls to appease her. 'I may go and have an early night. Maybe we both should?'

She nods and I help her to her feet as she complains about her bad back and how her chest is aching.

'Broken heart,' she says as I accompany her up the stairs.

It's only once we reach the top that I realise I don't know where I'm sleeping tonight.

'I thought I'd be in Charlie's room,' I say. 'But I see it's been turned into a storeroom.'

Iris waves her hand in the air as if it's not a problem.

'Plenty of space in this house,' she says. 'Sleep in Jacob's room. I haven't had a chance to change the bedsheets since he... but I know you won't mind.'

I stay standing in the hallway as she heads to her own room. With one hand on the door handle she turns to me.

'You know where Jacob's room is, don't you? After all, you spent plenty of nights there when you thought I wasn't watching. You always were a bit of a slut, Eva Walsh.'

TWELVE

Iris shuts her bedroom door quietly and I stay rooted to the spot. What just happened? Did Iris just call me a *slut*? A wave of nausea rolls over me as my headache begins to settle over the crown of my head.

I head for Jacob's room, the whole time peering over my shoulder expecting Iris to return with either an apology or another barrage of insults, but it's all gone eerily quiet. She's upset, she misses her family, it's understandable. My being here is probably dragging up a lot from the past. Just like with her outburst in the church, I'm sure she didn't mean it. Anyway, I only have twelve more hours under her roof then I can get away from Cragstone. Forever. I can manage that.

Jacob's bedroom door is shut. I turn the handle and step inside.

His room had been forbidden to me as a child. It was one of the first things Charlie told me when I visited her house for the first time aged twelve.

'It's locked,' she told me in a frantic whisper. 'My big brother doesn't let anyone in his room while he's away at school.'

I instantly decided that Charlie's brother had to be very cool and mysterious. We'd play board games in her room and watch the Disney Channel, and while she chatted away about the boys she liked and the girls she hated, I'd be thinking about Jacob. When she wasn't looking, I'd study the framed photos of him in the living room, or when Iris shared holiday snaps with me I'd imagine what Jacob's voice sounded like or fantasise about holding his hand. For years I never told my best friend that I had a wild crush on her older brother.

Entering Jacob's bedroom is like stepping back in time. In a flash it's beginning of summer and Charlie's enigmatic brother is finally home for good now his exams are over. The window is open and the air smells of mown grass and possibility. The garden below is full of butterflies, but not as many as the ones in my stomach. That summer my mother died. It was also the summer I fell in love with Jacob Donnelly... and he fell in love with me.

I shut the door quietly behind me and walk around in the semi-darkness, draping my hand over every item. His old history textbooks are still on the shelves beside a pile of smooth white stones. I pick one up and cradle it in my hand. I always found holding the stones he gave me a comfort. Jacob's desk looks exactly the same as it did back when he'd help me with my homework, and above it is another shelf full of the Star Wars figurines he got for his ninth birthday. His father had insisted Jacob keep them in their boxes but Charlie told me he'd taken them out so he could join in with her Barbie games. Barbie and Han Solo made a cute couple, according to her brother.

I sit on his bed, smiling at the memories. Still the same single bed he had as a child, the one I lost my virginity in. It looks so small, far too small for a grown man to sleep in comfortably every night. Why didn't he get himself a bigger bed?

I climb under the covers, wearing Jacob's pyjamas, realising it's the first time I've got into this bed without him in it. I don't have a toothbrush and I'm wearing no make-up, so I don't bother washing my face. As soon as I cover myself with Jacob's duvet, the rising nausea I've been pushing down for the past few hours abates a little.

I stayed the night a lot at the Donnelly house. Charlie had one of those beds that I thought was so fancy, the kind that had a mattress underneath that you could slide out. My mother never knew nor cared where I was half the time, and at least when I stayed at Charlie's house, I knew I'd get fed. We'd lie in the dark and talk and talk, and eventually I'd get her talking about her brother. My favourite subject. Charlie called him Star Boy because he got top grades in every subject. He was also the captain of the football team, the most handsome in his class, and even raised money for charity. No one had a bad word to say about Jacob Donnelly, least of all his family.

'Why did your parents send him away to school?' I asked her one night as we lay side by side, Charlie in her bed and me on the raised mattress.

I heard the squeak of her bed as she turned to face me. 'They didn't send him away. He got a scholarship and begged to go. He was really into Harry Potter when he was younger, so he probably thought his posh boarding school would be like Hogwarts. Dad said if it was free, and he enjoyed it, they would be stupid to stand in the way of his "academic success".' She was so close to my face I could see her make inverted commas with her fingers for the last two words. 'Wales is less than two hours from here, so he wasn't that far away. Star Boy got to fly, and I stayed here.'

It was too dark to see whether she was sad, jealous or proud of her big brother.

'How come I haven't met him yet?' I asked.

She shrugged and said he was meant to come home for the holidays and on the occasional weekend, but he always begged to stay at his rich friends' houses. Sometimes they'd pay for him to go skiing or spend a week on their boat; Jacob never said no to an adventure, so Charlie didn't see as much of him as she would have liked. And that's how her brother, Star Boy, remained the untouchable guy everyone talked about at our school but no one ever got to see.

When I finally met Jacob, I was crying. Even though I'd been best friends with his sister for five years, I presumed Jacob didn't know about me. But he did. He knew everything.

My mother had hit me with an empty vodka bottle that morning and cut my lip. I'd run to Charlie's house and found myself on the Donnellys' doorstep before I knew what I was doing. Iris had tended to my cuts and bruises, her lips pursed together so tightly they'd turned white. She never said a bad word about my mother to me, but I could tell by her face what she was thinking. Michael had gone to collect their son for the Easter holidays and that's how Jacob found me, sitting on the lid of his toilet, mascara running down my cheeks and crusty blood collecting in the corners of my mouth.

'This is the last straw, Iris! We need to report it this time,' Michael had shouted, pointing at my face. 'It's getting worse and worse.'

I'd begged him not to, but Iris had said we had to do what was best for my welfare because I wasn't safe with 'that woman'. I asked if instead I could stay at their house more often – not all the time, but when things were really bad. I told them social services would take me away otherwise, and that would be so much worse. Michael and Iris went to their room to talk about it, Charlie went to her room to get my bed ready, and everyone forgot about Jacob. He hadn't even taken his coat off yet, let alone had the chance to say hello to anyone, but none of my drama fazed him. He smiled, a slow, warm smile, and opened his arms until I was resting my head on his chest. He held me. That was all. I was seventeen, he was a year older. Star Boy the wonder kid held me, the pathetic daughter of a drunk, without saying a word and that's when I knew that it didn't matter where I lived... Jacob would always be my home.

Tears are wetting my cheeks and dripping into my mouth. I curl up under the bedsheets and bury my face into his pillow, breathing deeply, imagining I can still smell him. I can't. I said goodbye to that boy a long time ago when he broke my heart and took away the last shred of trust I had left in anyone. Then I said goodbye to him all over again yesterday. I thought I'd already mourned him but being back in his room is reopening old wounds.

After that Easter, Jacob returned to school, and I stayed the night at Charlie's house at least three times a week. Her parents promised not to report my mother, and no one asked me any difficult questions. At dinner we talked about school grades, and the parties Charlie and I were invited to, and whether either of us was dating anyone... but no one mentioned my mother.

Jacob didn't ask me about her either. He graduated from school, secure in the knowledge he'd get the highest grades possible in all of his A levels, then came back for the summer. He had a way of listening that made me feel important and interesting. When I talked, he smiled encouragingly; he'd nod along to whatever I was saying, his eyes always trained on mine. He made sure I got more potatoes than him at dinner, he cut me the largest slice of cake, and he'd slow down his eating so I wouldn't be the last to finish.

Then one hot night in July, I found myself at midnight in the Donnellys' hallway, sitting on the thick carpet with my back against the wall, staring. It was the last day of term and Charlie and I had spent the afternoon running around her garden having a water fight. She'd fallen asleep early because she'd had too much sun and felt dizzy, but I couldn't sleep.

Iris and Michael were away that night, a new hotel opening out of town, and Jacob had been holed up in his room all day. He'd said he had work to do, which was a lie because school was over and I'd caught him watching us play. I'd waved up at him then dissolved into a fit of giggles as he'd ducked behind the curtain. Looking at him made me feel ill sometimes, hot and sweaty like I had a fever, even though I never spent time alone with him.

My mother was the reason I couldn't sleep. I hadn't told anyone, but she was getting worse. The colour and texture of her skin were changing, she'd shake between drinks, and there were days when it was impossible to speak to her. She'd look at me, but her gaze went right through me.

So that's how Jacob found me, curled up on the carpet with my arms wrapped around my knees. He didn't say a word as he reached down and took me by the hand, pulling me up and leading me to his bedroom. I followed. Jacob was someone everyone followed without question. He stopped at his bed, pulled the duvet cover back for me and I got in. I didn't once feel unsafe or wonder what he was doing. He climbed in behind me and opened his arms so I could rest my head on his chest, then he wrapped his arm around me and held me. That was it. He didn't say a word, his hands never left my shoulders, he just silently held me. It wasn't much, but it was everything.

I slept better that night, in his arms, than I had for years. We didn't talk in the morning either, he didn't try to save me, he just held me for as long as I needed him to. The next night I waited for Charlie to fall asleep, and I crept into her brother's room. He was still awake, waiting for me. He held me all night that night, then the next, and that's all we did for months.

That summer I turned eighteen, my mother died, and I moved in. Jacob was meant to go to uni in October, but he deferred, declaring that he wanted to do a year of charity work. He said it made more sense for him to start university at the same time as his sister. His parents, who loved finally having him home, didn't try to convince him otherwise. No one argued with Star Boy.

The truth is he stayed for me. We finally kissed three months after I moved in, although by then I was completely and utterly, madly, deeply in love with him. He told me he'd never leave me. Then eight months later, after I was forced to flee Cragstone, he did just that. He left me and never looked for me again.

I'm so lost in the memories that I don't hear the door open until I look up and Iris is silhouetted in the doorframe.

'Oh dear,' she says, approaching the narrow bed and towering over me. She reaches out and I freeze, but all she does is place the back of her hand against my forehead. 'I came to check whether you have a temperature. You said you weren't feeling well, and I thought maybe you were coming down with something.'

'I'm fine,' I mumble. 'Are you still angry with me?'

She gives a little laugh. 'Angry? Why would I be angry with you? I'm worried, that's all. I wanted to give you these.'

She places a glass of water and two large pills on the bedside table beside me.

'What are they?' I ask.

'They'll make you feel better.'

I think about what Bianca said about her being crazy, but all I've seen from Iris is kindness and grief. Since her outburst at the church she's been lovely. I probably misheard her earlier. Iris wouldn't use a word like 'slut'.

'Thank you,' I say, giving her a shaky smile and picking up the pills. I pop them in my mouth, take a sip of water and pretend to swallow them down. I don't take medication I'm not familiar with, but I don't want to appear ungrateful.

'All gone,' I say, storing the pills inside my cheek like a hamster.

Iris kisses my forehead and pulls the covers up over my chest. 'There's a good girl,' she says. 'I'm here if you need me, just shout out if you feel unwell. I promise I won't let anything bad happen to you.'

I wait until she leaves the room before I spit the pills into my hand, throw them in the bin then go to lock the door. But the lock isn't there anymore. When did Jacob take the lock off?

'Sleep well,' Iris calls out.

The last thing I'm going to do tonight is sleep well.

THIRTEEN
23 DECEMBER

I open my eyes, look around me and groan. I never thought I'd be waking up in Jacob Donnelly's bed again, let alone two days after his funeral. My legs are aching, and I think back to running in the rain yesterday and falling over. I look at my knees, peeling back the plaster. Each knee is sporting a bright purple bruise, but the graze isn't too bad.

Today is the day before Christmas Eve. Or, as Charlie and I liked to call it, Christmas Eve Eve (we watched a lot of *Friends*). It used to be her favourite day because she decided that Christmas Eve Eve would be Christmas Day for best friends. We would exchange gifts – in my case make-up I'd stolen from the local shops. I didn't like stealing, but my mother had an uncanny ability to find any money I made from babysitting and keep it for herself. Charlie, on the other hand, would buy me clothes from my favourite brands and pretend they were in the sale and that we'd both spent the same amount of money. I would always wait to be invited to Christmas Day at the Donnellys, but I never was. Not until my mother died. That was the best Christmas I ever had.

I reach blindly for my mobile phone, patting my duvet cover

and leaning over to the bedside table, before realising it's still in my handbag downstairs. Just goes to show how stressful last night was that I didn't even check my phone before I went to sleep. I stretch, every bone in my body heavy and sore.

I have no idea what the time is but it's light outside, which means it's late because this time of year it's never fully light before nine, although it may be later than that. I jump up, swearing under my breath. I have a train to catch at ten twenty-three and I need to collect my bag from the hotel first. My jeans are dry now, albeit a little muddy, so I get dressed and open the door silently so as not to wake up Iris. A faint snore comes from her room, and a ball of guilt grows in my chest that I'm going to go without saying goodbye, but I couldn't bear her begging me to stay again. I creep downstairs as quietly as I can, looking up to where there used to be a wall clock, but there's only a faint circle now. Strange. Was the clock there yesterday? I peer into the kitchen, but there's no clock in there anymore either and the one on the oven says four thirty-two, so that's definitely wrong.

My handbag is hanging up with my coat by the door. I rummage around inside. My wallet is there, so are Amanda's house keys, but no phone. Without it I have no idea what the time is, or if I'm running late, and more importantly, I have no train ticket!

OK, no need to panic. Even if I don't find my phone, I can just print the ticket from a laptop.

I search for my phone in the kitchen, on the worktops and the table, in the living room between the couch cushions where we were sitting. I definitely had it when I went to the shops – I had a shopping list typed up on my Notes app – so it must be here somewhere. Iris still has a landline, a huge beige monstrosity with an old-fashioned round dial like something from the nineteen eighties. It's been in the hallway since I was a kid; she once told me it belonged to her parents. It takes me a while to remember how to use it. I dial my mobile phone number slowly, the dial whirring back into place with each spin, then I wait for it to connect so I can listen out for the rings. It goes straight to answerphone. *For God's sake!* So I've lost my phone *and* it's run out of battery. Great. My charger is in my bag at the hotel, so even if I find my phone, I'm still unable to use it unless Iris has a charger. Maybe I took it upstairs after all. I return to Jacob's room and shut the door behind me.

There's something almost illicit about rifling through the belongings of the dead. It was the same when my mother died, sifting through her clothes and jewellery like a burglar, touching the things I wasn't allowed to go near before, seeing all her private belongings she'd saved only for herself. After she died, I kept some photos and the simple gold chain and hooped earrings she always wore, but at that point she'd sold nearly all we had for alcohol. I think back to what Amanda told me about Mario having a box of my old childhood keepsakes, my diaries, Jacob's decorated stones, old photos. I hope she ignored me and didn't tell him to throw it away.

I'm moving piles of paper around on Jacob's desk in the vain hope I'll find my phone inexplicably buried beneath them, but deep down I know it's a waste of time. It's not here. I think of Jacob's accident and the irrelevant things he must have been doing the day before he died. The days he worked that he wouldn't get paid for. Making grocery lists of items he'd never get to buy. Paying bills when the next day none of it would matter. Silly, empty and ultimately futile are the things we fill our days with and like to call 'busy'.

I swallow down another gnarly rock of grief as I scan the paperwork: hospital appointments, bank statements and handwritten notes. I peer more closely at the hospital letters. Some are results of blood tests showing that Jacob was negative for anaemia, coeliac disease and Crohn's disease. One letter says that often stomach aches can be psychological, recommending he see a therapist for underlying anxiety or stress. The date they gave him is in nine months' time. A bubble of anger erupts in my chest. Anyone who is having a difficult time mentally doesn't have the luxury of waiting that long for help. I should have got back in touch with him. I could have helped him.

I look at the handwritten notes scribbled on paper ripped out of a notebook. That's not Jacob's handwriting. It looks like Iris wrote them.

Stop ignoring me.

You're not well, son. You need a second opinion.

Please come down and eat. I promise I haven't been taking your things.

Each sheet of paper is folded down the middle, as if it's been in an envelope. I look around the room and spot a similar one on the floor by the door. I pick it up and open it.

This is getting silly now. You have to open the door and talk to me, or I'll get rid of the lock.

How bad did Jacob get that his own mother was unable to help him?

Something feels off about Jacob's death but, like trying to cup water in my hand, my thoughts are slipping and sliding, and I can't grasp any of them. I can't get my head around the image of sensible, perfect Jacob doing anything as reckless as drink driving at night. He wouldn't do that.

I rummage through the rest of the paper and notebooks on his desk. He has a large, old-fashioned desk diary open to 29 November – the day he died. He's written in each segment of that week, boring reminders like 'plumber 9am' and 'get cash out' but nothing concerning. I keep scanning the pages, past appointments and future ones, and I realise what's off. He didn't have one social engagement in there. I flick back a few more pages but most of the dates are blank, except for dark pen marks where it looks like he'd been testing to see if his biro works. Then the page before that is torn, and the one before that is covered in his writing spanning the entire page with words like 'LEAVE ME ALONE' and 'FUCK OFF' written in large capital letters, the pen having pressed so hard into the paper it left an indentation. Who was that anger directed at?

I hold my head in my hands, trying to ignore the migraine flickering at the edges of my vision. I can't think straight, and I can't miss my train. There's no way around it... I have to wake Iris up. Maybe she knows where my phone is or took it thinking it was hers. The house is so tidy she probably picked it up and put it somewhere. And even if she can't help me find it, she must have a mobile phone I can use to log into my Gmail. I can forward my confirmation email to the hotel and get them to print it out when I collect my case. Or Iris can print it out here – Michael still has a printer in his old office. Yes, that's a good plan. I'll do that.

I knock gingerly on her bedroom door, but there's no answer. Judging by the bright light outside it might be later than I thought. I don't have time to waste. I knock again and when she doesn't answer the second time, I turn the handle and step inside, my eyes trying to adjust to the semi-darkness.

'Sorry to disturb you,' I whisper.

She has an eye mask on and at the sound of my voice sits bolt upright in one swift motion. Whatever backache she had before has clearly gone.

'What? What's going on? Is it my boy? Is Jacob OK?' she mumbles.

I close my eyes, my heart sinking to my toes. She must have been in a deep sleep.

'It's me. Eva.'

She rips off her mask and stares at me, her steely-grey hair matted and standing on end. Her eyes glow black in the dusky light of the bedroom. I stay in the doorway, not wanting to intrude on her space.

'Oh, no,' she says as reality catches up with her. 'Oh, my baby. He's gone.'

She flings her covers off and climbs out of bed. She's dressed in a frilly nighty that hangs off her bony skeleton like a Victorian ghost. Ten years ago, she would never have been caught dead dressed like a grandma. She looks like my mother did at the end of her life and it fills me with a mix of sorrow and fear. She's sobbing.

'Please, leave me be,' she says, pushing the door. 'I just want to be alone.'

'Sorry I woke you up,' I shout out. 'Have you seen my phone?'

She opens the door again and steps into the hallway.

'Your phone? You woke me up for *that*?'

I flinch at the sudden change of tone.

'I really need to know what the time is, Iris. I have to catch my train soon and my ticket is on my phone.'

She gives me a long stare, her mouth set in a straight line.

'Well, that's what happens when you rely on technology, isn't it? I always said to my children that everything began to go downhill when people stopped wearing watches. I never take mine off. Your phone shouldn't be your life.'

I suppress a sigh. She's probably right but I don't have time to talk about the digital revolution.

'Have you seen it?'

She crosses her arms and leans against the doorframe.

'No.'

'OK. Well, do you have a mobile phone I can borrow, please?'

She shakes her head. 'I have a house phone. That's all I

need. If anyone needs me, they can call me at home or they know where I live.'

Right. So no phone, then. I find it hard to imagine this once savvy career woman would go from designing her own website to a simpler life, but maybe she decided to slow down once she retired.

'Do you have a laptop?' I venture.

'Of course not! The internet is poison. I was always saying to Jacob that you can't trust anything online nowadays. I wanted him to get a nice job in one of the local shops, or maybe the bank, somewhere people would be able to see his lovely face every day. But no, he insisted on working from home and staring at that blooming computer all day.'

'Jacob had a laptop!' I cry. 'Would I be able to borrow it for a minute, please?'

Iris dabs at her eyes with the same red cloth she was using yesterday. She must have taken it to bed with her.

'He had his laptop with him the day he...' She looks away. She doesn't need to finish her sentence for me to know she's talking about his accident.

'So, what you're saying is that there's no way for me to go online.'

Iris shakes her head but looks far from sorry. I've wasted valuable time running around the house and I still don't know what the time is. Wait, Iris said something about always wearing a watch. I grab her wrist and squint at the watch face. It's ten past ten. I swear under my breath. I'm too late. Even if I ran all the way to the station, I wouldn't have time to collect my luggage or buy a ticket for the ten twenty-three train in the absence of my online ticket.

'What's the matter?' Iris asks.

I swallow down the lump in my throat. 'I've missed my train home. Again.'

There has to be another one this afternoon, surely. The

website said there were two trains a day to London on weekends and one during the weekdays. Or was it the other way around? I sniff and bite down on my bottom lip. I really don't want to spend any more time in Cragstone or in this house.

'You'll have to stay for Christmas,' Iris declares triumphantly. 'As I said before, I have a food delivery arriving today. I ordered it weeks ago, before... well...' She dabs at her eyes with the dirty red cloth again. 'Turkey, pigs in blankets, all the trimmings. You have to stay!'

I really don't want to, but I can't tell Iris that.

'I don't know. I need to pick up my bag from the hotel. Maybe they can check the timetable for me. There might a train this afternoon,' I say.

Her face falls. 'Don't leave me. Everybody leaves me.'

'I'm not,' I say as kindly as I can muster, rubbing her shoulder. 'I have plans and...'

'You owe me. After what you did.'

There's no malice in her voice; she says it like it's a fact. Like we're having a casual conversation about how I ruined her life.

'What did I do? I told you... I wasn't in contact with Jacob. Him dying wasn't my fault.'

Iris's face grows harder. 'I'm talking about what you did to my family all those years ago.'

'I didn't do anything!' I cry, my voice squeaky like a young child's. 'You know the rumour Bianca spread wasn't true. I would never do such a thing!'

She didn't listen to reason back then either. She still threw me out of her home and turned her children against me.

'If you go, then I'll end it all,' Iris says, her eyes rimmed red and her chin wobbling. 'There's nothing left to live for anyway. If you don't stay for Christmas, I might do something stupid.'

And just like that I understand why Jacob never left home, and why he chose his mother over me.

FOURTEEN

It takes another hour until Iris stops crying and allows me to go back to the hotel.

'I have to get my belongings. I've not brushed my teeth in over twenty-four hours,' I say with an attempt at a playful smile.

'You could use Jacob's toothbrush. He left it behind.'

I hide my disgust and pat her on the arm. 'I'll only be an hour or so. Then I'll be back.' *To say goodbye*, I want to add. *Because I'm never returning to Cragstone again.*

'At least have a coffee before you go,' she insists, running into the kitchen and reappearing with a cafetière like the one the hotel had yesterday morning. 'I only use freshly ground beans.'

I'm tired and I'm hungry, so maybe a coffee and a biscuit will do me good. She's elated that I ask for a cookie as she still has some left from the last batch she baked. I eat and drink as fast as I can. Today is going to be another long, difficult day. They're the only kind you get in Cragstone.

. . .

It's a lot colder today than it was yesterday, and Iris made a big fuss about my borrowing a scarf. Probably so I'm forced to return it and have to see her before I leave.

I walk briskly towards the high street, my gloved hands in my pockets, head down against the relentless wind that's managing to find every exposed part of my body, biting at my ears, up my sleeves, winding its way around my ankles. A few wisps of snow have started to fall like ash from a burning building. I wrap the scarf tighter around my neck, the faint scent of cedarwood and black pepper making me wonder whether I'm wearing one of Michael's old scarves. Did he take *any* of his belongings with him? Or was he so desperate to leave that he started afresh in every way?

It's a Saturday and the high street is busier than I've seen it since I got here, with locals getting the last of their Christmas presents before everything shuts. There's a queue outside the toy shop and the supermarket has no trolleys left outside. I won't be going back in there. The last person I need to see right now is Bianca.

I feel a tap on my shoulder, and I spin around with a gasp. It's not her though, thank God. It's a postman. He whips off his woolly hat and I try to keep the expression on my face as neutral as possible when I realise who it is.

'Harry!' I say, forcing my lips into a smile.

He smiles at me sheepishly, his cheeks ruddy from the cold and his eyes the colour of glaciers.

'I thought you'd be long gone by now,' he says.

'So did I. I missed my train. I didn't know you were a postman,' I add lamely. Why would I know what his job is? Why am I initiating small talk?

He pats his bright red satchel proudly.

'Been doing this job since I left school. Keeps me fit. Hey, listen. I don't suppose you've seen Bianca today, have you?'

'No,' I say. I don't add the *thank God* I'm thinking.

'Strange, because she didn't turn up for work this morning and no one can get a hold of her.'

'I saw her at Sainsbury's yesterday,' I say. 'Around five in the evening.'

Harry's face is so pale his freckles make him look like he's been splattered with paint. 'She hasn't been seen since. She was meant to go to Orla's house last night.'

'Oh,' I reply because I don't know what else he's expecting me to say.

'I don't suppose you saw anything strange in town after you spoke to her last night?'

A slow, creeping dread washes over me and I tighten my scarf around my neck, but it does nothing to warm me up. Do I tell him about the person in the hood? The man I thought called out my name? I don't know if there's any point. Nothing actually happened and I wouldn't be able to give a description of their face anyway.

'Isn't Bianca's brother a policeman?' I ask.

Harry rolls his eyes, as if that makes any difference. 'Yes, but he's useless. He said they've already checked nearby CCTV but they didn't see anything unusual. Anyhoo...' He claps his bright pink hands together. 'I'm sure she's fine!'

I nod along, looking around me, waiting for him to say goodbye. His thick hi-vis coat looks warm but he's wearing no gloves and long shorts. Why is there always that one guy, no matter the weather, who loves to wear shorts?

Harry remains beside me, staring at me, waiting for me to keep the conversation flowing. I need to make an excuse to get away, tell him I'm on my way to catch another train or something.

'Sorry about Thursday,' he says after a few more seconds of silence.

It takes me a moment to realise he's talking about the

funeral, and the whisky, and possibly the fact he was being mean while also awkwardly trying to hug me.

'It's fine,' I say quietly. 'It was a tough day for everyone.'

The snow has started to fall faster. I rub my hands together, thankful I'm wearing gloves, and blow into them for warmth. In the awkward silence, Harry's comment about Bianca is nagging at me. I should report what I saw last night. Maybe I should tell Ryan, Bianca's brother, about the hooded man. I'll get his number from the receptionist at the hotel.

'I had a killer hangover yesterday,' Harry finally says.

My legs are growing numb from the cold and my knees are still stinging from my fall yesterday.

'Me too,' I reply. 'I stayed at Iris's, but I'm hoping to get back home today.'

If you'll let me!

'You were at Jacob's house?' Harry exclaims. 'Wow. I didn't expect that. Iris hates you.'

Hate? That's a bit strong. Don't let the truth stand in the way of manners, Harry.

'Well, that's all water under the bridge,' I reply. 'We're fine now. It was just a stupid childhood rumour that got out of hand.'

'No, I mean what she said in the church. Blaming you for Jacob's death.'

Right. So everyone heard everything, then.

'She was just upset,' I say. 'She's been lovely to me since.'

I'm not being entirely honest, but I don't need to add fuel to the fire. I cover my mouth with my hand, my gloves cold and damp against my lips. I feel like I'm going to be sick.

'You know she's not the only one who thinks Jacob died because of you.'

'Because of *what?*' I explode. 'What am I being accused of exactly?'

'Because you were in touch with Jacob, and he was on his way to see you when he died.'

'No, he wasn't!' I shout. 'And if he was, I knew nothing about it.' I can feel tears gathering in my eyes. I bat them away angrily with the back of my sleeve. 'I don't understand why everyone in this town thinks I'm a liar. Why do they all hate me so much?'

Harry shrugs. 'Because you broke up Iris and Michael's marriage,' he says under his breath.

An icy puddle forms in the base of my stomach. That one lie ripped a family apart and ruined my life. And now, a decade later, I can't believe everyone is still talking about it.

'You know full well the rumour Bianca spread was fake!'

Harry raises his eyebrows at my outburst.

'Bianca saw you kissing Jacob's dad. She even took a photo.'

'She saw him kiss someone who *looked* like me. But it *wasn't* me, it was Amelie, the woman he ended up marrying. You've seen her. She looks exactly the same as me from behind, same hair and height and everything. Except she was an adult, and I was barely eighteen. Yet you all chose to believe Bianca over me and treated me terribly!'

'You weren't the only victim, Eva. Imagine how Charlie felt hearing her best friend was having an affair with her dad, and Jacob knowing his creepy dad had a thing for his girl.'

'*But he didn't!*' I cry out. 'Michael confessed about his affair with Amelie and once everyone saw what the other woman looked like, they knew I wasn't lying.'

Harry makes a face and I shove his shoulder.

'For God's sake, Harry, Michael isn't a pervert! He was like a dad to me.'

'Even if it wasn't true, that kiss destroyed the Donnellys' marriage.'

I rub my face, my stomach spasming so hard I have to lean

forward. It will never matter what I say: Cragstone never forgets. But Harry hasn't finished yet.

'I don't know why you still have anything to do with that family,' he says, sorting through his satchel and picking out a selection of envelopes. I follow him as he turns into a side road and walks up the garden path, popping them through the letter box.

'I *don't* have anything to do with them,' I say for the hundredth time on this godforsaken trip back to hell. 'I haven't returned to Cragstone since Jacob broke up with me.'

Harry makes a dismissive face again and I keep following him door to door.

'What?' I say, shoving his arm lightly again to get his attention.

'I saw the photos, Eva,' he says. 'It's hard to believe anything you say when Jacob showed me proof that the two of you were back in touch.'

I recoil at his ridiculous statement. 'What do you mean?'

Harry stops in the middle of the pavement and turns to face me. 'Just stop lying. I saw the photos. Jacob showed me. He showed a lot of people.'

'*What photos?*'

'The ones you sent him of you. Oh, come on, no need to look so shocked. It doesn't matter now, anyway, I guess.'

Yes, it does!

It all matters. It's bad enough they didn't believe it wasn't me in the photo of Michael cheating on his wife, but this time I don't even know what photos Harry is talking about. I grab him by the arm and force him to look at me.

'Whatever photos Jacob showed you of me, I didn't send them,' I say. 'How do you know Jacob wasn't making stuff up?'

Harry looks down at the floor, making circles in the snow with the tip of his trainers.

'Maybe you're right. Jacob wasn't doing very well,' he says.

'Anyway, I have to get going. I need to ask more people about Bianca.'

Harry turns to leave but I reach out for him, making him slip on the icy pavement. He rights himself and I let go.

'Please, tell me what the hell is going on. I need to know, Harry! What do you mean Jacob wasn't doing well?'

I think about what I saw in Jacob's room. The folded-up messages of concern from his mother. The frantically scribbled notes of desperation in his diary. Was Jacob depressed? Was he... suicidal?

'He wasn't well,' Harry says, his gaze fixed on the shapes his feet are making in the newly settled snow. 'And I don't just mean the strange stomach aches he had or all those hospital trips. He wasn't a happy bunny. Bit gone in the head, in my opinion.'

'You mean he was struggling mentally? How?'

Harry shrugs, his ears now as red and sore-looking as his frostbitten cheeks. 'I'm always out and about, with my job. I see and hear things. Sometimes I'd see Jacob early in the morning sitting on a wall or a bench staring into space. Sometimes he was drinking too. A bit like us two the other night, knocking back booze like a couple of cute lovesick teenagers.' He laughs lightly but I don't join in. There was nothing 'cute' about sitting on a damp wall, eating soggy chips with Harry. 'We all love a bit of whisky in these parts.'

Jacob didn't. Jacob hated whisky. Harry doesn't know what he's talking about.

'Do you think he was unhappy?' I ask.

'I know he was. Iris has always looked after him, she's a great mother, but you can't blame the guy. First you left for London and broke his heart...'

I didn't break his heart. He *dumped* me *after I left!* I want to scream, but Harry is still counting on his fingers.

'... then his dad and sister left home, then he broke up with Bianca, and then you started leading him on.'

I let the last ridiculous comment slide because I want to know more about Jacob's mental state.

'Why did he turn to drink?' I ask. 'Jacob was the calmest, happiest, healthiest guy I knew.'

'Probably the meds,' Harry says with a shrug.

'What medication? How do you know all of this?'

He shifts uncomfortably and takes another bundle of letters from his bag. 'I've said too much. I hold a position of trust and authority as a postman; I can't discuss the things I see or the letters I deliver to people. I'm just saying he got a lot of post from the hospital and packages from health food companies. Iris did her best to keep him well, but it made no difference. She really did spoil her little prince. Now look where all that fussing got her... nowhere. Anyway, I must get on now.'

'Of course,' I mumble. 'I hope you find Bianca.'

'What? Oh, yeah. I'm sure she's fine,' he says, still standing there.

'Bye then, see you around,' I say, hoping I can turn around now.

I can't. Harry's eyes have lit up and he's taking a step towards me. 'Wait. Are you staying here for Christmas?'

I supress a sigh. I bloody well hope not.

'I don't know. Why?'

'A group of us are meeting at the pub tomorrow evening,' he says, pulling his woolly hat back on. 'We always meet up Christmas Eve. Want to join us?'

I can't think of anything worse, but I nod along anyway. Harry looks happy with himself and holds up a bright pink hand to wave goodbye as if he hasn't just delivered a massive blow to me along with his festive post.

I turn on my heels and head back to the hotel, the entire

time thinking about Bianca and the hooded man and these so-called photos I was meant to have sent Jacob. What does everyone in Cragstone think they know about me? What lies are they all believing now?

FIFTEEN

Orla jumps up and squeals my name as I enter the hotel.

'I'm so happy to see you!' she says, running around the reception desk and giving me a big hug.

I pat her back but she's one of those people who hugs for at least five seconds too long and after a while I have to let my hands drop to my sides until she stops.

'We've been so worried. Did you hear about Bianca? No one has seen her since her shift finished at six last night and then you didn't get your bag yesterday. When I saw it was still here this morning, I started imagining the worst!'

'I stayed the night at Iris's,' I tell her as I unwrap my scarf and undo my coat. It's so stuffy in here and my head is starting to ache again.

'I heard. Kitty, who lives around the corner from Iris Donnelly – you don't know her, she's one of our cleaners – she told me this morning that she saw you going into the Donnelly house with shopping last night. I couldn't believe it. So I checked the trains today, and I thought to myself, "Don't worry, Orla. She'll be back for the bag in the morning," because your train was at ten twenty-three this morning, yet here you are, five minutes to one. I'm so confused. I nearly went over to Mrs Donnelly's house myself with your rucksack. But thank goodness you are all right. I'm waiting for Steve to call me back; Bianca's brothers are insane with worry but I'm sure Ryan will track her down.'

I don't know if it's the heat from the open fire, the instrumental rendition of 'Jingle Bells' that's playing through the speakers or Orla's high-pitched voice, but another wave of nausea hits me and I have to grasp the edge of the reception desk to stop my knees from buckling beneath me. I really hope I haven't caught the flu.

'Can I have a glass of water, please?'

Orla looks at me properly for the first time since I walked in and lays her hand upon mine. 'You look ever so peaky. Not pregnant, are you?'

She finds that comment extremely funny and laughs as she heads for the kitchen. Why do people think pregnancy is something to joke about? She doesn't know me well enough to joke about that. She has no idea how all I've ever wanted was a big family, and now I'm no longer with Mario I'll probably never get that. Anyway, I had my period last week, I'm definitely not pregnant.

'I'm just stressed. I missed my train,' I say, taking a sip of the water she's handed me. 'I overslept and couldn't find my phone this morning, so I was too late to catch my train. The entire day has been a disaster, to be honest.'

Orla is now standing behind the desk, nodding like a little dog on a car dashboard.

'How's Jacob's mum doing?' she asks. 'I heard she's gone a bit mental, but I don't like to gossip.'

I doubt that.

'Mental how?' I ask.

'I'm just saying what I heard,' Orla replies, holding her hands up in surrender. 'Bianca told me that Jacob told her that his mother was controlling and always guilt-tripping him. Bianca is adamant that's why he dumped her and didn't join her in Scotland. You have no idea how loved up they were.'

I don't want to know how loved up my dead ex-boyfriend and my childhood enemy were, thank you very much.

Bianca thinks Iris is crazy, and Harry thinks Jacob was crazy... maybe this whole town is crazy. I wish everyone would mind their own bloody business. I'm coming down with something and I have neither the time nor energy to yet again be the antagonist in Cragstone's latest drama. Which reminds me...

'I saw someone acting strangely last night. Would I be able to call Ryan on your phone?' I ask.

Orla's brow creases with curiosity. 'Give me your mobile and I'll put his number in it for you.'

'I still haven't found my phone.'

'Oh dear. I'm sure it will turn up.'

Orla dials a number on the hotel phone, listens while it rings, then holds it out to me. 'It's Ryan's answerphone. Tell him what you saw.'

I'm not prepared. I don't know what to say that doesn't make me sound stupid.

'Errr, hi, Ryan. It's Eva. Eva Walsh. You don't know me, I came back for Jacob's funeral... Anyway, I saw a man in a hood. I think it was a man. Last night, around five thirty-ish, after I left Sainsbury's. That's when I last saw Bianca, your sister, and afterwards I saw a man in the street acting a bit shady. I don't know if that's helpful. Sorry. Err, bye then.'

Orla looks at me like I just passed wind in public, and I can feel the heat rising in my cheeks. I drink the last of the lukewarm tap water she gave me.

'Oh,' she cries. 'I meant to say, you got a phone call yesterday after you left for Mrs Donnelly's house. From a man.'

My stomach lurches. The only man who knows I was staying at this hotel is Michael, but Orla would have mentioned him by name. Unless... My hands start to sweat, and I grip my empty glass of water tighter to stop it slipping out of my grasp.

'Did he leave his name?'

Orla consults the Post-it notes on her desk and picks one up. 'Mario Florentine? Florentina?'

My stomach spasms again and I clench my teeth together, swallowing down the saliva filling my mouth.

'What did he want?'

She shrugs. 'He was looking for you. I said you'd checked out and were going back to London yesterday afternoon, because I thought you were, then he hung up. Did I do something wrong?'

'No,' I say. 'You did everything right.'

I'm going to vomit and my arms and legs are beginning to feel heavy. My chest is getting tight and I'm struggling to take a deep breath, I'm definitely coming down with some kind of flu. I just want to leave this town once and for all, but what if Mario is waiting for me to turn up at Amanda's? He knows where she lives – he's dropped her off when we've had nights out before. She said he was accusing me of having cheated on him with Jacob. It makes no sense. Has someone been spreading lies about me here *and* to my ex? I can't go back to Amanda's house. I'll have to go straight to her mum's instead.

'Could you do me a favour please?' I ask Orla, leaning against the reception desk and focusing on my breaths. 'Could you check when the next train leaves for London? Without my phone I'm a bit lost.'

Orla gives me a beaming smile and I wonder how bored she must get in this job. She's a naturally helpful, chatty person, yet the only time I've seen anyone in this hotel was that family checking in yesterday.

'Of course! But the train station is closed now,' she says, still smiling.

'What do you mean?'

'No trains.' She taps away at her keyboard and turns the computer screen towards me. 'See? This morning's train was the last one. No more until Wednesday the twenty-seventh.'

I put down my glass and grip the edge of her desk, my legs weakening beneath me. That's four days away. That can't be right. I can't stay here one more night, let alone four!

'Are there trains to anywhere else?' I ask. 'I don't mind changing.'

Orla shakes her head. 'No trains anywhere. It's Christmas, Eva!'

I know it's Christmas, Orla! Shit shit shit!

I rub my face, swallowing down the acid climbing up my throat.

'How about a taxi?' I ask.

She laughs. 'To London? That would take over five hours. Even more so in Christmas traffic.'

'I don't care. Call the taxi company. Please?'

She shakes her head again. 'I'm sorry, Eva. But Cragstone Cabs is shut for Christmas.'

If she says the word 'Christmas' one more time I'm going to scream.

'How can a taxi company be closed?' I shout. 'This is literally the one time of year everyone goes out and gets drunk and needs a taxi home!'

Her eyes widen at my outburst, and she shrugs again. 'Ali and Ian are the only drivers in Cragstone, and they like to be home with their families this time of year. Ian's daughter is dating Ryan, actually. You know Ryan, Bianca's brother, the policeman you just left the message for. At least they were dating the last time I checked, but Ryan's a very private person, so I don't have the latest.'

Oh my God. I don't care. I don't care about the love life of a man I don't know.

I can't take this town one more bloody second.

'What about an Uber, then?'

Orla makes a face.

'What?' I say, doing my best to keep my voice steady. 'Ubers come out to Cragstone, don't they?'

'But you can't book one without your phone, Eva.'

For crying out loud!

'Right. Yes. Can you take a look at costs on *your* Uber account, please, Orla, if you have one? If you book it, maybe I can transfer the money to you. I need to get back to London.'

She appears dubious but looks it up anyway. 'It says here it will cost you five hundred and twenty-six pounds. I don't have that much in my account to book it and I don't think they take cash.'

I sigh. I don't have a spare £526 anyway... but neither do I want to stay at Iris's house for another four nights.

'I might be able to get you a hire car,' Orla says. 'I don't mind dropping you off at Leighbury – you can rent them from a place there. Fiveacres has a rental car company too, I think.'

'I can't drive.' She raises her eyebrows in surprise.

Why did I never get my licence? I've never needed a car in London, that's why! 'I'll just book a room here until the twenty-seventh.'

I might just about survive Christmas if I'm on my own with movies and takeaways for company. The Black Lion doesn't charge a lot per night – I can put it on my credit card. It will still be cheaper than a taxi home at any rate.

Orla shakes her head again. 'Sorry, but we're fully booked until the second of January. Christmas is our busiest time of year,' she says.

How can it be their busiest time of year when I never see anyone here?

I want to bang my dizzy head against the hotel's exposed brickwork wall adorned with tinsel and fake mistletoe.

'I'm sure Iris will be happy to have you a few more nights,'

Orla adds, like she's just had a bright idea. 'I know she can be a bit... up and down, at times, but she could probably do with the company.'

I nod silently as Orla's chattering voice grows far away, like my head is under the bath water again. How can this be happening? I planned to come here for one short church service and now I'm trapped back in my past over Christmas, surrounded by people who hate me.

My mouth feels like it's stuffed with cotton wool, making it difficult to speak. I go to take another sip of water, but the glass is empty. 'Yes,' I hear myself saying. 'It's fine. I'll have a lovely time with Iris. It's not a problem. I'm lucky to have somewhere to stay.'

Orla hands me my rucksack. I don't want to go back to Iris's house. I don't want to sleep in Jacob's bed again tonight, surrounded by all the things that made him want to die.

I head for the door, but Orla calls out my name. She's tottering over to me while holding an envelope out. 'Crikey, I did it again. I nearly forgot to give you this!'

'What is it?'

'A card.'

'Oh, thank you.' She's giving me a Christmas card. That's nice. I don't know anyone who gives out Christmas cards anymore. 'Sorry. I don't have one for you.'

She laughs. 'Oh no, silly. I sent my Christmas cards out weeks ago. If I'd have known you'd be here, I would have written one out for you too, but this one isn't from me. I found it on the desk earlier with your name and room number on it.'

'Who's it from?'

'Goodness, I don't know. I didn't open it. It feels like a Christmas card.'

Who, other than Orla, knows what hotel room I was staying in?

I hover by the hotel exit, waiting for her to walk away, but she continues to stand there.

'Merry Christmas, then,' I say.

'Oh. Right. Yes. Merry Christmas.'

'And I hope you track down Bianca,' I add, my hand on the door handle so Orla takes the hint. 'I'm sure she's fine.'

'Yes. Of course. Her brother is on the case, and he will have received your message, so I'm sure he'll get to the bottom of it.' She hovers for a moment, takes a deep breath and keeps talking. 'I was thinking... and feel free to say no... but now that you're staying a little longer, would you like to join us at the pub tomorrow night? It should be fun. We always meet up Christmas Eve. The whole gang.'

Why is everyone obsessed with me joining them at the pub tomorrow? Shouldn't they all be out there looking for Bianca? The hotel phone starts ringing, and Orla runs over, giving me the opportunity to open the envelope unwatched. I pull out the card but it's not a Christmas card; it's a postcard of Cragstone's market square. I turn it over. Something has been handwritten on the back in big, black capital letters.

NOW YOU'RE BACK I'M GOING TO MAKE SURE YOU NEVER LEAVE

A shooting pain grips my belly again and my hand shoots to my mouth, but my stomach is too empty for me to vomit. I look around me, as if whoever sent this might be hiding behind the yucca plant or the sofa in reception. Is this a threat? What do they mean by 'never leave'? It's too hot in here with that open fire. My underarms have grown sticky and clammy. I pull at the neck of my jumper and wipe my hands on my jeans, but it doesn't help. I need some fresh air.

'Everything OK?' Orla calls out from behind the desk.

'Yes. All good.'

Do I say something? Maybe the person watching me sent me this? Maybe they have something to do with Bianca's disappearance? I don't even like Bianca, but I seem to be the only one concerned that she's been missing since yesterday.

I push the door of the hotel open, savouring the gust of fresh air flowing through the gap, but Orla is still talking.

'That was Iris on the phone,' she calls out. 'She was checking you were OK because you were taking a long time. I explained you were on your way back to hers because there are no trains. She's ever so happy you're staying for Christmas.'

'Thank you,' I mutter, turning back to the exit and forcing one foot in front of the other. This can't be happening. My throat is closing up. I can't breathe. The snow is falling faster now and it's hard to see. I gulp down the frigid air; it helps my head clear a little but not enough. The snow has settled on the pavement, walls and benches, making every sound soft and muffled. The streets are emptying, people rushing home to start their preparations for a family Christmas. I can't do it. I don't want to go back to Iris and that house and her constant cakes and biscuits.

I start to walk, wishing there was somewhere else to go. A figure in the distance emerges from the white mist, walking towards me. I swing my backpack on to my shoulders, but it feels like I'm carrying a sack of rocks, weighing me down, making it impossible to push through the flurry. I try to speed up, but the person is getting closer. They have something in their hand. What are they holding?

I want to run, but another shooting pain darts through my guts, making me double up, my knees still stinging from falling over yesterday.

'Fuck off!' I shout. 'Leave me alone.'

They're getting closer. I shrug my bag off my shoulders and hold it up in front of me, as if it will protect me from a knife or a gun or a punch in the head. But when I look up all I see is Harry's pale face, and in his fist is a handful of post.

'Only me,' he sing-songs. 'Sorry to startle you. Orla just told me the good news, so I wanted to say hurrah! You're staying! We'll see you at the pub tomorrow then, yes?'

I swing my bag back on to one shoulder, but I can't speak. I don't know what to say. All I can think about is that Bianca is missing and I just received a threatening postcard... in an envelope just like the ones Harry is holding.

SIXTEEN

It takes me double the time to walk back to the Donnelly residence as it did to get to the hotel from there. The snow is relentless and blinding and the ground slippery, forcing me to shuffle so I don't slip. When I look behind me, I've left a trail like a snail. If anyone wanted to follow me, then I've just made their job a damn sight easier. I've lost all feeling in both hands and my breaths are coming in sharp wheezes, although whether that's from my impending flu or the freezing temperatures I don't know.

As usual the high street is half empty, the doors closed even though the shop windows still twinkle with Christmas decorations. The only movement is a queue forming outside the fish and chip shop. It's the perfect weather for hot chips and battered cod.

I keep my head bowed as I walk past people shifting from foot to foot in the snow, hoping there's no one there I know. The windows are steamed up and through them I can see three women wearing hats, rolling up fish and battered sausages in white paper. It's gone lunchtime and my stomach is growling. If I eat something substantial I might feel less jittery. I peer through the doorway and check out the prices above everyone's heads.

'There's a queue,' a man in overalls shouts out.

'I'm just looking.'

One of the women behind the counter stops what she's doing and glares at me, mid-roll. I notice she only has three fingers on one hand.

'I know you. You're that Eva girl,' she says, pointing at the door. 'Out!'

Everyone turns to stare at me. I tighten my now damp scarf around my neck and scurry back into the cold. What did I do?

Ten minutes later I'm trying to gather myself on Iris's doorstep before knocking, but she must have been eagerly awaiting me because she swings the front door open and ushers me in.

'Come along,' she says, taking the rucksack off me and pulling at my woollen coat. 'My, my, you really should have brought a thicker coat with you. Looks like we're getting that white Christmas after all. Oh, Eva, I'm so happy you're staying a few more days. The food delivery arrived while you were out, and I have some lovely treats for us. It's going to be a magical Christmas!'

Iris is out of her pyjamas and dressed in a loose green dress with matching eye shadow. She's even washed her hair and styled it neatly. She pulls me into the kitchen, sitting me at the table.

'How are you feeling?' she asks, taking a thermometer out of its case. 'Orla told me you were under the weather. Do you think it's the flu? It might be. Vicky next door had it last week. Nasty business.'

I don't have a chance to answer before she's sticking the thermometer in my mouth.

'Now, you're not on one of those silly diets are you? Only that I ordered lots of stuffing and pigs in blankets.' She dabs at her eyes with the ratty red cloth she's always carrying around with her and takes a long sniff. 'Jacob loved sausages.'

'I'll eat anything.'

'How about some of my biscuits?' she says.

'No, thank you. I'm feeling a bit queasy and—'

'Nonsense. You must be famished,' she says, placing some cookies on a plate before me. She opens the fridge and takes out some butter and ham. She wasn't lying. Even from here I can see the fridge is groaning with food. As she busies herself making me a sandwich I didn't ask for, I think about the postcard Orla gave me. It had scenes of Cragstone on one side and writing I didn't recognise on the other. But it was the message that won't stop haunting me: *I'm going to make sure you never leave.* Is that a threat, a promise or someone's desire? Who would have sent that? What do they want with me?

'Bianca Clarke is missing,' I say to Iris.

'I don't know a Bianca.'

'Jacob dated her.'

Iris has her back to me, but I see her stiffen, the buttersmeared knife hovering in mid-air. 'She was a slut,' she says in a monotone voice.

That's what Iris called me last night. Slut. So I wasn't imagining it. Is that what she thinks of all her son's girlfriends? Harry said Jacob showed him photos of me. Maybe I have a fever and I'm overthinking this, but it all seems to be connected – the postcard, the funeral text, the photos, the man in the hood and Bianca going missing. I don't know what any of this means, but I do know Jacob's death was not a straightforward accident. He was on his way to see me, and for some reason everyone thinks we were in touch. Whoever sent the postcards and text doesn't want me to work out the truth!

'... and I do like to watch the King's speech after lunch.' I didn't realise Iris was still talking. 'They always show such good films Christmas evening. Ooh, I'll have to crack open the fancy chocolates.'

I haven't been listening to a word she's saying.

'Here you go, love,' she says, placing the sandwich before me. My stomach contracts but I don't know if it's hunger, nausea or good old-fashioned dread. How am I expected to sit here, planning my Christmas Day TV viewing, when someone nearby is out to get me? Maybe not just me... maybe they've already found their latest victim.

'I don't feel well,' I say. 'I should go and unpack my things and rest for a bit.'

There's nothing to unpack. All I have is the funeral outfit that's too formal to wear anywhere else and the jumper and jeans I'm wearing right now. I guess I'll be in the same outfit for the next four days. Good job I brought extra underwear.

'You're being very rude,' Iris says.

The change in her tone makes me look up.

'Thank you for the sandwich,' I say. 'I really appreciate it, and the fact you're letting me stay. I just feel a little weak right now.'

'Don't leave me on my own. Please.' She's sitting in the chair opposite me, staring at her hands as she twists that red rag of hers into a rope. She uses it to dab at her eyes again. 'I started to believe Jacob when he said you'd changed and that you were a good person again.'

'He talked to you about me?' I say, taking a bite of my sandwich to show Iris my gratitude for my lunch. It turns to wet cardboard in my mouth and takes me three goes until I'm able to swallow it. I need to understand what Jacob knew, or thought he knew, about me before he died. 'What did Jacob tell you?'

'What do you care?' she snaps.

I'm not rising to the bait.

'I care a lot. I really did love him,' I tell her. 'Back when we were kids. I need you to know that. He broke my heart when he split up with me. I'd thought we'd be together forever.'

Iris looks up at me, her eyes bloodshot and her eyeliner so smudged her eyes look like dark empty sockets in a cracked skull.

'I'm not talking about ten years ago. I'm talking about your secret love affair!' she spits. 'Jacob tried to hide it from me at first, but I know my boy better than he knows himself. He can't keep anything from his mama.'

She keeps slipping into present tense, but that's not the part that's disturbing me.

'What love affair?' I ask, my voice wavering.

Iris heaves herself out of the chair and takes something out of a drawer, slapping it on to the table. It's a photo. A photo of me. I slide it along the table towards me. I recognise the image: it's a close-up of the photo my work took of me for their website. The same image I use on LinkedIn. It's been cropped so it's just my face. I turn it over, and in handwriting not dissimilar to mine it says, 'To my darling Jacob, I can't wait to see you soon. I love you so much!'

'That's not me,' I say, pushing the photo away from me. 'I mean, the photo is of me, but it's been taken from the internet. I never sent that to anyone and that's not my writing on the back.'

'Liar!' Iris shouts, using the dirty rag to wipe her face again. 'He told me everything. It's not the only picture. Look!'

She hands me another one. This time it's me standing in front of the Eiffel Tower. Except it's not me because it's the same face from the LinkedIn photo, superimposed on to someone else's body. On the back is more writing. This time it says, 'Next time it will be me and you in France. Together. I'll always be yours xx.'

My mouth fills with saliva and I swallow it down, pulling my collar away from my neck. Someone is making photos of me and forging my writing. I take a deep breath but no air is going into my lungs.

'That's not me either,' I stammer.

'Do you think I'm blind or stupid?' she shouts, jabbing the photo with her finger. She's bitten her fingernails down further, the edges of their beds now red and bloody. 'I can see it's you. You're just like his sister, making up lies and trying to get him to run away. Well, you succeeded in the end, didn't you? If he hadn't been on his way to see you, he'd never have crashed his car.'

I scrape the chair back as I jump to my feet. 'How many times do I have to tell you? I never saw or spoke to Jacob again after he left me all those years ago. I've never been to France, let alone Paris. That is definitely not me. It's not even a good Photoshop job. Look!' I point at the face in the photo. 'It's the same face as the other picture.'

'Of course it's the same face. Wavy brown hair, green eyes, little impish nose. *Your* face,' Iris exclaims. She points a finger at me, her jagged nail so close that it scrapes the tip of my nose. 'You're nothing but trouble, Eva Walsh. First you broke up my marriage and then you killed my boy!'

SEVENTEEN

I should never have returned to Cragstone. I wish I knew who sent me that text about the funeral because whoever it was has created utter chaos. I want to storm out of this house, tell Iris to fuck herself and never return to this terrible town ever again – but I can't because I have nowhere else to go. I'm out of options. I have to stay silent, stay calm and stay put.

'Where did you find the photos?' I ask gently, trying not to escalate things.

Iris sniffs and looks away like a petulant teenager. I close my eyes and count to three.

'Iris?'

'I found them in Jacob's jacket pocket the week before the accident. He tried to deny it at first – he knew I didn't trust you. But he told me everything eventually.'

He knew I didn't trust you? How can this woman harbour a ten-year grudge over something I didn't do? It's *Michael* she should hate for cheating on her, not me for having the same bloody hair colour as his new wife!

'What did Jacob tell you?' I ask.

'That he was in love with you.'

A pain in my chest blooms bloody, like someone has punched me in the heart. Jacob was in love with me? As in... recently? I've thought about Jacob nearly every day since I left this dreadful place. I was too scared to get in touch with him after he finished with me; I couldn't bear to be rejected a second time. The year we were together defined my life and I never let him go. Not fully. Even years after we broke up, every time I cried, I imagined Jacob holding me. Every time something good happened, he was the first person I wanted to tell. Sometimes I talked to him in my head, sought his opinion, told him my dreams and my fears before going to sleep at night. And now his mother is saying he loved me all this time too.

When Mario proposed to me, Jacob was the first person I thought of. Mario took me to Mauritius; it was the talk of the office. The lowly interiors buyer snagged the boss's son. We'd been dating a year and I'd already moved in with him. I really had it all back then: the handsome man, a job I loved, a beautiful home we shared. Then on the last night of our holiday, as the neon sun began to melt over the sparkling waves, Mario and I walked to the end of the jetty, where he got on one knee and presented me with a two-carat diamond ring from Tiffany's. It was what Instagram dreams are made of. Yet all I could think about was Jacob. It wasn't the waves I could hear lapping beneath us or the call of the parakeets as they flew overhead, but my ex-boyfriend's voice echoing the words he used to tell me as we lay curled up together in his single bed. *When I ask you to marry me the engagement ring will be white gold, because you only wear silver, and it will have a stone the same colour as your eyes when the sun is shining. And I'll propose somewhere special. Not some cheesy beach at sunset but a private place known only to us. Somewhere you can return to time and time again because it will be the place where you said yes to our forever together.*

I looked at the gold ring Mario was holding out to me, which probably cost double what I made in a year, yet I yearned for something different. This handsome, successful man was presenting me with the perfect future yet all I could think about was my past and everything I'd lost.

'So is that a yes?' Mario asked. 'My knee is hurting.'

I nodded and jumped up and down, and he swung me around, smiling at the camera I hadn't realised he'd propped up against the railings. Ten minutes later strangers on his TikTok account were commenting how happy they were for us, and women I didn't know said they were jealous, and men told him he was smart to 'snap her up' and all the time I could hear Jacob laughing at me, saying, *What the hell are you doing, Eva? This isn't you. These are the losers we used to laugh at.*

'Jacob told you he was in love with *me*?' I say to Iris. 'After all this time?'

She nods, solemnly. 'He never stopped loving you.'

'But he dated Bianca.'

She scoffs. 'So? She was nothing. He never stopped talking about how you broke his heart.'

'How did I break his heart?'

'By leaving.'

I didn't leave Cragstone because of Jacob. I left because Iris and everyone else drove me out of town. He was meant to follow me... not break up with me.

'I went to university!' I cry. 'Jacob was meant to go to Oxford, and we were going to keep dating. That was the plan. Then *he* dumped *me*. But what does any of that have to do with these photos?'

'Everything!' Iris shouts in my face, making me flinch. 'My boy was weak. Weak of body, mind and heart. As soon as you left, he started to get those awful stomach aches and dizzy spells. He was once bedridden with migraines so strong he couldn't see for days. And where were you, Eva? Where were his father and sister? Nowhere. It was *me* who cared for him, *me* who made sure he went to the doctors and drove him to his hospital appointments. Everything was going so well until a year ago when he started to act peculiar. And that's when your little tryst must have begun.' She holds up a photo, pushing it into my face. 'That's when you started sending him these!'

This conversation is going nowhere. Iris will never believe that I haven't spoken to her son for ten years, the same way she refuses to believe I had nothing to do with Michael cheating on her.

She's gnawing on her stubby fingers, pulling at the hangnail on her right thumb and making it bleed. 'This isn't doing my heart palpitations any good,' she says with a shaky voice. 'I need my tablets.'

She waves her hand in the direction of the kitchen cupboard. I walk over and take them out. 'Here,' I say, passing her the packet with a glass of water. She takes two but stays silent.

'What are they for?' I ask.

'My nerves.'

I could do with a couple myself. She goes back to working her thumbnail between her teeth as I try to make sense of the last three days.

'It's all Michael's fault,' Iris says.

I sit back down. I'm tired and I still feel really sick. I don't know how much more of this I can take.

'I tried so hard, Eva. I tried so hard to keep him. I never looked like this back then. I was curvy and beautiful and so energetic. He was satisfied in every way. I even wore sexy negligées and perfume to bed.' I really don't need to hear this. 'Do you have any idea how hard it was seeing you walk around the house in your little shorts and crop tops, with your luscious hair and tight, youthful body?'

'I was just a kid!' I exclaim. What is the matter with this

woman? 'I never saw Michael as anything but Charlie and Jacob's dad. I was crazy about your son, for Christ's sake.'

'I know, but I felt like you just being under the same roof highlighted what an old bag I was. And then everyone started talking about that kiss and I didn't want to believe it. My Michael? Betraying me like that? With the girl we'd done our best to save?'

'It wasn't me!' I say through gritted teeth.

'*It didn't matter who it was!*' she yells. 'He'd finally found someone better than me. I was both not enough for him… and too much.'

I don't know what she wants me to say. At the time she called me every name under the sun. She packed my bags and threw them out of the window. Michael stormed out and Charlie stayed in her room crying and Jacob didn't know which way to turn. No matter how much I protested my innocence, the die was cast. Even after Michael told his family about his new work colleague, Amelie, and announced he was leaving his wife for her, all of Cragstone had already decided the original rumour was way more entertaining.

'Do you and Michael speak anymore?' I ask tentatively, already guessing the answer.

She shakes her head. 'He was angry at me for throwing you out and upsetting our children. He refused to collect his belongings, said I'd lost my mind. Poor Jacob. All of the arguing made him so stressed. It's why he put off going to uni. His father made him ill.'

I doubt it was his father who made him anxious.

'What did Michael say about Jacob's sickness?'

Iris grunts dismissively. 'He blamed me. Said I was mollycoddling him. Charlie was angry too. I stopped her from getting on a train to see you in London, you know. Literally pulled her off it. Stupid girl. I said you don't chase after bad news.'

I bite my tongue. Literally. My mouth fills with the taste of copper and my throat starts to ache. Were it not for Bianca Clarke's gossip and Michael's bad decisions, I'd still be part of the Donnelly family. Jacob loved me, and Charlie didn't hate me either, she wanted to stay friends. But Iris ruined all of that. I shake my head at the thought of how different life could have been for eighteen-year-old me back then. I lost my mother, my boyfriend and my best friend in one year, and there was nothing I could have done about it.

Two weeks away from my nineteenth birthday I took my two bags of meagre belongings and caught the first train to London. I wasn't due to start uni for another three weeks, and I had nowhere to sleep, no friends or family outside of Cragstone, so I used my savings and found student lodgings. That's when I met Amanda. She helped me find a job in a sandwich shop near campus, and I slowly rebuilt my life. I studied interior design, as planned, and I eventually got a job as a buyer, specialising in textiles and ceramics. I'd always wanted to design restaurants, but this was close enough. I worked my way up, making friends and bad dating choices, enjoying nice holidays and earning more and more money, until I was assistant to the head buyer for the home interiors chain Florentino. The company established by Mario's father. Then just as I had it all, Mario cheated on me, and Jacob died, and I lost everything. Again. I'm back exactly where I was a decade ago. The poor, pathetic girl with nowhere to go, the girl everyone hates, still wishing Iris Donnelly would believe her.

'I never changed the locks after Michael left, you know,' Iris continues. I look up. She's dabbing her face with that old cloth again. Two of her fingers are bleeding, the blood dripping on to the fabric and disappearing into the red. 'It's silly, I know, but a small part of me thought maybe he'd come back. That he'd get bored with that little harlot and see the errors of his ways.'

'I never threw my door key away either,' I say quietly. 'I

have it in a box with my old school diaries. I should have brought it back with me.'

Iris laughs. It's the saddest sound I've ever heard. 'How ironic that the only person who's here with me during my hour of need is the only person I never wanted to see again.'

We sit in silence, both of us reliving every moment over the years that has led us here. But none of it explains why someone is making fake photos of me and sending them to Jacob, or who sent that weird postcard or the text message inviting me to the funeral.

'That's not me in those photos,' I say again quietly, placing a hand on hers. She lets me. 'I'm not lying to you, Iris. I don't know who sent them to Jacob, but it wasn't me.'

She pulls her hand away from mine and lets out a long, angry sigh. 'It doesn't matter. He was coming to see you. If he hadn't been driving that day, he'd still be here.'

'It was an accident. He was driving over the limit,' I say. 'There were empty bottles of whisky in the car.'

'Not my boy. He wouldn't do that.' Iris shakes her head, her greying hair moving limply from side to side like a dirty mop. 'He was unwell. He should have stayed home with me.'

'He was a grown man!' I say, louder than I mean to. 'There comes a time when you have to let people go.'

Iris jumps up and looms over me, making me flinch. 'He was my baby,' she says, spittle landing on my face. 'He was sad. I got him pills but he wouldn't take them. I tried to make him happy, but he wouldn't listen to me.'

I stumble as I stand up. 'What if it was *you* who was making him sad?'

Iris's mouth hangs open, her eyes dull and lifeless. 'What? All I ever did...'

But I'm too fired up to care now. I'm too angry, too sick and tired of her nonsense.

'What if your obsession with keeping your son near caused

his depression?' I yell, poking her shoulder with my middle finger. 'What if you controlled him and trapped him to the point where the only way to get away from you was to escape?'

Her face pales and grows slack. 'But I didn't stop him going anywhere,' she says, stumbling over her words. 'He had weekends away. He went out in the evenings. He was poorly and I kept him safe, but he could come and go as he pleased.'

'What if it wasn't an accident?' I'm pushing harder now. I want her to feel the pain I'm feeling. 'What if Jacob drove off the cliff on purpose?'

EIGHTEEN

I've gone too far this time.

Iris has been in her room crying for hours and all I can do is sit on Jacob's bed listening to her wailing through the wall. If I had my phone, I could call Amanda and ask her what I should do. Would she offer to pick me up? It's a ten-hour round trip. It doesn't matter. I can't call her anyway because, even though Iris has a landline, I don't know anyone's telephone number off by heart and there's no laptop to look anything up online.

I hit Jacob's pillow with my clenched fist, then punch it again and again and again until I'm pounding his bed and screaming silently into his duvet. I'm trapped, over Christmas, with my dead ex-boyfriend's unstable mother.

I look out of the window at the moon, wondering what the time is. Does it work the same way as the sun? If it's in the centre of the sky, does it mean it's midnight?

The street is bathed in a silvery glow, frost settling on the pavement at the front of the house like everything is dusted in icing sugar. I'm wearing Jacob's pyjamas again because they're warmer than mine. I wrap my arms around myself, imagining it's him and that we're looking out on to the frosty night together. We used to do that when we were younger. He would stand behind me, a whole head taller than me, and he'd wrap his arms around my middle as he'd whisper our future into my ear.

'We'll have a house like that one,' he'd say, pointing at the biggest house on the street. 'And we'll decorate it however you want. Would you like a turquoise front door with a golden octopus door knocker?' He knew my favourite colour and my favourite animal. He knew everything about me. I'd giggle and he'd kiss my neck. 'I'll give you the world, Eva. Everything I have I will give to you. Where would you like to go?'

'The forest,' I'd say. 'I don't want anything grand. Just you, me and a cabin in the woods.'

'Then that's what you'll have,' he'd say.

But we were children, and children think everything is easy. There's nothing romantic about a cabin in the woods at Christmas: it's cold and isolated. The same way that I never did get a golden octopus door knocker – I got a room-share in London's Zone Two with just one toilet for four adults. Then when Mario proposed we talked about nice houses in the suburbs, close to work but near to parks and places for our children to play. Children that will never exist now.

But standing here it's easy to feel the hope I did as a teenager. Maybe it's easy to be happy when you're young because you imagine things can only get better – that life works in a straight line that only ever goes up.

Christmas trees twinkle in the windows of all the houses, happy families inside with sleeping children dreaming of Christmas morning. The only thing I liked about this time of year as a child was that my mother was hardly home. It's a lot more socially acceptable to be drunk every day in December than the rest of the year. She'd go to any local event where there was cheap booze: watered-down vodka and Coke at the bingo hall or free boxed wine at the local bookshop hosting a launch for a local writer. She had no shame when it came to getting an easy drink.

Jacob was the only one who knew all my stories. I told Mario some, the sanitised version as to why I don't have a large, happy family like he does. He loved to play out my rags to riches story for his friends, romanticising my past. I was his tough Cinderella, and he was my dashing prince who'd rescued me from ruin. But I noticed the way he'd watch me as I poured the wine at dinner, weighing up whether he'd taken a risk with me, whether I'd turn into an unpredictable lush like my mother. A disgrace. A potential gold digger. Well, I guess I saved him from that pain. It wasn't very Cinderella of me to run away from him, leaving no clue as to how he could find me. Maybe that's why he's so obsessed with bringing me back my box of belongings – the veritable glass slipper.

Has he been reading my old diaries and creating stories in his head of me cheating to excuse what he did? Or perhaps it's more than that and this is about him winning.

A shiver runs through me. I hold my hand against the radiator beneath the window. It's stone-cold even though it's turned up to the highest setting. Iris must have the heating timed to turn off at night. Was Jacob cold at night? He must have been contributing financially to the home, but I wonder how much of a say he had in how he lived.

A thick navy-blue dressing gown is hanging on the back of his door. I put it on and continue to stare out of the window at the street below. I sometimes wear glasses for distance, when I'm travelling or at the cinema, so I'm having to squint through the window to make out some of the shapes in the grey light of the night. Small trees look like people staring up at me, and bushes like children squatting on the side of the road. All is quiet and empty outside, but I can't ignore the creep of uncertainty climbing up my spine as I imagine that somewhere, out there, is someone who wants to scare me. Maybe even wants me dead.

I walk over to my rucksack and dip my hand in the front pocket until I find the postcard of Cragstone that was left for me at the hotel. It's made up of four squares, each one with a scenic picture of the market square with its winding streets and creepy statue. *Now you're back I'm going to make sure you never leave*, it says on the back in thick black capital letters. It was personally addressed to me and hand-delivered to the hotel. Whoever is after me is still out there. Whoever lured me to Jacob's funeral has me trapped in Cragstone now. I sigh. No, that's not true. I chose to miss my first train, and no one forced me to oversleep and miss the second one. Yet... I can't find my phone or shake the feeling that someone is watching me.

A wave of fear, cold and slick, washes over me. *Bianca!* We both dated Jacob and now Jacob is dead, and Bianca is missing. That can't just be a coincidence. Everyone seems far too relaxed about not being able to track Bianca down, even Orla and Harry laughed it off, but that's because they don't have the full picture. They don't know what I know. I think back to the garbled message I left Ryan. God, I hope he listened to it and shared it with his police colleagues.

A piercing ring cuts through the air, making me jump. My phone! It's outside the room. I run to the door then stop. That's not my ringtone. The phone stops ringing, and I wait and listen.

'What do you want?' Iris is shouting from her bedroom.

The walls are so thin in this house I can hear everything she's saying.

'I've told you before not to call me,' she shouts. 'Yes, I texted you but that doesn't mean I want to hear your voice, you traitor!'

I hold my breath, my body rigid, my hand still on the door handle.

'I'm fine!' she continues shouting. 'Why do you always act

like I can't look after myself? If you really cared so much, you'd be here. Leave me alone. I don't want to speak to you!'

Iris must have a mobile phone, which means she lied to me. If she lied about that, then what else has she been keeping from me? I wrap the dressing gown cord tighter around my middle, pulling up the collar until my chin is covered. I'd be warmer and more comfortable in bed, but I'm too anxious to rest, my mind whirring with every new discovery.

I'm still holding the postcard and I don't realise my hands are shaking until I hear the thick paper fluttering against my thigh. Why did Iris lie about not having a phone? I could have accessed my train ticket instead of wasting so much time searching for mine. I could be back in London by now. Angry tears collect in my eyes, and I rub at them with one hand, placing the threatening postcard in Jacob's dressing gown pocket. But the pocket isn't empty: there's a piece of card in there. I pull it out and stare at it in confusion. It's a postcard. I step closer to the window, studying the picture in the faint light of the moon. It's a postcard of Cragstone with four photos, similar to the one I received today. One image is of trees in a forest, another a field full of sheep, and the next two are photos of a sandy beach and cliffs looming over still waters.

I flip it over, my hand flying to my mouth as a scream threatens to clamber up my throat. I clasp my hand more tightly over my lips, keeping the fear locked inside. On the back of this postcard, written in thick black marker pen, are two words.

KILL YOURSELF

NINETEEN
24 DECEMBER

My dreams are plagued with nightmares and I wake up coated in sweat. The heating is on full blast and I can hear voices. I jump out of bed, noticing it's the first time since arriving at this house that I haven't felt ill. Maybe I'm not coming down with the flu after all. Someone is talking downstairs. Is Iris on the phone? No, it's the voice of an older woman and she's calling out Iris's name.

I grab Jacob's dressing gown and step out of the bedroom quietly. Peering down the stairs, I accidentally catch the eye of an elderly lady wearing a purple anorak and a woolly hat with a pink bobble on the top. Her wiry grey hair is escaping like candy floss around the edges and on her right hand she only has three fingers. It's the woman from the fish and chip shop, the one who shouted at me to get out. What's she doing here?

'Eva Walsh,' she says, her throat raspy. 'Look what you've done.'

Me? I walk down the stairs slowly, the carpet thick beneath my bare feet. Through the wooden banisters I can see Iris lying on the couch, fanning herself with a piece of paper. At first I think it's a postcard, but it's not. It's a takeaway menu.

'Oh, Vicky,' Iris says, holding out a hand for the woman to help her up. 'Thank God you came.'

Vicky is clutching a bunch of keys in her five-fingered hand. I must be looking at her strangely because she holds up the keys, her face stony cold.

'I live next door. I have a set. Iris just called me.'

'Is everything OK?' I ask.

Iris makes a big fuss about getting off the sofa, grunting and moaning. Her face is drawn and pale, and she's clutching at her chest. I descend the stairs and stand in the hallway, looking on at the commotion like a small, helpless child.

'My heart,' Iris says in a weak voice. As she goes to get her coat the older woman closes the space between us, bringing her face close up against my own.

'You have some cheek coming back,' she says. There's something familiar about her pale eyes, something about the way they crease at the edges as she speaks. 'Poor Iris is in a right state. Why don't you leave this family alone?'

Iris must have told her neighbour about what I said. About Jacob feeling so trapped by her that he killed himself.

'What a vicious tongue you have!' Vicky says.

There you go.

'You should be ashamed of yourself,' the old lady continues. 'How dare you say such an evil thing to an ill, grieving mother? Jacob was a lovely boy and if he'd stayed home that night then none of this would have happened.'

I can't do anything but stand there, my mouth opening and closing uselessly, thinking about the postcards in my dressing gown pocket, one of which is telling Jacob to kill himself. Maybe what I said wasn't that far-fetched. Maybe he was struggling or getting bullied or...

The neighbour is still pointing at me, her gnarled hand with its three fingers twisted with age. 'When my Harry told me you were back, I said that girl will bring nothing but trouble. I told him to keep away from you. You're a curse on this town, young lady.'

I know where I've seen those empty eyes before.

'Harry's your son?'

She gives me a filthy look as she helps Iris put on her shoes.

'Yes, my youngest. He's a good lad, just like Jacob was, so don't you be getting any ideas. Harry has an important job, lots of money in his savings, and a nice little flat. I know what women like you are like, coming back here and taking advantage of our men. Now come along, Iris. A&E on Christmas Eve is going to be a bloody nightmare, but best we get you checked out. Again.'

Vicky ushers Iris out of the door and I follow.

'Can I help?' I ask. 'Is there anything I can do?'

Vicky turns around faster than I thought she was capable of and jabs me in the chest with her crooked finger. 'I want you gone when we get back,' she says. 'You're just like your mother. Rotten to the core.'

And with that they hobble over to the red Fiat parked outside, the two of them shooting me snide looks and whispering to one another. As soon as Vicky helps Iris into the passenger seat and shuts the car door, Iris stops clasping at her chest and smiles at me. A slow, malevolent smile that sends ants crawling beneath my skin. Vicky gets into the driving seat and Iris switches the theatrics back on again, groaning and clutching at her chest. There's nothing wrong with her. No woman who can scream and shout as loudly as she did last night is having a heart attack. I wonder who she was talking to and whether she took her phone with her.

I wait until they drive off before shutting the front door and racing upstairs. If Iris took my phone, then it has to be somewhere in this house. She wouldn't let me into her bedroom when I woke her up yesterday and always keeps the door closed. Maybe my phone is in there. I glance out of the hall window, checking the little red car has definitely gone, then head for her room.

As soon as I open the door I gag, physically recoiling at the stench. It smells bad in here, *really* bad. I switch on the light and gasp. Unlike Iris's meticulous kitchen and living room, Jacob's bedroom and Michael's office, which hasn't been touched in a decade, Iris's room is a festering pit. Her pillows are yellow and have no pillowcases, the floor is covered in litter, and dozens of mouldy coffee cups and dirty plates cover every surface. There are stains on the parts of the carpet I can actually see, and all the drawers are open with clothes hanging out like lolling tongues. My first instinct is to start tidying, but I can't do that or she'll know I've been in her bedroom. No wonder she didn't let me in here yesterday. How long has she been living like this? Some of the plates look like they've been there longer than Jacob has been dead.

I don't know how long I've got so I don't have time to question anything; all that matters is finding my phone. I hold my breath and start by looking under the bed, instantly wishing I hadn't. It's rammed with bags and boxes.

Using my fingers like pincers, I pull at a bin bag. It's covered in dust and loosely tied. This is like something out of a horror movie. I'm almost too scared to look inside, imagining the carcass of a dead fox writhing with maggots or Jacob's leftover dinners that Iris couldn't bear to throw away. I slowly undo the ties and open the bag, keeping my face as far away from it as I can. There's no further smell, so that's something. I look closer and breathe a sigh of relief. It's just a pile of musty old books. I pull them out and flick through them. It's Jacob's old school reports and textbooks from when he was a child, along with his football kit and trainers. It may not be as bad as I feared, but why keep all this? And where are Charlie's old things? I tie the bag back up and push it under her bed, then pull out a box. Inside is a mix of cables, including phone chargers and a laptop charger. Are these old ones belonging to Michael and Charlie? Or does Iris have a laptop too?

I leave the bed and look inside her wardrobe next. Most of the clothes aren't on the hangers properly, just folded over or looped over the rail. At the bottom of the wardrobe are some Christmas gifts, large boxes wrapped in gaudy paper complete with ribbons and bows. I look at the tags. One has Charlie's name on it and the other three are made out to Henri. Everything is wrapped in different festive paper, most of them with Santa and holly prints and one wrapped in expensive-looking glossy black and green paper. Something behind my ribcage squeezes. So she does still care about her daughter and grandson. I imagine her hiding these gifts away, planning for a Christmas Day alone, wishing she were with her grandchild but being too stubborn to make amends. What on earth did she do that made Charlie keep away from her? Maybe that's who Iris was shouting at last night.

I close the wardrobe door and move over to the bedside table. It has three drawers. I rummage through the bottom one, which contains old chocolate wrappers and empty packets of paracetamol and ibuprofen. There's a notebook in there full of her writing. I know it's wrong to look, but I flick through it anyway, noting the dates she's written down go back five years. Next to them is a list of symptoms: nausea, vomiting, diarrhoea, migraines, shortness of breath. In another column she's written medications and remedies, along with hospital appointments and notes to herself like 'lower the dose' and 'too high'. If Iris is a hypochondriac, then that would explain her sudden 'bad heart' this morning and her comment to me about having pills for everything.

In the middle drawer I find a Kindle, and a laptop case but no laptop. I'm now convinced she has a laptop. Iris is not an old lady; she was computer-literate enough ten years ago to manage her social media accounts and run Facebook ads for her business, so I don't believe for a second she's been living a tech-free existence. In which case, why hide it from me? Why not help me get back to London? Is she really that lonely that she'll do whatever it takes to keep me, someone she clearly dislikes, in her home?

The final drawer I look in is full of little boxes, the kind you keep jewellery in. One contains earrings, another a brooch. None of them are big enough to hide my phone in, but I'm curious now so I keep opening them one by one. I choose one that rattles, prising off the lid and immediately dropping it to the floor with a yelp. Dozens of teeth fall like yellowing pebbles on to the carpet. Good God. Who keeps a box of teeth in their bedside table? I don't want to touch them, but I can't exactly leave them scattered all over the stained carpet. I pick them up one by one and place them back inside the box. They're tiny, so I'm guessing they were Charlie's and Jacob's baby teeth. Vile. I'm nearly too scared to look inside the other boxes, but I do. One is full of hair, taped into a neat swatch, and the last box contains a dummy, the teat brown and cracked. Next to it is the red cloth Iris has been using to wipe her face with. I pick it up and shake it out. It's a tattered Babygro. She's been mopping up her tears using her dead son's baby clothes from thirty years ago. My entire body grows cold as I slam the last drawer shut. This is too much. I want to stop but I need to find my phone. I have to ring Amanda and let her know I'm stuck here or she'll be worried.

The smell in this room is making me want to heave. I cover my face with Jacob's dressing gown and take a deep breath into it; the smell of washing powder mingles with a faint scent of his deodorant. It's like he's with me, which makes me feel a little braver.

I have to think this through properly. If I were a deranged hoarder who hated her son's ex-girlfriend, where would I hide her phone? Maybe it's in a bag somewhere. Did she leave the house with a handbag?

There are three bags hanging on the outside of her wardrobe: a plain black leather handbag with a gold clasp, a tote bag with a picture of a cat on it and a small clutch adorned with pink and green beads. The beaded bag and tote are empty, but the black one has a zipped-up compartment inside containing a brown paper bag. I take it out and plunge my hand inside, my heart quickening as I feel two postcards. I steady my breaths. Was she receiving threatening notes too? I pull the pieces of card out of the paper bag, instantly relieved to see they aren't postcards but photos. That's fine. Photos are normal.

I flip them over and a strange sound escapes my throat, something between a squeak and a gasp. The two photos in my hand are of me... in my underwear.

TWENTY

I can't stop staring at the photos. This isn't me. The face is my face – one is from my latest Facebook profile picture and the other is that LinkedIn photo again – but the body isn't mine. Why does Iris have fake photos of me, semi-dressed, hidden inside her handbag? Did she find them with the others in Jacob's jacket pocket, as she claimed? Or... No. The alternative is too awful to think about.

I leave her bedroom, taking the photos with me, and lean against the wall in the hallway. I'm struggling to breathe, my heart hammering in my chest and every inch of my body fizzing, telling me to run, go, get as far away as possible. But I can't. I have nowhere to go and no way of getting there. I go back into Jacob's room, shut the door and sit on his bed. I don't know what the time is, but I wasn't in Iris's room that long. Fifteen minutes, maybe. Twenty tops. The hospital is half an hour away, more with traffic, and there's always a long wait to be seen. She won't be back for a while yet.

I place the sordid photos beside me on Jacob's duvet then take both postcards from his dressing gown pocket. I compare the writing on the postcards – they were definitely written by the same person. I gather the notes from Iris on Jacob's desk and compare the writing to the postcards. It's different.

Are the photos and postcards linked? Why would someone send Jacob photos of me, pretending to be me, then threaten us both? And why would Jacob think we were in a relationship if he'd not spoken to me in ten years? And Bianca... is her disappearance connected to all of this?

If I'm going to find any answers, then they have to be in here, in Jacob's bedroom.

I pull open his desk drawers and dump the contents on top of his desk. Unlike with Iris's room I don't have to worry about anyone noticing I've been going through his things. I sit at his desk and start leafing through each sheet of paper. There are letters from the bank, bills, more hospital appointments, a folder marked 'work stuff'. I don't even know what he did for a living. I pull out the paperwork... but it's not work stuff. It's dozens of sheets of paper that appear to be a printout of an email conversation. I scan my eyes over them, my head making small shaking motions and my mouth so dry I'm struggling to swallow. The conversation is between me and Jacob – but I haven't been emailing Jacob. EvaWalsh_gf01@gmail.com is not my email address.

I pull out one of the sheets of paper and search for the date. It was sent on 10 April – that's eight months ago. I read the message that's supposedly from me.

> Hey Jacob, how are you feeling today? I hope the sickness has stopped. You poor thing. I wish I were there to look after you, to mop your brow and hold you as you sleep. I miss you so much, baby. But it won't be long until we're together. I think about you all the time, and how amazing life is going to be when you're finally able to leave that monster behind. Just run away... I'll be here waiting for you. Always. Eva xxx

I re-read the printout five times. Who the hell sent him this pretending to be me? It doesn't even sound like me! 'Baby'? I've never called anyone 'baby' in my life. And is Iris the 'monster' this fake Eva is referring to? I read another email, this one dated October, but it says more of the same about Jacob being ill and how we will be together soon. I keep scanning through each page, email after email, each one connected to the last like one long conversation. Looking at the time stamps, there were some days when he can't have got much else done but speak to the fake me. Every email is telling Jacob to be careful, to keep putting his money aside, to escape from Cragstone because he isn't safe. One reminds him that we can't text or speak on the phone because his mother checks his phone at night and his bills, so emails are the only way to communicate until we can meet in person. There are more photos of me amongst the printouts, some sexier than others, most of them with writing on the back. Writing that isn't mine...

Who was tricking Jacob? And more importantly... why?

I check his other desk drawers and rifle through his bookshelves, shaking books out and searching behind them, even though I don't know what I'm looking for. Clues, perhaps, as to who this weird stalker is. Evidence that none of these emails or photos came from me, that someone has been for a year, maybe longer, impersonating me.

I re-read the emails about Jacob putting money aside.

> You need to save your money, baby. We will need it when we run away together. Remember where I told you to put it. It will be safe there. I don't love Mario, that's just a ruse so no one suspects us. Be patient, baby. Nothing will tear us apart this time.

Was Jacob paying money into a dodgy bank account? Was

he being scammed by someone preying on his biggest weakness – me?

I wish Jacob's laptop was still here. How much money was he putting in this account? And where was he going the day of the accident? What if he *was* on his way to meet me? Or, at least, in his mind he was. My throat is itchy, and my eyes are stinging. I rub my face, but it doesn't help. I want to cry. Not just out of fear and frustration but for Jacob. My darling Jacob, who was in love with a lie.

I put the printouts in date order and scan through the last one. It's from late November, two days before Jacob's death.

> We'll finally get to be together soon in our special place. Don't say goodbye to anyone, just pack your bags and drive. We're nearly there, baby. Stay safe and stay healthy. I love you. Eva xxx

His reply simply says...

> I know what I have to do now. It's over. I'll finally be free.

A loud knock at the front door makes me jump, the papers scattering to the carpet like dead leaves at my feet.

TWENTY-ONE

That can't be Iris at the door. Even if she forgot her keys, I saw Vicky had a set, so she'd let her in. I pick the papers up off the floor, hands shaking so much I keep dropping them, but I don't have time to tidy them up because the knocking is getting louder.

'Hello? Eva?'

That's a man's voice. The only people who know I'm here are women.

I wrap Jacob's dressing gown around me more tightly and look down the stairs. The glass in the front door is frosted and warped, so all I can make out in the gloom of the winter light is an outline of a man in a hood.

'Is that you, Eva?' he's calling out. 'I can see you at the top of the stairs. I have something for you.'

On the doormat are four envelopes that weren't there earlier. I hurry downstairs and pick them up. They look like Christmas cards, or maybe condolence cards for Iris.

'It's me... Harry,' the voice says. 'I have a package for you.'

I breathe out in relief and wait for my heart rate to slow down before opening the door. As soon as I do a gush of wind hits me in the face like an icy slap. Harry is standing on the doorstep in his postman uniform, although this time, along with his unseasonal shorts, he's wearing an elf hat with a bell on the top. He laughs and shakes his head from side to side, making the bell jingle, then stops abruptly when he notices I'm still in my nightclothes.

'Oh, I didn't get you out of bed, did I?' he says, his eyes lingering too long on my clavicle. I tighten the dressing gown even further and cross my arms.

'It's gone eleven,' he says. 'It's nearly lunchtime. Are you ill?'

My breaths are coming in long shudders and my heart is still racing, but at least I know what the time is now.

'Have you seen Bianca?' I ask.

Harry's face screws up. 'I didn't think you and Bianca were friends.'

'We're not... It's just, you said yesterday she was missing. Is she OK?'

He shrugs. 'No idea. Not heard anything. No news is good news, I guess.'

Not necessarily. I thought he'd be more worried about her than this. They should be out there searching for her!

'You don't look well,' Harry says. 'Your eyes have dark circles under them.'

I'm shaking. Can he tell I'm shaking? I can't stop thinking about the emails I just read, scattered all over Jacob's desk, along with the postcards and the photos of me in various stages of undress. Who was sending all of this to Jacob? What if Bianca isn't OK and it's all too late? What if I'm next?

Harry is still staring at me.

'What do you want?' I bark at him.

He balks at the tone of my voice. 'I have a parcel.'

'Iris isn't home.'

'I know. My mother told me she was taking her to the

hospital and that you were here. She said to bring the parcel to you quickly because you'll be leaving soon,' he says.

Well, Vicky's wrong... I'm not going anywhere.

'Is Iris OK?' Harry continues. 'Mum says she gets ill a lot. She's so caring, my mother, never has a bad word to say about anyone.'

Boys and their perfect mothers – they never see what's right in front of them. I shuffle on the spot. My feet are bare, and the cold wind is turning them to ice.

'The parcel?' I say, widening my eyes expectantly.

'Oh, right. Yes. Of course! It's for you, by the way. It has your name on it.' Harry's pale eyes crinkle at the edges as he searches through his red satchel. 'Here you go. Here's the package I have for you.' He pulls a flat box out of his bag and hands it to me. 'I mean, I have it and it's for you but it's not *from me*. Obviously I don't know what it is, but if it's a fancy Cartier necklace you can pretend it *is* from me. Haha.'

It takes all my willpower not to roll my eyes.

'For me?' I repeat.

Harry nods enthusiastically and stays standing on the doorstep, as if I'm going to open the gift in front of him. Why is everyone in Cragstone so damn nosy?

'I put the letters through the letterbox, but the package wouldn't fit so I knocked. I thought maybe it was for Iris – she's gotten quite a few cards since, you know, Jacob dying and all that. But then I saw it's addressed to you. Which is nice. I didn't think anyone knew you were here.'

They don't. A shiver runs from the top of my head down to my bare feet and it's not just from the cold. Something is happening right now and I'm not sure what it is. The only people who know I'm here are Orla, Iris, Harry, his vicious mother and Bianca. I thank Harry and go to shut the door, but he stops it with his thick boot.

'One more thing... Still on for tonight?'

'What about tonight?'

He shakes his head again so his silly hat jingles. 'It's Christmas Eve, Eva! Christmas Eva, haha.'

Oh my God.

'And?'

'Drinks at The Swan. Dear me, you have the memory of a goldfish. We'll have to start calling you Dory!'

I swallow down every emotion I'm feeling right now and give Harry the smile he's so desperately seeking. 'I'll be there.'

He throws his hands in the air and whoops. He actually whoops. I close the door while he's still talking, saying something about carrying on where we left off.

'Yes. Lovely. Can't wait,' I call out, finally exhaling one long breath as the door clicks shut.

I leave the letters for Iris on the hallstand and stare at the package in my hand. It's square and flat and wrapped in brown paper, the address scrawled in thick black capital letters. My heart skips a beat. It's the same writing as on the postcards. I can't see a postage mark, so there's no clue as to where it was sent from. I peel back the paper slowly, my shoulders sagging with relief when I see it's just a box of chocolates. They must be from a fancy shop because there's no brand name and they aren't covered in cellophane. I open the lid carefully, praying the contents are what they should be. They are. It's just chocolate. No note, no indication of who it's from, but at least it's nothing threatening.

Unless there was a note mixed up with the cards on the doormat!

I sift through the four envelopes: there's a pink one and two thick cream ones for Iris, and one plain white envelope for me. It has my name on it, scrawled in the same writing as the package, but no stamp. Whoever sent me this card put it through the letterbox themselves.

I open the envelope, expecting to see a Christmas card, but

it's not a Christmas card. It's another postcard. This one depicts beachside scenes of Cragstone, with sunny images of the cliffs full of wildflowers, and a panoramic view of the town. I keep staring at it, my hand trembling, my head tight like a balloon ready to explode. I don't want to turn it over. I don't want to see what it says on the back. But I have to.

I flip it over.

I KNOW WHERE TO FIND YOU NOW

TWENTY-TWO

I shower in a daze and wash my hair, not that it makes me feel any cleaner because I only have one outfit and it's getting grubby. Luckily, I packed spare underwear but I'm going to have to do a wash load soon. I hope Iris doesn't mind. Maybe I should offer to do all her washing. I keep thinking about the state of her bedroom and bedsheets. She's been gone a while now. Is she going to be angry I'm still here? Or will she be secretly relieved I never left?

I'm filling my head with inconsequential things because I can't think about the postcards and the photos and the chocolates and the emails on Jacob's desk. I don't know what they all mean, except that I'm not safe. I lean my hand against the bathroom wall as the water cascades down my back. I'm dizzy and my stomach is rumbling. I can't remember the last time I ate a decent meal. I can't think straight.

Back in the kitchen I'm no longer met by empty cupboards – every shelf and the fridge are packed with food, everything from biscuits and chocolate to vegetables and at least five different cheeses. Iris wasn't exaggerating about over-ordering for Christmas. I make myself a cheese sandwich using the fresh bread and a new packet of cheddar, taking a small bag of crisps out of a bigger bag, careful not to use anything too fancy that Iris may be saving for Christmas Day.

That's tomorrow. Christmas is tomorrow, and I haven't told Amanda that I won't be meeting her at her mum's house. I wish I knew where my bloody phone was.

I stare out of the kitchen window as I eat my boring sandwich, chewing slowly as a million questions crowd my mind, none of which I have the answers to. The hedges and pavement look like they've been sprayed with glitter, cars glistening like giant sugar plums. The sky is low and white, clouds hanging heavy with snow.

I keep re-reading those emails in my mind and my mouth turns sour, my sandwich no longer having any flavour. All those proclamations of love and talk of saving up money. Who was Jacob emailing all this time? Was it just money the scammer wanted from him, or something more sinister?

I'm washing up my plate, knife and chopping board when a phone starts ringing. I drop everything into the sink and race out of the kitchen, convinced it's my mobile, until I realise the sound is coming from the hallway and the ringing is Iris's landline. It's a loud, old-fashioned trill of a ring that sends me straight back to my childhood. Should I answer it? I stand in front of the ancient home phone, staring at it for what feels like an eternity before I snatch up the receiver with my soapy hands.

'Hello?'

Silence.

'Hello?' I say again.

There's breathing on the other end. My breath catches in my throat. It might be him, them, the person sending the threatening messages.

'Have I dialled the wrong number?' a woman's voice says after a short pause.

It's OK. Everything's fine. I need to calm the hell down.

'I don't know,' I reply. 'Who are you looking for?'

She laughs. I know that laugh.

'Charlie?' I say, just as she says my name.

'Eva? What on earth are you doing at Mum's house? You were the last person I expected to answer.'

I drop to the floor and sit cross-legged, cradling the phone between my ear and shoulder. Suddenly I'm eighteen again, remembering how Jacob would call the house when he went out, and I'd answer. He'd tell me how much he loved me, and all the ways he wanted to kiss me, and I'd sit on the Donnellys' swirly carpet listening to how much he adored me as his parents looked on unknowingly. Jacob and I loved one another so hard, in full view of everyone, for such a long time until his family realised we were together. Those were the best of times.

'I'm staying here over Christmas,' I tell Charlie.

There's an intake of air, followed by more silence. 'Oh, Eva. Please don't do that,' she finally says.

'Sorry. I didn't have much choice. I wanted—'

'No. You don't understand. You have to get out of there.'

'What?'

'Leave! Don't stay for a chat or eat any food, just go home.'

'I can't,' I reply, my voice high and tinny as my throat begins to close up. 'I'm trapped in Cragstone. The trains aren't running until the twenty-seventh, and I have no other way to get back to London.'

'Have you been feeling ill lately?' Charlie asks.

'Well, yeah, but it's been a stressful time, what with the funeral and being back in here and—'

'Headaches? Nausea? Dizziness? Has your stomach been aching?'

'Yes. What is'

'Listen to me,' Charlie says in an urgent whisper as if Iris can hear her all the way from France. 'My mother is not well.'

'I know,' I reply quietly. 'She's been struggling a lot over the last few days.'

Do I mention Iris's bedroom? Do I tell Charlie her mother is at the hospital right now?

'She's been like this for a long time,' Charlie says, her voice still just above a whisper. 'At least ten years, maybe longer. It's why Dad left her – erratic mood swings, constant lies, fake illnesses.'

'About that,' I say. My head flops forward and I run my fingers through my damp hair. 'Your mum is in A&E right now with chest pains. I'm sure it's nothing, but I thought you should know.'

'No!' Charlie cries out.

Oh dear, I've really upset her. 'Sorry, if I'd had your telephone number, I'd have—'

'No,' she says again, not letting me finish my sentence. 'I'm not worried, and I'm not upset. There's nothing wrong with her.'

'Yeah, I think she's a bit of a hypochondriac.'

'It's worse than that. I've been looking into it for a long time, and I think my mum has Munchausen syndrome.' The line goes quiet, then I hear a faint sound that might be Charlie sniffing. 'Actually... I think she has Munchausen by proxy.'

I frown. That's ridiculous. Charlie is making Iris sound like one of those crazy women from a true crime podcast.

'Munchausen by proxy?' I say. 'What do you mean?'

'Munchausen is when—'

'I know what it is,' I cut in. 'I'm just saying it's all a bit far-fetched. Are you seriously telling me that you think *your mother* was making Jacob ill? On purpose?'

'Yes,' Charlie says. 'I do.'

'Why?'

'For attention. To make him dependent on her. Control.'

I thought mothers with Munchausen by proxy hurt their young children, poisoning them or causing injuries that looked like accidents. Or they prey on the weak and vulnerable. But Jacob? He was a grown man; a smart, strong man who planned to study medicine. He wasn't weak or naïve.

'But Jacob wouldn't ever let anyone treat him that way,' I say.

Charlie gives a long sigh. 'You'd be surprised. After you left and Dad walked out, Jacob and I started to get ill. The doctor said it was anxiety from all the stress, which made sense, I suppose. Everything at home was a mess and Jacob and I were meant to be starting uni after the summer. Then I realised I always felt better when I was away, like when I stayed the night at a friend's house, so I presumed it was something to do with the house. Maybe I had an allergy to damp or a specific plant or maybe the washing detergent. Dad even got a plumber to check for carbon monoxide poisoning, but it wasn't that. Although it *was* poisoning.'

I'm glad I'm already sitting on the floor because my head is fuzzy, and my legs have gone hollow. I have to hold the phone receiver with both of my clammy hands as they are now slick with sweat.

'What kind of poisoning?' I manage to say.

'Cyanide.'

I let out a nervous laugh. 'That's crazy. Where would Iris buy cyanide from?'

But Charlie isn't laughing. 'I don't know. I left for France, and a few days after I got there I felt fine. Then I came home to see Jacob because he was really poorly, and I fell ill again. I got my blood tested in France when I got back, presuming I'd caught whatever it was from my brother, and that's what the

French doctors said. Cyanide. It's why I never returned to Cragstone until Jacob died. I can't trust my own mother.'

I try to take a deep breath, but I can't. My lungs are filling with concrete, and I have to shake my head a little until all the little grey dots clear from my vision. The shortness of breath, dizziness, stomach cramps...

'I thought I was coming down with the flu,' I say. 'Are you saying the cyanide is in the food I've been eating?'

'Yes.'

The cookies and cake! Iris never ate them but always insisted I have more.

'Does your mother have a laptop?' I ask Charlie.

'Of course.'

'And a mobile phone?'

'Yes. I tried calling it earlier but it's turned off. I spoke to her last night. It's why I'm calling today because she was threatening to kill herself again. She sent me like twenty text messages.'

'I knew she was lying,' I say. 'She convinced her poor neighbour to take her to the hospital.'

'Don't feel sorry for Vicky,' Charlie says, her voice dripping with disdain. 'That interfering old bag loves the drama. People like her encourage my mother; they bring out the worst in her.'

'Did Jacob know all of this?' I ask.

'I told him what I told you, but he refused to believe our mother would hurt us. I even called his GP but they said they couldn't discuss their patients' records. Jacob blocked my number in the end, saying he could no longer trust me. Although I sometimes managed to get him on the landline.'

I can hear the pain in her voice, the years of regret that she didn't do more for her brother. That she didn't push harder.

'Why didn't your dad do anything?' I ask. Michael was the saviour, the hero, the one we all turned to when a teacher was mean to us, or when there was a spider on the ceiling. Where was Jacob's father in all of this?

Charlie lets out a hum of frustration. 'He went over to the house so many times,' she says. 'My mother keeps the downstairs neat and tidy, so no one would guess she has issues, but Dad saw she'd started to hoard things upstairs. He begged her to see a psychologist, told Jacob he wasn't helping her by staying there and listening to all her vicious lies about us. But Jacob believed our mother – he really did think he was ill – even though the doctors kept telling him there was nothing wrong with him. There was no way of convincing him that our mum was behind it all because anything we said just fed into her stories about how we didn't believe him and that she was the only one he could trust. It's why Dad never collected his things, so he had an excuse to keep going over there. But it made no difference what we did: Jacob refused to listen.'

'And the blood tests didn't show cyanide poisoning?' I ask.

'I have no idea. He said our mother opened all the post from the hospital so he wouldn't get stressed. He actually told me that like he was indulging her, knowing how much she enjoyed looking after him. You know what my brother was like. Star Boy had to be the good guy, the only one who remained to save our mother from herself. Until he got back in touch with you, that is.'

My stomach plummets like I've dropped twenty floors in a lift. I can't take it all in. Poison. Lies. A broken family. And now Charlie is saying she also believes the nonsense about me and her brother being together. Why wouldn't she? Jacob did. In his mind we were emailing every day.

'Your brother and I were not a couple,' I say. 'Not since we were kids.'

Charlie goes quiet. 'What do you mean? I spoke to Jacob in October and he sounded really happy. It was so strange to hear him upbeat and hopeful that I got worried; I thought he was on drugs.' She chuckles sadly. 'But then he said you two were back together, and that you were convincing him to leave home, and I figured that could only be a good thing.'

'That wasn't me.'

Poor Jacob thought I loved him, thought I was going to rescue him from this hell, and there I was far away in London, with a man who never truly knew me, completely unaware of the horrors Jacob was enduring. I would have rescued him had I known. I would have come back and begged him to leave, and maybe there would have been more. Maybe I would have had the courage to tell him I still loved him, and he'd love me, and everything would have worked out. We will never know.

'What do you mean that wasn't you?' Charlie says. 'He told me about the emails and the photos and how you broke up with your ex for him.'

I swallow down a sob, all the words I want to say a garbled mess trapped in my throat. 'It's all fake.'

'You're not making any sense!' she shouts. 'Tell me the truth.'

'I am! I'm not lying,' I shout back. 'I don't know who texted me about his funeral, but I think it has something to do with the fake photos of me he received and the emails he was sending to someone who also wasn't me. I'm sorry, Charlie. I wish it *had* been me. I wish I'd known how much he was suffering at the hands of your mother, but I didn't. I didn't know anything.'

I'm crying hard now, and I can hear Charlie on the other end of the line sobbing too.

'You think he was catfished?' she asks.

'Something like that.

'What do we do?'

'I don't know. It's all too late. What if your mother made him so ill that he killed himself?'

Charlie's crying is so loud I can't make out what she's saying. I dab at my nose with the sleeve of my jumper.

'It's not your fault,' I tell her.

'I couldn't prove anything,' she says. 'I tried. I begged Jacob to search the house. He said he did but there was no strange medication or cleaning products, or anything that could be poisonous. He said Mum was right, that Dad and I were making awful things up about her. I know I was poisoned but I've not been able to prove it was her who did it, so please be careful. Don't accept anything my mother gives you to eat or drink. Better yet, leave now and never come back.'

'I'm staying,' I say, realising in that moment what I have to do. 'I need to know who sent me the text and who's been pretending to be me. And Charlie... there's something else you should know.'

'What is it?'

I have to tell her. I can't keep it inside anymore.

'I think someone is out to get me. I've been receiving weird postcards and Bianca is missing and... I'm scared to leave the house and now I'm scared to stay inside the house. What do I do?'

'Eva, this is serious. You have to tell the police,' she says. 'Ryan. He's a policeman, and a decent guy. Speak to him.'

I think back to the stupid voice message I left him yesterday. I should have told him to call me at Iris's to follow up.

'OK. I'll track him down.'

I give Charlie my mobile number, explaining that it's gone missing, and write hers down on a piece of paper, which I put in my pocket. I'll put it in my bag later so I don't lose it.

'Stay safe,' she says.

'I'll try.'

'And keep me updated when you find your phone,' she adds. 'If you find any evidence at all, go to the police. Iris may be my mother, but Jacob was my brother and I'm certain she hurt him.'

We say goodbye but those three little words keep circling my mind.

She hurt him. She hurt him. She hurt him.

The box of chocolates is still on the hallstand. I push it away and go upstairs. It's time to start playing this game my way.

TWENTY-THREE

It's dark outside by the time Iris returns home. It could be five o'clock, it could be seven – I have no way of knowing because the watch she's wearing is the only timepiece in the house. Vicky looks exhausted as she helps Iris inside, muttering something about how she hadn't planned for this on Christmas Eve, her husband isn't happy, and she hasn't started on the sprouts yet.

'All OK?' I ask, descending the stairs.

'What are you still doing here?' Vicky barks, pointing at me with her twisted hand. 'I thought we told you to leave?'

'I couldn't possibly go knowing Iris is ill,' I say. 'She shouldn't be alone over Christmas with no one to look after her. Unless you want her to stay with you, Vicky?'

The look on the neighbour's face is priceless.

'I told you Eva's a good girl,' Iris says, beaming up at me. 'Like a daughter to me, she is. Didn't I say that in the waiting room, Vicky? Didn't I say Eva's an angel?'

'Not quite,' Vicky replies, sitting Iris down in the armchair and patting her hand.

Iris smiles up at her neighbour. 'Thank you. You're a good woman, Vicky Hilborn.'

The old lady nods curtly and walks past me without a backwards glance. 'Merry Christmas,' she shouts over her shoulder before slamming the door behind her.

I join Iris in the living room and give her a long hug. She wasn't expecting that either. Well, she better get used to surprises because I have a few more up my sleeve.

'What did the doctor say?' I ask, my voice oozing with concern.

Iris plumps up the cushions behind her, enjoying every moment of my attention.

'Just a scare this time,' she replies, patting her heart. 'He said I was to keep away from stressful situations and I mustn't overexert myself.'

'Of course,' I say. 'You sit there and watch your game shows and let me do all the hard work. It's the least I can do for letting me stay. We'll have a lovely Christmas together, just you and me.'

She closes her eyes and leans back in the armchair, cooing with delight when I place a cushion on a stool and insist she puts her feet up.

'You know you hurt my feelings when you said I drove Jacob away. It's not true. I loved my boy so much.'

'So much,' I echo. 'More than any mother I know.'

I bite down on my inner lip, doing my best to keep my face in a neutral smile. If Charlie is right, then I want this woman to pay for what she did to her children. If Iris had only left Jacob alone to live his life, he may have stood a chance of leading a happy, healthy existence. Instead, she gaslighted him, made him ill, convinced him that he had no choice but to stay under her roof. She's not going to get away with this.

'I got you these,' I say, handing Iris the box of chocolates I received. I'm expecting her to react in some way, to look wary or surprised, but instead she beams with delight and calls me an angel again.

'It's gone six, you know,' she says, taking three bon-bons in one go and popping them into her mouth one after the other. 'You might want to start thinking about dinner.'

I count to ten in my head, the whole time smiling beatifically at her as she stuffs her face with the expensive chocolates. Well, at least that rules Iris out as the sender of my gift. I wait a moment, and once I see she isn't keeling over or choking, I leave her to finish off the box while I head to the kitchen to prepare dinner. A dinner I won't be scared to eat because I made it.

Iris says I can use whatever I want except the turkey because that's for tomorrow, so I set to work making minestrone soup and chicken pie. Everything I use I wash first, or I take it out of plastic wrapping so I'm confident none of it has been tampered with.

As soon as I got off the phone to Charlie earlier, I searched the entire kitchen and bathroom for poison or strange substances. I have no idea what a bottle of cyanide looks like, but I opened every packet and pot and smelled every liquid and lotion I found. I had images of Snow White's evil stepmother injecting apples with green poison, but I didn't find anything that could cause serious harm. Maybe Iris was crushing her anxiety medication into powder and sprinkling it on Jacob's food, or stirring it into his coffee? Would he have noticed? Would it have been enough to convince him and everyone around him that he was too ill to function?

I insist that Iris and I eat our soup and pie in the living room, in front of an airing of *The Sound of Music*, mainly because I don't want her in the kitchen or near my food. She talks about Jacob throughout the film, telling me how Christmas was his favourite time of year and how he always bought her such thoughtful gifts. She tells me how he would write lovely messages in her card, telling her how much he loved her, promising he would never leave.

'But he left me in the end anyway,' she says. 'Life can be so cruel sometimes, taking away the only person who ever truly loved me. He loved me more than he loved anyone else in this world, you know. He loved me more than his father, his sister... even you.'

I struggle to swallow down my pie, every inch of my body tense and prickling like barbed wire is being dragged through my veins. *How dare she!* Her so-called love stifled him, trapped him and ultimately killed him. That wasn't love Jacob was showing her, it was obligation. He was scared of her and her actions. It was me he loved until his dying day. No wonder she's hated me all these years. No wonder he was so vulnerable and easy to scam.

'You have me now,' I force myself to say. 'I'm here.'

Her eyes fill with tears, but I don't feel an ounce of remorse for tricking her this way. I'm going to stay as long as it takes to prove Iris was making Jacob ill, and to discover who was behind the death threats and the catfishing Jacob endured. He didn't deserve any of this. People should have noticed what was happening – as far as I'm concerned all of Cragstone killed him!

'I'm going to the pub tonight,' I announce. 'I hope you don't mind but I think that's what Jacob would have liked. Me spending time with his friends, for us to celebrate him at this time of year.'

Iris's eyes narrow and her face turns stony, her right cheek twitching. She stays silent as she stands up with her nearly empty dinner plate held aloft.

'Let me take that,' I say with a saccharine smile. I rush over to her, but she pulls her plate away.

'I can do it,' she says, trying to get past. She barges into me, causing her plate to tip and the remnants of her chicken pie to dribble down my jumper and only pair of jeans.

'Oh dear,' she says without feeling. 'That's going to stain dreadfully.'

She did it on purpose. The conniving cow has dirtied my only set of clothes.

'Why don't you change into Jacob's PJs?' she says. 'We can have a nice night in.'

'Good idea. I'll put my clothes in the wash first,' I say through gritted teeth.

I leave her to deal with the plates as I run upstairs and strip off my jeans and jumper. I get a cheap thrill walking around the upstairs of Iris's house in my underwear. A part of me wishes she was watching me right now, semi-naked in her ex-husband's office and her dead son's bedroom, so she'd doubt everything she knows to be true. I want her to envy me. Hate me. Fear me. I was never a threat to her as an eighteen-year-old; the rumour about me and Michael was nonsense. But now? Now all I care about is that she suffers and pays for what she did to the boy I loved.

I need to find something to wear because I'm going to the pub whether Iris likes it or not. This is my only chance to speak to those who saw Jacob last. I need to know if Bianca has been found and what they know about all the threats and lies surrounding Jacob's death.

Michael's office contains nothing but dusty paperwork, and Charlie's old clothes are too small for me. I rifle through more items in the piles where Charlie's bed used to be but all I can find are Michael's corduroy trousers and Iris's old work dresses. Maybe Jacob has something I could wear.

Back in his room I open his wardrobe and instantly burst into tears. Nothing has changed. I recognise so many of these items: the t-shirt we bought at a music concert at the beach, the smart shirt he wore for his interview at Oxford, the jeans he was wearing when I first saw him. Before I know what I'm doing I'm grabbing at his clothes, pushing them into my face, inhaling his scent like I'm holding on to all our memories for dear life. For years I mourned him, bereft that he wanted nothing more to do with me, until slowly I healed and made a life for myself. But now I know what he looked like as an adult, I know he remained handsome and kind because I've seen the things he said to me in his emails, and I know he never stopped loving me. The pain hits me so hard I stagger backwards, his clothes still clutched to my chest. I never stopped loving Jacob. I would have loved him back. If he'd got in touch with the real me, I'd have come back for him. I would have.

I sit down on the bed, Jacob's clothes in a tangled pile on my lap, and take a shuddery breath. I didn't want to admit this to myself at the time but Mario never gave me the twist in my belly Jacob did, or the ache in my chest. He never caused that desperate tugging inside of me that I'm feeling right now just by holding his old clothes. Maybe it's knowing I will never see Jacob again that's making me yearn for him, for what we had and could have had. Or maybe it's simply safer to love someone out of reach. I take comfort in the thought of Jacob believing I loved him the day he died. Or maybe he discovered the truth and the accident was because he learned the only good thing in his life was pretend.

It's too late to save him but it's not too late to get justice for him. I can give him that much.

I pull his old jeans off the hanger and try them on. They're too long in the leg, but if I roll them up they're fine. The waist fits. I find a light blue jumper that I've never seen before in his drawer and put that on too, rubbing the cashmere against my cheek and inhaling his scent. I tie my hair back and close my eyes as I make a promise out loud.

'I'm not going to let you down, Jacob,' I whisper.

Iris is calling for me downstairs.

'I'm just putting a wash load on,' I shout out. The utility room is next to Charlie's bedroom. I'd never seen a house with a separate room for the washing machine before I came here. Like Iris's bedroom this space is a mess, full of empty detergent bottles and powder all over the floor. I wipe the inside of the machine with an old rag before I load it and wipe the tray out too.

Back downstairs I find Iris in the living room, her eyes glazed over as she stares at the screen. Someone on TV has won a speedboat and is laughing because they get seasick.

'I took my pills,' she says, her mouth drooling on one side. 'They help me sleep.'

She looks up at me wearing her son's clothes and her eyes widen a little.

'Jacob?' she says, reaching out for me.

'Iris. It's me, Eva,' I say.

'My darling Jacob.'

I step back but her hands grab out for mine, clasping it tightly.

'Oh, son. What have I done?'

TWENTY-FOUR

I've never been happier walking out of a house than I was ten minutes ago when I left Iris snoozing in her armchair in front of the TV. The conversation with Charlie keeps running through my mind as I dissect every word she said. She was adamant her mother tampered with Jacob's food, and possibly mine over the last few days. I haven't eaten or drunk a thing Iris has made in over twenty-four hours and my head is clear again. Or maybe it's psychosomatic and I'm losing my mind as well. It sounds far too outrageous that Iris would invite me to her home in order to feed me a cake she poisoned. Middle-aged, middle-class women from Cragstone don't do that. Or do they?

The walk to the pub is more pleasant than I expected. The snow has stopped, its icy remains squeaking underfoot. My lungs are able to pull in the fresh air fully for the first time in days and Jacob's jumper, so soft against my skin, is like a secret hug from him.

But I don't feel buoyant for long because when I arrive at the pub it's heaving. I don't know why I'm surprised to see it this full on Christmas Eve – it's not like there's much else to do around here. At first, I'm worried that I'm too early, but then I see Orla waving at me from a crowded table at the back of the room.

'You made it!' she cries, squeezing herself past the others and weaving her way towards me. According to the clock above the bar it's only eight thirty yet Orla's already drunk. Have they been here all day?

'Look who it is!' she cries out to the others, holding my hand up in the air like I've won a race.

Someone at the table mumbles, 'Whoop-de-doo.' I glance over Orla's shoulder and there's Bianca, glaring at me.

'Oh my God!' I cry, running past everyone and hugging Bianca before I realise what I'm doing. She's as surprised as I am, jumping to her feet and pushing me off her.

'What the hell?' she shouts. Everyone is watching, some of them whispering to one another.

'I thought something awful had happened to you.'

She looks at me like I'm mad.

'You went missing,' I explain. 'Everyone was looking for you.'

Bianca makes a contrite face, avoiding the eyes of the two men at the table who I presume are her brothers.

'I got lucky,' she says.

'You definitely did. Did someone take you? Did you get away?'

'Are you taking the piss?' Bianca holds her mobile phone up to my face. 'I got lucky on Tinder. I connected with some guy from Leeds who was housesitting for his sister in Fiveacres. He picked me up after work and I had a little minibreak. Why is that your business anyway?'

Oh God, I feel so stupid. There I was imagining Bianca being attacked by that man I saw lurking in the shadows, but instead she was getting her end away with some random stranger. One of the men at the table is laughing. I think that's Bianca's younger brother, sitting next to a blonde woman. Oh.

The policeman. My face heats up as I remember the ridiculous message I left him.

'Hey,' I say to everyone at the table.

Some I recognise, most I don't, although I do notice Harry isn't here. I'm not going to ask after him, though, in case word gets back to him and he takes it as a sign that he should keep trying to befriend me.

'Sit! Sit!' Orla says, dragging me over to the table.

Everyone makes space for me, and Bianca sits back down with a huff. She's now opposite me, her brothers flanking her, and Orla is pressed so tightly beside me her thigh is rubbing against my jeans. She reaches out for the hand of the man to Bianca's left, who must be her husband, Steve, which confirms that the one pouring me a glass of Chardonnay is definitely PC Ryan. I look around the table, wondering if any of them sent me the chocolates, the postcards or the funeral text, or if I'm mistaken about all of that too. Whatever is going on, someone here knows something.

'Thanks for the invite,' I say to them all.

'*I* didn't invite you,' Bianca replies.

'Don't be mean,' Ryan says, passing me the wine with a wink. 'The rest of us are happy to have Eva here. She clearly cares a lot about you.'

I give him a tight smile and swallow down the wine, grateful it's still cold as the pub is really hot. I shrug off my coat and drape it over the back of my chair.

'What the hell are you wearing?' Bianca shouts, leaning over the table and knocking over an empty pint glass. She's slurring and her eyes are bloodshot, although at least this time she's put on fresh make-up.

'Jeans and a jumper?'

'The jumper I bought Jacob!' she screams. The pub falls quiet, and no one at the table says a word until the hubbub returns. Bianca's brothers pull her back and she lets them, slumping back against the bench with a thud.

'Did he give you that jumper?' she says, her voice shaky and fists clenched.

I lean away from her. I didn't realise I'd pushed my chair back already. Bianca has been itching for a fight since I arrived in Cragstone but I'm not rising to the bait.

I take a deep breath and keep my voice steady. 'I found it in his wardrobe literally half an hour ago. I'm staying at Iris's and I had nothing to wear.'

Bianca deflates against the bench, her red eyes growing glassy.

'You've properly got your feet under the Donnelly table again, I see.'

'What choice do I have? I'm sure Orla already told you all there are no more trains to London until the day after Boxing Day.'

'Convenient,' Bianca replies. 'Move into a dead man's home then wear his clothes and befriend his friends.'

'He never had any friends,' I spit. Everyone looks at one another nervously. 'Don't pretend you all liked Jacob. You didn't, not in the end. He was escaping from this place when he died. Although he clearly didn't think much of you, Bianca, or he would have taken this jumper with him.'

She looks like she's going to launch herself across the table again, but I hold my ground. I'm not letting her win.

'I was going to ask if any of you sent me chocolates today, but I guess you didn't.'

They all give one another looks as if to say that between my being happy to see Bianca and the chocolate comment, I'm definitely losing my mind.

I'll take that as a no, then.

'Has Iris given you the gift yet?'

I look up. Ryan is smiling at me encouragingly. Isn't he the one dating the taxi driver's daughter? I wonder if that's her next to him, the mousy blonde who hasn't said a word yet.

'What gift?' I ask.

He tops up my wine. I didn't realise I'd already drunk it all. Is he talking about the gift Orla mentioned Iris had for me the day after the funeral? With all the concerning revelations over the last two days, I totally forgot about this.

'What is it?' I ask him.

He looks like he regrets having said anything. 'Nothing. It's not important.'

'Do you know what Ryan is talking about?' I ask Orla, who knows everything about everyone and never minds sharing.

She shakes her head beside me. She has hiccups and I don't think she's going to last much longer before she either falls off her chair or vomits.

'Someone was looking for you today,' she says to me, bopping me on the nose.

'Isn't she Little Miss Popular?' Bianca says. I ignore her.

'Looking for me at the hotel?'

'No. You got another phone call.'

'From whom?'

'*Whom,*' Bianca mimics.

'Marlo,' Orla replies. 'No, Marco. No... wait up.' She closes her eyes and for a minute I think she's fallen asleep, then she sits up and opens her eyes wide. 'Mario! That was it. That Mario Florentino fella who called the other day. Sexy name. Sorry, babe,' she adds, patting her husband's hand. 'Don't worry, it was Eva he wanted not me.'

All heads swivel in my direction. Orla may not have heard of the Florentino family, but the others clearly have. Especially the mousy blonde and Ryan, who are looking at one another with wide eyes.

'Don't look so impressed,' Bianca says, nudging her brother. 'Eva bagged her boss's son then he dumped her.'

'I didn't "bag" him, we were engaged,' I reply, doing my best to sound calmer than I feel. 'And he didn't dump me, I dumped him.'

'Because he cheated on you,' she says with a smirk. 'Harry told me. You might be pretty, Eva, but men clearly get bored of you eventually.'

The comment doesn't hurt as much as it should do, which tells me all I need to know regarding my ex-fiancé and Bianca's opinion of me.

'What did Mario say?' I ask Orla.

I knew he was persistent, but this is getting ridiculous.

'He's coming to pick you up.'

'What?' I shout at the same time as Bianca and a few others at the table. Orla holds her hand back up in the air, her head hanging limp like a pumpkin about to fall off a scarecrow.

'He asked if you were at the hotel, and I said no. Then I told him you'd lost your phone and were staying at Jacob's – I mean, Mrs Donnelly's – and you had no way of getting back. So he said he would come and get you tomorrow.'

'But tomorrow's Christmas Day,' I say. 'He's in Italy for Christmas.'

'I know. He told me that. He said he'd fly back from Milan and get you tomorrow night. I think it's very romantic.' She reaches a hand across the table to her husband. 'Would you fly back to get me if I was stranded in a little English village at Christmas, babe?'

Steve doesn't have time to answer before Orla slips off her chair and lands giggling in a crumpled heap on the filthy pub floor.

'Time to get you home,' Steve says, rolling his eyes at his brother and sister as he picks his wife up off the floor. 'We don't get out much, so she's hit it a bit too hard tonight. Getting three kids to bed on my own on Christmas Eve is way more heroic than flying over from Italy if you ask me.'

Everyone chuckles affectionately and says goodbye as Steve struggles to the door with a floppy, giggling Orla. I want to stop them from leaving, chase after them and ask Orla more questions, but what's the point? I'm not going to get any more sense out of her tonight.

I have to leave this awful town, and Mario would be a way to do that, but I need answers first. I don't want Mario here. I can't deal with all of his drama too right now.

Why can't he just wait until I'm back in London? I know why... Because Mario always gets what Mario wants, which means I now have one more person in Cragstone to worry about. And, thanks to Orla, he knows exactly where to find me.

TWENTY-FIVE

Orla and Steve have only been gone a few minutes when the two women beside Ryan get up at the same time and wave goodbye to us. Ryan nods in response but hardly looks up, so maybe that wasn't his girlfriend after all. I look behind me as they leave the pub and notice they're hand in hand. OK, so that was definitely not his girlfriend.

Ryan is saying something but all I can think about is that Mario is coming to Cragstone. What the hell am I meant to do now? I'm going to have to talk to my ex whether I like it or not.

'And then there were three,' Ryan says. 'Sometimes it's nice to not have anyone to rush home to. The night is all ours. Another bottle?' he asks me.

'I'll get it,' Bianca says, shooting me a dirty look as she leaves the table and fights her way to the bar.

Fine by me. I didn't want to be stuck at the table with her either.

Ryan moves up a seat, so we're face to face, and leans closer to speak to me.

'I got your message,' he says. 'I wanted to talk to you, but you didn't leave a number.'

'I lost my phone,' I say. 'Sorry I wasted your time. It was probably nothing.'

'It wasn't nothing. You sounded scared. Why did you think something bad had happened to Bianca?'

I bite my lips together. Today has been too much; if this nice man starts showing me an ounce of kindness, I'm going to start crying.

'I don't know, my mind has been all over the place lately. You know, coming back here and Jacob dying... I was just being paranoid.'

Ryan may seem nice but that doesn't mean I can trust him. He's Bianca's brother after all. I'm not telling anyone anything until I have proper evidence of what's been going on.

'You probably don't remember me,' he says. 'I was in the year below you at school.'

Ryan has the same plump lips as his sister, except he also has dimples and lighter hair. He's not traditionally handsome like Jacob, or chiselled and brooding like Mario, but... he's sweet. Like that Hollywood actor people say looks like a capybara. Glen whatshisname.

'Of course I remember you,' I say, even though I don't.

His smile widens and his dimples deepen. I don't have to tell Ryan anything, but getting to know the local police might be useful right now. I need to get as much intel about Jacob's death as I can before Mario turns up and my visit is cut short.

'So,' I say, leaning closer. 'Have you always wanted to be a cop?'

'No, for a long time I wanted to be a pastry chef.' He chuckles softly. 'Damn, I've never told anyone that before. I actually make a pretty mean croissant.'

'Very impressive.'

He gives me a crooked smile, lowering his eyes bashfully even though he's clearly enjoying the attention. I look behind me and check Bianca is still at the bar. I can only imagine how she'd react if she saw us talking like this.

'Seriously, though,' I continue. 'Is it difficult, being a policeman?'

'Not really, just doing my duty. It's normally quiet around here. Nothing too dangerous.'

'Jacob's accident must have been tough on you and your colleagues, then.'

He looks up and the pain in his eyes takes me by surprise. 'Of course it was hard. Jay was family... at least for a year or so.'

Jay? Of course, how insensitive of me. I'd totally banished the image of Bianca and Jacob together from my mind. But I can see it now, Jacob being part of the Clarke family and Ryan looking up to him. Ryan wanting to be in Jacob's inner circle, bathing in the warm glow of Star Boy's light.

'Jay was a good guy,' Ryan adds. 'We all wanted to be Jacob Donnelly when we grew up.'

I smile. I like that Ryan calls Jacob 'Jay' and that he saw in him what I used to.

'I'm so sorry you had to go through that,' I say. 'Were you on the scene? Did you have to identify the body?'

He shakes his head slowly as he fiddles with a cardboard coaster.

'I never saw the body. I saw his torn clothes though, and all his belongings scattered over the rocks, covered in blood. That was bad enough. Then my colleague found a couple of teeth in a rockpool, and Jacob's dentist confirmed the teeth were his. The blood and hair found at the scene were tested too, which all helped to confirm his death. Sorry, is this too much for you?'

I shake my head even though I'm having to grit my teeth so as not to cry. 'Are you saying they didn't find Jacob's body?'

He's not making any sense. How can you confirm someone's death without a body? What was inside the coffin they buried three days ago?

'Well, not exactly. But there were enough... *bits* of his body for the coroner to be certain it was him and that he was definitely dead. There wasn't much left of his car, and that coastline is treacherous. No one would survive hitting those rocks, and even if they did, they would have been washed away immediately.'

I sniff and Ryan squeezes my hand. I don't realise I'm crying until he wipes a tear from my cheek with his thumb.

'Was it on that awful bend where it falls down to the little beach?' I ask.

He nods and my stomach knots. Jacob and I used to love walking along those cliffs, wishing there was a way down to that secluded patch of sand so we could be alone. The other beaches were always busy with families, but that tiny rocky patch would have been the perfect hideaway. Except it was inaccessible by foot or boat.

Ryan is now staring at the cardboard coaster, now stripped of all its paper.

'Just getting access to the cove and bringing the car up took all day,' he says, his own eyes swimming with tears. 'There was no way Jay would have survived that fall. It was awful, Eva. I'll never forget the scene. Especially the Christmas present sitting there, all wrapped up, next to his blood-stained clothes.'

'What Christmas present?'

He sighs and goes to drink from his wine glass before remembering it's empty and that his sister is at the bar.

'That gift I was talking about earlier. I knew Iris wouldn't give it to you. When I was collecting Jay's belongings from the scene there was a box with a tag on it and it was addressed to you. No stamps. I think he planned to give it to you in person. It was all wrapped up in glossy black Christmas paper and ribbons, like he'd made a lot of effort. Anyway, my boss said I should add it to the belongings being returned to his mother. I pointed out that it had your name on it, but my boss said as next of kin it was up to Iris to give it to you or not. I guess she didn't.'

'No. She didn't.'

'Maybe she's waiting until tomorrow,' Ryan says with a hopeful smile. 'You know, give it to you on Christmas Day. I'm sure that's what Jay would have wanted.'

Iris hadn't been pretending; there *is* something from Jacob she planned to give me, just as she'd said in the message she left with Orla. I wonder why Iris changed her mind. I wonder if it's the package I saw at the back of her wardrobe wrapped in different paper to the others.

Bianca returns to the table and Ryan sits up, creating some distance between us. I still have so many more questions for him, but now his sister has returned the atmosphere has turned icy and awkward.

'So... what are your plans for Christmas?' I ask Bianca. I notice she only has two glasses in her hand. 'Are you seeing that guy from Leeds?'

She gives me a derisive look, hands Ryan a glass of wine, then rummages around in her handbag.

'I'm going outside for a smoke. You joining me, Ryan?'

He shakes his head. 'I gave up in the summer, remember?'

She rolls her eyes, grabs her own glass of wine and stomps outside.

'Don't mind her – she's just grumpy because Harry Hilborn isn't here,' Ryan whispers.

I'd forgotten all about Harry.

'Bianca and Harry?' I whisper back.

'Yeah, she's been into him for a while now.'

'But I thought she hooked up with...'

'I think she was trying to make him jealous. I doubt there was even a Tinder man; she probably just stayed home with her phone off and didn't answer the door, trying to make Harry worried.'

Harry didn't seem at all worried to me.

'Is that why he isn't here?' I ask. 'Is Harry avoiding your sister?'

Ryan smiles and sits back on the bench, sliding his untouched glass of wine over to me. 'No. Harry's completely oblivious. He's volunteering at some kids' thing at the church hall. Bianca thinks it's all magnanimous of him, but I know it's because his mum made him. God, I'm so sick of this pub and everyone in it. Want to get out of here before Hilborn catches up with us?'

I like this guy. Harry made out that Ryan was stupid, but he's not. He's not only easy on the eye but he's astute, caring and funny. Crazy to think he shares a bloodline with Bianca.

'OK,' I say. 'Let's finish this drink between us then I'm sure we can find a classier joint to hang out in.'

Ryan laughs. 'Nice thought, but I doubt we'll find anything classy in Cragstone. Actually, there's a new wine bar by the beach if you don't mind the walk. My house overlooks the sea. The little group of houses next to the ice cream shop.'

'Perfect.'

I know where Ryan lives. It's near the site of the accident. I take a sip of wine and consider how I'm going to phrase my next question before we leave.

'Ryan, um, was Jacob OK before he died?'

He lets out a sad laugh and runs his hands through his thick hair. 'No, Jay wasn't OK. Not at all. He wasn't even OK when he was dating my sister, although he seemed to be getting better before they broke up.'

I think back to what Charlie said about her mother, and Bianca also said Iris wasn't to be trusted, yet I haven't heard anyone else say she's a terrible person. Could one woman have so much control over her adult son?

'Do you think Jacob's mum made him ill?' I ask Ryan.

I like that he doesn't instantly dismiss me and takes his time answering.

'Iris Donnelly is a complicated character,' he says finally. 'She changed a lot after you left, we all noticed. She began to keep her kids on a really tight rein, especially once Michael moved out. She acted like Charlie and Jacob were her possessions, like they were the final thing her ex was trying to take away from her. I felt sorry for Jay at first – he was a sweet guy trying to be kind to his mum. I get it, family is everything. When Mum struggled after Dad died, we all tried our best to be there for her. I could see that's what Jay was doing – as a son you feel extra protective of your mother – but then things got a lot weirder about a year ago.'

I sit up in my seat. 'Weird how?'

'Jacob wouldn't stop talking about you.'

'Talking about me is weird?' I say with a light laugh.

'No, I don't mean that. It was the things he was saying about you. He kept showing everyone these photos of you that he said you'd sent him, telling us how you were both still madly in love with one another and had been emailing back and forth for ages. I only got a glance at the pictures, but they were strange. Not in a lewd way, but... I don't know. The way he spoke about you was really intense too. Something felt off.'

I must look as shocked as I feel because Ryan reaches out and pats my arm.

'Are you OK?'

I shake my head, doing my best to keep my tears at bay.

'He was wrong, wasn't he? You weren't together.'

'No. We weren't. How did you know? Everyone else believed him.'

Ryan shrugs. 'Call it a hunch. I'm a policeman, my job is to question everything, and I didn't buy it. Then I did some digging.'

My breath catches in my throat, and I lean forward. I want

to take Ryan's hand and pull him towards me, block out everything and everyone else around us so it's only his voice I can hear. Ryan is the first person I've spoken to in Cragstone who's been seeing what I'm seeing. That none of this is straightforward. I knew there was more to Jacob's accident than meets the eye.

'I found you on LinkedIn and Facebook and saw straight away that his pictures were fake – his photos were the same as the ones of you online. It didn't make sense to me because, although I knew you hadn't sent those photos, I do believe he believed you were talking to one another. Which means he was either delusional or someone was tricking him.'

'That's what I think too!' I exclaim. Finally, we are getting closer to the truth. Maybe I *can* trust him. 'But no one in this town ever believes a word I say. He was being tricked via email by someone pretending to be me, although I can't work out why. I also think Iris was hurting him. She was making him ill to keep him close.'

'Whoa. Eva. Slow down,' he says. 'Tell me everything from the beginning.'

Ryan's soft and friendly face grows hard, his pupils widening like a cat on the prowl. This man takes his job seriously and is far from stupid; he may actually be the only smart person in Cragstone.

I take a deep breath and speak as slowly and clearly as I can. 'Charlie told me that she believes Iris poisoned her and Jacob. She thinks it was Munchausen by proxy. It's something parents, usually mothers, do to their children... usually young children. It's a control thing; they make their kids ill for attention. That's why Jacob was always sick. It wasn't some mystery illness, it was poison. And the person Jacob was emailing wasn't me. He was being conned by someone. All I can think is that he was being conned out of his savings.'

'That's quite a hypothesis,' Ryan says. 'Do you have any evidence?'

I nod vigorously. 'Back at the house. Plus I've been getting threatening postcards with strange messages written on them since I arrived here. That's why I was scared for Bianca – I thought I saw a man watching me and I was worried I was being stalked. Perhaps whoever that was, whoever sent me the postcards, is also the person who was targeting Jacob. What if all this is connected to his death?'

Ryan is already on his feet. 'You can't go back to that house,' he says, working his way around the table towards me. 'Let's go to the wine bar and you tell me everything again in as much detail as possible. You can stay at mine if you feel safer there.'

Hold on. That's a more dramatic response than I was expecting. I thought he was going to call me Nancy Drew or ask more questions, but he's taking it seriously. Which means it's not as far-fetched as I feared. But that doesn't mean I'm going to spend the night at the house of a man I don't know and wake up with him on Christmas Day! For all I know Ryan could have been the one sending Jacob those emails.

'I can't stay with you. If I leave Iris's house, she won't let me back in,' I say. 'And that's where all the email printouts, photos and postcards are.'

Ryan places his hands on my shoulders and looks me so deep in the eyes that my mouth dries up and my throat closes over.

'Are you sure?' he asks.

'Yeah,' I reply. 'It's getting late. I should head back now or Iris will worry.' I'm not being entirely honest, though. The truth is that if we leave this pub and go somewhere else, I won't want to go back to the Donnelly residence. And I need to.

Ryan nods. He gets it. 'Come on, I'll walk you back.'

'You can't.' I think back to Iris's actions tonight, the way she tried to sabotage my evening out by making my clothes dirty.

She's a lot more compos mentis than she makes out. 'If Iris sees me with you, she'll have loads of questions. You don't know how she gets. I'll be fine on my own. It's not far.'

Ryan hesitates then nods again, although I notice his jaw is tense and twitching.

'Stay in touch, OK? Give me your number and...'

'I don't have a phone, remember?' I remind him. 'Iris has a landline though.'

A cloud passes over his face. He's thinking the same thing I am – someone in Cragstone doesn't want me to leave. He dips his hand in the pocket of his coat on the back of the chair and scribbles something down on a piece of paper. 'Here's my number. Keep it safe, and if you need me, call me. I know where the Donnelly house is. Use Iris's home phone if you can and let me know you got home safe. Then call me tomorrow. If I don't hear from you by tomorrow afternoon, I'll come and find you, OK?'

'But my ex-fiancé is picking me up tomorrow,' I say quietly.

'Don't leave with him. Stay,' he says, his hands grasping the tops of my arms.

'Yes, stay!' a voice booms from the door as a man in a Santa outfit bursts into the pub. 'The party has just got started!'

TWENTY-SIX

A gush of cold air fills the pub as a man strides towards our table dressed in a cheap Santa suit complete with floppy hat and tummy padding. He pulls down his cheap synthetic beard, making Ryan groan under his breath so quietly only I hear him.

'Harry. You made it,' Ryan says with zero enthusiasm.

'Call me Ho Ho Harry tonight,' Harry says, putting his beard back in place and punching Ryan lightly on the arm. He turns to me and gives me a big hug, seemingly unaware that I'm not hugging him back. I want Ryan to know I'm as elated as he is that Harry has joined us.

'Doesn't he look cute?' Bianca says, stroking Harry's beard. Her cheeks are flushed from the cold and her hair has been mussed up from the wind. 'Hey, Santa,' she coos. 'I think it's my turn to sit on your lap. Although I can't promise that I've been a good girl.'

'I heard,' Harry replies, straight-faced.

Bianca blushes and steps aside as Harry takes a seat and pulls at my arm. 'I think Eva was first in line, actually. Jump on, Christmas Eva. There's nothing to be scared of. Santa only comes once a year.'

Bianca laughs loudly, the way only the drunk can do comfortably in public, but Harry isn't even looking at her. I've changed my mind, I *do* want Ryan to walk me back now because I have so many questions for him but he's used Harry's entrance as an excuse to escape to the bar. I don't blame him.

'No, thank you,' I say to Harry, sitting on the chair next to him. Just in time Ryan approaches our table with a tray of drinks, and I give him a look of gratitude.

'A wine for you,' Ryan says, handing me another Chardonnay. 'Wine for my sis, and a pint for Father Christmas.'

'Cheers, m'dears!' Harry holds the glass aloft then takes a long, slow slug without taking his beard off. Foam mats the white fabric, making his moustache stick to his top lip like a dead rodent left out in the rain. I turn away from him as Ryan squeezes himself back on to the bench behind the table and picks up his old glass, the wine probably warm by now. He beckons his sister to join him but it's obvious she wants my seat.

'I better be going,' I say, getting up.

Bianca steps forward, poised to jump into my chair beside Harry, but Harry pulls me back down.

'You haven't even drunk your wine yet.'

'I have a headache,' I lie.

'Come on, Eva,' Harry says. 'I've only just got here.'

Bianca reluctantly joins her brother on the bench, and I sip at my drink. I don't have a headache yet, but I know I'm going to have a killer one tomorrow. As if Christmas Day with Iris won't be hard enough. I have to stay focused, go through all the clues again and gather all the evidence for Ryan so we can discuss things further.

I check my jeans pocket – Jacob's jeans pocket – where Ryan's telephone number is folded up and hidden away. Mario is going to have a wasted trip tomorrow because as soon as Christmas dinner is over, I'm making my excuses and going straight to Ryan's house. I'm not leaving Cragstone until a proper investigation against Iris, and Jacob's stalker, is under way.

'Looks like we'll be spending Christmas next door to one another tomorrow,' Harry says. 'I'll be at my parents' house all day. I don't suppose you fancy popping over, do you?'

'Yeah, maybe,' I say, avoiding his intense gaze.

'Working your way through the entire town, are we?' Bianca says.

I look up with a start. What's she talking about now?

'Not enough to get with Jacob *and* his father, but now you're flirting with my brother *and* Harry three days after your dead ex's funeral, all while your rich fiancé is on his way to rescue you.'

'You were flirting with Ryan?' Harry says beside me.

I ignore him. 'What exactly is your problem?' I say to Bianca. 'Absolutely nothing happened between me and Michael, yet your vicious tongue ruined my life. And now you want to start more rumours?'

'Just saying what I see.'

'You've always been spiteful and jealous,' I say. 'I wouldn't be surprised if you were the one sending the postcards.'

'What postcards?' she says.

Ryan leans over the table and places his hand over mine. 'Eva. Leave it.'

'What's going on between you two?' Harry says, edging his seat closer to me but glaring at Ryan. He's still wearing his beard, speckles of beer landing on my cheek every time he speaks. Ryan takes his hand away from mine like he's been burned.

'What do you care, Harry?' Bianca says. 'Eva has been back five minutes and you're already chasing after her like a lovesick puppy, just like you did at school. You were the same with Jacob, desperate for him to be your friend. When I was dating him, you hung out with us all the time. I thought it was *my* company you enjoyed but of course not, it was *him* you were obsessed with.'

Harry was obsessed with Jacob? Ryan catches my eye and the hairs on my arms stand on end. This might explain why Harry keeps popping up unexpectedly. It wouldn't be difficult for him to pretend to be me over email, enjoying having power over perfect Jacob, the man he envied. I bet he even faked those photos of me for his own kinky kicks. I shudder at the thought. Plus Harry's mother said he had savings. I wonder if Jacob contributed to them, somehow thinking he was putting money aside to escape Iris.

'Admit it, Harry,' Bianca taunts. 'You've always been obsessed with Eva and Jacob.'

Harry's face, partially hidden beneath his cheap beard, has turned as red as his Santa suit.

'OK, time to cool down,' Ryan says, making his way around the table and standing behind me.

Bianca's eyes flash with anger, her top lip turned up in a sneer. 'Great. Now my own brother is jumping to the rescue of the little whore!' she shouts out. 'Look at you both, fighting over Jacob's cast-offs.'

'Enough, Bianca! You're drunk and you need to go home,' Ryan shouts.

I'm impressed. I didn't have him down as the commanding type.

'I'm not drunk,' Bianca shouts back. 'I'm the only one brave enough to say what no one else wants to admit. Eva is a whore, just like her mother. She's always had stupid boys falling over themselves for her and that's how she's ever got anywhere. She's a calculating bitch who manipulates everyone around her to get what she wants. She's probably back to see if Jacob had any money she can trick Iris out of. We all know he wouldn't have driven off the cliff if it weren't for that slag!'

The entire pub stills, everyone looking at us. My face stings with the humiliation of what she's saying because I get it now. This is what everyone has always thought of me. I saw myself as the hard-done-by daughter of an alcoholic while they all saw me as the pretty temptress who bewitched innocent men and took advantage of kind-hearted women. Everyone is gawping at me. I recognise faces from school, from church, from the various shops on the high street. There are no strangers in Cragstone – I'm the most foreign person here. And now I know exactly what everyone thinks of me.

Bianca's goading me, waiting for me to throw my drink over her or say something back so she has the perfect excuse to hit me. Nothing has changed since school. Nothing but me. I'm smarter now, and stronger, and all she's doing is confirming my fears that Jacob's death was not straightforward and there was more than one person here who was angry with him and seeking revenge.

'I'm not listening to this anymore,' I say quietly, grabbing my coat and handbag. 'Jacob's death was the result of something bigger than you realise. He was being persecuted by someone, and I'm going to find out who.'

I don't care that I have an audience or that the entire town thinks I'm a crazy, stuck-up, conniving slag. All I care about is getting answers. I shrug my coat on and head for the door.

'Want to walk with me?' I ask Ryan.

He looks at his sister, then at me, and makes an apologetic face. 'Sorry. I need to make sure she goes straight home and doesn't cause any more trouble,' he says to me quietly. 'There's no calming her down when she gets like this.'

As disappointed as I am that I won't get to speak to him further tonight, I like that he puts family first. That's how it should be.

'I'll walk you home, Eva,' Harry says, scrambling to his feet and adjusting his damp beard, now yellow from the beer. I wish he'd take that awful thing off. 'I'm staying at my mum and dad's tonight, remember, so I'm going that way anyway.'

How could I forget? The last thing I want to do is wander the streets with Harry, but I think of the last time I walked home alone in the dark and how the hooded man was watching me. Maybe it's safer to be with someone – even if that someone is a creepy idiot dressed as Father Christmas.

Ryan's fingers squeeze mine as I walk past him, and I bite my bottom lip to stop myself from crying. I know it's pathetic but I'm so relieved to finally have an ally. Relieved there's at least one person in this awful town who believes me.

It's a bitterly cold night and I'm thankful I remembered to wear the scarf Iris lent me. I wrap it tighter around my throat, breathing in the familiar scent of peppery cedarwood. I wish I'd worn a hat though because my ears are stinging from the wind.

'You look chilly,' Harry says after a few minutes of walking silently down the high street. The shop lights are twinkling, and every house is lit up with trees in the windows and decorations in the gardens. I really did think that one day I'd be an adult with a big house and a family and windows framed with fairy lights. Maybe even a sea view. I can't see any of that happening for me anymore.

'I'm fine,' I say to Harry, crossing my arms and tucking my chin into my scarf.

'Wait up,' he says, pulling on my coat sleeve. 'Take this.'

He pulls his Santa hat off and places it gently on my head. It makes a bigger difference than I thought it would, the tips of my ears immediately tingling as they thaw out. I thank him and he grins.

'Hey,' he says, slowing down as we reach Iris's house. He pulls on my arm and I stop walking. 'I meant what I said about you coming over at Christmas. I'd really like to see you.'

A wave of exhaustion hits me. I can feel the sharp acid of the Chardonnay climbing back up my throat and the inevitable headache beginning to linger behind my eyes. I don't have the energy for Harry at the moment, or any moment in fact.

'Thanks,' I mumble.

'I don't suppose you like me very much, do you?'

No, I don't. I feel bad about that. Harry's harmless, but why must he be so overbearing? What does he want from me?

'You're lovely,' I say, doing my best to appease him. I find it's much easier to lie to men like him than let them down gently.

'Really? You think I'm lovely?'

Shit. I should have gone for blunt.

'What I meant was that—' Before I have a chance to finish my sentence Harry's wet beard is on my face and he's trying to kiss me. The fluffy, beer-soaked polyester makes me want to gag. I turn my face away, but I can't step back because he's gripping the tops of my arms tightly.

'Stop,' I say quietly.

'Eva, oh Eva, I've wanted you for so long,' he groans, his lips moving along my cheek towards my mouth. 'Jacob never deserved you. I knew you'd be back, and now you have to stay.'

What did he just say? A cold chill washes over me. I try to squirm out of his grasp, but he's holding on too tightly. 'Get off me. I can't breathe!'

He pulls his beard down and kisses my neck, his lips wet and his breath heavy.

'Oh God, Eva.' He inhales my collarbone and behind my ears. 'Jesus, you smell so good.'

I pull his stupid Santa hat off my head and hit him with it until he stops. 'That's enough!' I cry out, pushing him off me.

He looks up, his eyes bleary and his lips red and blotchy.

'You're right,' he says. 'We don't want Iris or my mother catching us. Neither of them would approve. But I'll be over tomorrow. I have to see you again, Eva. I'm not letting you get away this time.'

I run to Iris's front gate, rushing down her path towards the door. It makes no difference what I say to Harry because I know men like him: he will purposely misconstrue it and convince himself that we're destined to be together. He's unhinged, possibly dangerous, and exactly the kind of person to be deluded enough to mess with Jacob's head and send me those postcards. I need to get inside the house, call Ryan and tell him everything.

I'm rummaging around inside my handbag, trying to find the door keys as fast as I can before Harry follows me up the garden path, when I realise I don't have a key. *Shit!* Now I have to knock on the door and risk waking Iris up.

'Do you need a hand?' Harry calls out from his parents' front door on the other side of the low wall. 'My mum has a set of spare keys. I can go and get them for you.'

In that moment the front door flies open. Iris is standing before me in her dressing gown, her face red and swollen from crying.

'There you are!' she cries, pulling me inside by the scruff of my neck. 'I thought you were dead.'

TWENTY-SEVEN

'It's gone eleven o'clock,' Iris says, shutting the door and tugging my coat off me. 'You have no phone, so I called the pub, but the barman wasn't very helpful. He said he didn't know the names of everyone in there and that this wasn't nineteen ninety-two. I've been at the window waiting for you for hours. How could you go like that? How could you leave me when you know I have a bad heart?'

Iris is slurring, one side of her mouth drooping. I look over her shoulder into the living room. The packet of pills she came back from the hospital with is on the coffee table, half of them popped out of their blister pack.

'Did you take more of your meds?' I ask.

'The doctor said I was to take them when I felt anxious. But I feel anxious all the time.'

'Let's have a cup of tea,' I suggest, pulling off my trainers and bracing myself for whichever version of Iris we're getting tonight. My face is humming from where Harry pushed himself against me; I can still taste the beer from his fake beard. I wanted to call Ryan, but I can't now with Iris looming over me.

I'll call him when Iris goes to bed, then I'll take all the evidence to his house tomorrow. Mario won't find me there either.

I left the kitchen tidy after cooking earlier, but now it's covered in dirty pots and pans, washing up in the sink and splashes of something on the walls.

'I've been cooking,' Iris says, following my gaze. 'I was getting ready for tomorrow.'

I'm too dazed to say anything more than, 'Let me put the kettle on.'

'No, no. I'll make the tea,' she says, fussing with mugs and teabags and a white ceramic pot of sugar I haven't seen before. Jacob always took two sugars in his tea. I'd joke that they'd catch up with him eventually, but if anything he died looking better than ever.

Iris pours the boiling water in both cups, adding a heap of granulated brown sugar into mine.

'Oh, I don't take sugar,' I say.

'Go on. It's good for you,' she says, stirring it in. I notice she doesn't put any sugar in her own tea, just milk, enough so her tea resembles bath water. So much for her dairy intolerance.

I try to look inside the sugar pot, but she moves it away.

'Did you have a nice night?' she asks tersely, her lips stretched into a disapproving straight line.

'Yes, it was lovely,' I say, lies rolling off my tongue with ease now.

'I saw you with that Harry boy. He was being very touchy-feely outside.'

I repress a shudder at the memory of him grabbing me. 'He had too much to drink.' I hope she didn't see him try to kiss me.

'Vicky says he has terrible taste in women.'

OK, so she saw everything.

'I find him rather tiresome,' I say. 'A little on the pushy side.'

'Indeed,' Iris replies, watching as I stir my tea. She's waiting for me to drink it. I'm not stupid – I'm not eating or drinking anything she prepares for me. I change the subject.

'Ryan Clarke, the policeman, was at the pub tonight. He mentioned a package was found at the scene of the... At the cove. When they collected Jacob's belongings. It was addressed to me.'

'I looked but I can't find it.'

Liar.

'You must have it somewhere. All the items they found were signed over to you. Ryan said it was wrapped in black paper with my name on. He asked whether you had given it to me yet.'

'Drink up,' Iris says. 'Your tea is getting cold.'

I pretend to sip it and she smiles.

'I think it was a Christmas present from Jacob. For me.'

Iris puts the sugar pot back in the cupboard and places the milk in the fridge. 'I don't think so. The only person my son ever bought presents for was his mama. Have you seen all the packages under the tree? They are all for me, from my son. Such a good boy. I'm saving them for tomorrow. Christmas morning was his favourite time of year. He loved me so much.' Iris starts to cry again but this time I don't comfort her. I know she has the gift and I know she's keeping it from me. What I don't know is what's inside and whether it will help me get to the bottom of whatever the hell is going on.

I pretend to drink my tea again then fake a yawn. 'That was lovely,' I say, taking my mug to the overflowing sink and tipping the contents down the drain when she's not looking. 'I better get to bed, though. Busy day tomorrow. You will let me do all the hard work tomorrow, won't you? All the cooking?'

Iris isn't listening; she's staring into the distance, dabbing at her eyes with the tatty red Babygro. I pat her on the shoulder.

'Want me to help you tidy up?' I ask even though I'm so exhausted I can hardly stand.

'No, no, you get to bed. Jacob does all the cleaning,' she mutters. 'Have you seen him? Is my boy coming home soon?'

I can't sleep. I spent hours combing through all the notes from Iris that I found in Jacob's room, re-reading the email printouts and scrutinising the photos and postcards. Everything I gathered together is now in an A4 envelope, ready to give to Ryan. It's too late to call him now, I'll have to call in the morning if I get the chance.

I found other things too – strange notes Jacob had left to himself, subscriptions for anxiety, nausea and depression medication, and photos of Jacob with his mother, her face scratched out. He was such a handsome man with his long-lashed brown eyes, strong jaw like his father, the same wide smile as his mother, and something that was all his own. I wish I'd known him as an adult. I also found some half-finished letters he'd written to me but never posted: declarations of love and promises of a future together. My chest aches at the thought of him believing we were in touch and that I felt the same way about him.

What would I do if he walked into this room right now? I'd forgive him, that's what. I'd tell him I understood that him breaking up with me was never about me. Then I'd rescue him right back. Love doesn't die just because the person has.

I stuff the A4 envelope into my backpack, still thinking about all the letters to me Jacob failed to finish. What was his plan? Did he have my London address? Did he really intend to send love letters to a house I shared with my fiancé? What if he managed to send one after all?

I climb into Jacob's bed, dressed in his pyjamas, imagining how that would have played out. Mario often opened my post, mainly bills and important-looking letters. It never felt strange at the time; he liked to look after me and that included ensuring my bills were paid. He was generous and could afford to look after me. Who wouldn't like that? But perhaps he wasn't being that generous, not now I know how jealous he is. I imagine a scenario where one of the letters Mario opened was from Jacob. What would it say? My guts curdle at the thought of Mario reading Jacob's innermost feelings about me. I can see it now, Mario's thick brows meeting in the middle, trying to make sense of the words. The way he'd rub the stubble on his chin as he re-read the letter a second time, scratching the back of his neck with frustration, the colour in his cheeks rising from anger and humiliation.

Maybe that's why Mario cheated on me... for revenge. And that's why he's driving all the way here tomorrow because he thinks I cheated on him with Jacob and wants to check my ex is really dead. My mind is a tornado of every scenario imaginable spinning around and around until I cover my head with the pillows and scream into the mattress.

For weeks I've been mourning the loss of Mario, and the life I could have had, and now all of that feels like somebody else's life, one that was never mine. Everything that has happened in the ten years since I left Cragstone doesn't feel real anymore. This place, my childhood and everyone who is still here from my old life, that's all that exists for me. I think back to tonight – Iris crying, Ryan's fingers brushing mine, Bianca's cold glare, Harry's hot wet lips on my neck. All these people I knew as a child are now adults wanting a piece of me. Insisting I stay, or that I go, or that I owe them something. I feel like I'm in one of those time-travelling movies where I've been transported back into the body of my eighteen-year-old self, yet I can't go back to who I was in London because she doesn't exist anymore.

The room is pitch-black. It's a cloudy night with no light from the moon. The house is old, with tired floorboards and plumbing that hums, the wind rushing through the spindly trees outside the window. I hear movement through the walls, and I imagine Iris tossing and turning in her bed, confused, thinking her son is safe asleep in the room next door. Was that sugar she put in my tea? Or was it something that would have made me ill enough that I'd not be able to leave the house again for a while?

I hear it again, a creak on the stairs. It must be her, wandering around or going to the bathroom. The bedroom door handle turns slowly, and I wait for her to come in like she did on the first night I stayed here. Maybe she'll ask how I'm feeling, take my temperature again, insist I take more pills. I bet she was like that with Jacob, making him sick then making him better in a confusing, relentless, maternal loop.

The door creaks open a sliver then stops. No Iris. It must be the wind outside making the windows rattle and the doors blow open. I get out of bed and go to shut it, then I stop. I can hear Iris gently snoring to my right, and the soft thud of someone walking. Where's it coming from? It sounds like someone's downstairs. No, surely it's just Harry or his parents next door. I open the bedroom door wider, just a crack, and squint into the darkness of the hallway. Nothing. I step out and peer down the stairs. Silence. It's not until I shut the bedroom door behind me, pushing it until it clicks, that I hear the unmistakable sound of the front door closing.

I run back to bed and pull the covers over my head the way I did as a child when I'd hear my mother coming home after a night of drinking, her uneven steps on the stairs, her voice thick with alcohol and calling out my name. I make a mental list of everyone who has a set of keys to this house, to the lock that hasn't been changed in decades: Harry and his mother, Michael, Charlie. There's even the old set of door keys in the box of my belongings Mario still has. Would any of them let themselves into the house then leave again?

It's Christmas Eve. I don't believe in Father Christmas... but I do believe someone is out to get me.

TWENTY-EIGHT
CHRISTMAS DAY

I'm awoken by loud banging and the smell of bacon. Once again, I have no idea what the time is but it's fully light outside. I pull the curtains back and can't help but smile at the sight of children riding their new bikes along the pavement outside, coats over pyjamas, and families through the windows bustling about, preparing for the arrival of their Christmas Day guests.

I think of my friend Amanda and how I never got to tell her I wasn't joining her at her mum's house. Has she been trying to call me? Is she worried? Of course she'll be worried. Damn it, I'm so stupid! I should have asked to borrow Ryan's phone last night, logged into my email account and sent Amanda a message.

I sit back down on the bed with a thud and rub my eyes. I don't want to go downstairs. I told Iris I would do all the cooking today but – surprise, surprise – she didn't listen. I massage my temples, scrunching my eyes at the headache forming like a Christmas crown around my head. Why did I drink so much again last night? One way or another, today is going to be hell.

My clothes are drying on the airer in the hallway where I hung them last night, but they are still too damp to put on. I pull the A4 envelope out of my bag, fold my clothes up anyway, stuff them in my rucksack and add the envelope full of evidence back on top. There's no way Ryan won't look into it further when he sees what that creep was sending to Jacob pretending to be me. I'll grin and bear it through lunch, then when Iris inevitably falls asleep, I'll escape to Ryan's house. I'll call him from Iris's landline. Failing that I'll just walk to his house. The coast is twenty minutes from here and there are only four or five houses by that ice cream shop he mentioned. I'll find him.

I'm stepping out of the shower, a towel wrapped around me, when Iris shouts up the stairs.

'Eva! Are you awake?'

'I'll be down in five minutes,' I call out.

I finish getting dressed in Jacob's jumper and jeans from last night, add some make-up and earrings, and attempt a smile in the mirror. It's more of a grimace.

'Well, don't you look lovely,' Iris says as I descend the stairs, running over and embracing me in a warm hug. She's dressed in festive green today, complete with a red hairband made of tinsel and earrings shaped like holly wreaths. 'Merry Christmas, my darling.'

A lump forms in my throat at the thought of this woman all alone on the most magical day of the year. Jacob, Charlie and Iris's grandson should be here instead of me, but she drove them all away. I'm still wary of her, and I'm still angry, but I also pity her. Hopefully Ryan can help me get her the support she needs.

'Merry Christmas.'

The kitchen table is laden with food. Didn't she say she was cooking last night as well? I really don't want to eat anything she's prepared but, equally, I'm hungover as hell and starving. She follows my gaze.

'Bacon, hash browns, pancakes, smoked salmon, pastries, fruit and I'm doing some poached eggs.'

My stomach grumbles but I keep hearing Charlie's words of warning. Will this food make me ill? Will not eating it make Iris upset? I don't know which is the safest option.

'You've made such an effort,' I exclaim. 'It looks wonderful!'

She beams at me, her sunken cheeks rosy and bright. 'It was the least I could do after all your help last night. I came downstairs and the kitchen was spotless. Thank you.'

What does she mean? I didn't do anything. I went upstairs before she did last night. She said she was going to clean up.

'Tea?' she asks. 'Or should we have a cheeky mimosa? It's nearly eleven o'clock, which is practically lunchtime. The turkey is in the oven, and I thought maybe you could peel the potatoes?'

I nod along without really listening and set to work preparing vegetables while she finishes the eggs and chatters away about Jacob. Once seated, I wait to see what she eats then do the same, picking at the toast and fruit, reasoning they will be the least likely things to be tampered with. She doesn't notice that I haven't touched my drink or that I'm copying her; she's far too animated about us opening our Christmas presents.

'Jacob always bought me such personal gifts. It must have taken him all year to plan my presents. Seeing my reaction was always his favourite part of Christmas Day. He loved to give more than receive.'

My stomach is swirling, and I don't know if it's from anxiety, the hangover or what I've eaten. I excuse myself and rush to the bathroom, where I sit on the toilet, my head in my hands, taking one deep breath after another as my stomach spasms.

I'm not safe here. I'm not safe from Iris, nor from whoever has been watching me, and I have no idea when Mario is getting here and what that showdown will look like. I stare out of the bathroom window, the edges tinted with frost while outside the white sky looks like an unfinished canvas. Tiny specks of dusty snow have already begun to float through the air, the grass no longer green but white as if icing sugar has been sprinkled over the back lawn.

'Eva?' Iris is shouting up the stairs. 'Are you unwell?'

'I'm fine. I'll be down in a minute,' I call out. It's just an upset stomach from too much drink, too much stress and not enough sleep.

'Let's do presents,' she says, her high-pitched voice eager as a child's.

I flush the loo and take my time washing my hands, then gulp down some water straight from the tap before opening the door. I only have to get through a few more hours of this then I can walk to Ryan's house. Preferably before it's dark and Mario tracks me down.

'Ah, there you are,' Iris says, clapping her hands with glee.

'Sorry, I felt a bit poorly but I'm OK now.'

'Hopefully not something you ate. Best you stay home for the next few days,' Iris says, rubbing my stomach like I'm expecting. 'Let me look after you.'

She insists we leave the breakfast things on the table, explaining that in this house Christmas lunch is around four o'clock anyway so there's plenty of time to tidy up and put the potatoes on. The turkey will take some time anyway.

'Come,' she says, bustling us into the living room, where the Christmas tree lights are twinkling, their glow illuminating the presents beneath. I notice Iris's gifts to Jacob are gone and the only ones left are those addressed to her.

'Let's sit on the carpet, in front of the tree,' she says. 'That's how we used to open the presents with the kids when they were little.'

I'm not quite sure what we're doing right now, but the only gifts I can see under the tree are the ones Jacob bought his mother. Oh no, I hope she's not expecting something from me.

This is such an unnecessary farce, but I have to play along. I have to keep Iris sweet until I can get out of here.

She sits on the floor cross-legged and beckons me over, indicating that I should hand her each gift one by one. As soon as she gets the first package in her hand she rips at the paper in a frenzied hurry, her face split open in a demonic grin.

'Bath salts!' she cries out, holding it up as if she's a contestant on one of her game shows. 'Lavender scented. My favourite.' She opens the box and pulls out the jar, popping the cork and smelling the grains of lilac-coloured salt inside. 'Oh, Jacob, you sweet boy. Thank you.' She puts it back inside, kisses the packet of cheap bath products and places it beside her. 'Come on. Pass me another one!'

I do as I'm told, and she rips into the paper again, pulling out something shiny.

'Cookie cutters! Look, Eva. He bought me tree-shaped cookie cutters. Thank you, Jacob. You always did love my baking. What's next?'

She proceeds to open a box of After Eights that nearly make her cry, a small tube of hand cream she puts on right away and a cheap wooden picture frame without a photo in it.

'Weren't they all so special?' she proclaims, signalling at the pile of gifts that look like they were purchased in five minutes from the discount shop on the high street. 'My baby was always so thoughtful. He clearly spent a long time choosing them. Wouldn't you say, Eva? Wouldn't you say my boy knows his mama so well?'

'Absolutely,' I reply. 'Oh look, there's still one left.'

Another gift is tucked behind the arm of the sofa. I pull it out and recognise it immediately as the package at the back of Iris's wardrobe that was different to the other gifts. It's wrapped in black shiny paper with green Christmas trees on it, thicker and glossier than the paper he used to wrap up hers. But I have no idea how it got here.

'Hand it over, then,' Iris says.

I look at the label and my breath catches in my throat. I was right. 'It's addressed to me.'

'What?' Iris's head jerks in my direction like a nervous lizard. 'Oh, yes, I bought you a little something,' she says slowly.

I read the label out loud. 'To my dearest Eva. Merry Christmas, our first of many together. Love Jacob.'

Her face falls. 'How did that get there?'

'I don't know.'

'It wasn't there yesterday,' she says. 'I know that because I took the things I bought Jacob back upstairs. There were no presents under the tree for you yesterday. My son only bought gifts for *me*.'

'It has my name on it,' I say, showing her the package. She tries to snatch it out of my hand, but I pull it away. The edges of the gift are a little scuffed and dented, like it's been dropped. The gift found at the scene of the accident. The gift from Jacob that Iris has been hiding from me.

'It's mine,' I say like a petulant child. 'It's for me, from Jacob. It's his writing with the same holly-shaped tags as the ones on your presents. This is the present you've been looking for, isn't it?'

Iris's face turns red as she twists the cheap wrapping paper from her presents into a rope. 'Yes,' she mumbles.

'I'm so glad you found it. Thank you!' I cry, enjoying every moment of her discomfort.

I go to unwrap it, but one end is already unstuck. 'Did you open it already?' I ask.

She shrugs. 'I had a little peek when the police gave it to me. You know, in case it was food, and it might go off. But it's not, so I figured it was safe to give it to you at a later date.' She keeps twisting the paper in her hand, tighter and tighter. 'I kept it for today. I wanted to surprise you!'

Liar. I open the box slowly, hesitantly, wondering what gift was so important to Jacob that he wrapped it a month before Christmas and was possibly on his way to deliver it to me in person. I peel the paper away from the box and pull it off. It's bath salts, the same cheap brand as his mother's set, except instead of lavender, this one smells of lemons. That's strange. Jacob knew I hated anything lemon scented; he even stopped wearing his favourite citrusy aftershave because of me.

'Oh, look,' Iris says. 'The same bath product as mine. Very thoughtful. Although he bought me a lot more gifts than just that one, of course.'

I don't get it. Did Iris replace Jacob's gift to me with this one and put his tag on it? Surely this isn't what he wanted me to have. Why would Jacob drive five hours to London to hand-deliver bath salts?

'Right,' Iris says, hauling herself off the floor. 'Let's finish peeling the vegetables and start on lunch.'

I stay seated on the floor, a surge of disappointment keeping me rooted to the carpet. I haven't received a gift from Jacob in ten years, yet this one has crushed me. He knew me so well. I'm being silly, it's not worth getting upset over, but none of this makes sense.

I open the flap and put my hand inside, expecting to find a small glass jar, but there are no bath salts – the box is full of screwed-up tissue paper. I pull a handful out, then another, until there's nothing left and the box is empty.

'Stop making a mess,' Iris says. 'You're lucky you got anything at all.'

I ignore her as I dig my hand inside, deeper and deeper until the tips of my fingers touch a velvety object. I smile. Jacob *did* know me well... and he knew his mother well too. He was keeping the real gift hidden. I pull out the contents as Iris stares down at me, her face slack with horror. She slumps on to the sofa as I examine my gift. A red velvet box.

'What's that?' she cries.

'My real Christmas present from your son.'

I look over at the tree, at the fairy lights illuminating the angel perched on the top. Behind it, through the window framed by heavy curtains, snow has begun to fall in thick, fluffy balls. Cragstone got its white Christmas after all. I swallow down the lump in my throat as I slowly open the box.

'What is it?' Iris screeches. 'What did he buy you?'

I gape at the open box, unable to say anything. Inside is a white gold ring with an emerald stone. Jacob always told me my green eyes shone like gemstones in the sun, and that one day he'd propose with a ring that matched them. He wasn't on his way to London to give me a Christmas present; he was on his way to ask me to marry him. Me, the woman he thought he'd been talking to for a year, the woman who told him to run away and come to her. But that woman wasn't me, and he died trying to get to her.

I wipe away the tears rolling down my cheek then slip the engagement ring on to my ring finger. It's the perfect fit. Jacob never failed at anything.

'No,' Iris says, reaching out for my hand. 'Take it off!'

I scramble backwards, clambering on to my feet.

'You tricked him!' she screams, trying to stand but so incandescent with rage she keeps falling back on to the sofa. 'He didn't love you, he loved *me*! You enticed him. Bewitched him. I always knew you would take him away from me in the end. That's why I pretended to be him and broke up with you.'

What did she just say?

TWENTY-NINE

'What are you talking about?' I stammer.

We are both on our feet now. Iris is inches from me, scowling defiantly with her hands on her waist.

'You heard me,' she says. 'I split you both up. It was getting out of hand, and I wasn't going to let you win.'

'Win what?' I shout.

'Him!'

I run both of my hands through my hair. It's like I'm standing on quicksand; every time I think I understand what's going on something else shifts and has me flailing. Is Iris telling me that *she* broke us up? That after I left for university it wasn't Jacob who dumped me... it was *her*? If she is, then she's re-writing history, everything I know to be a fact slowly morphing into a different picture. Jacob didn't hate me. He didn't choose his mother over me. *She* did. We could have been together for the last ten years. Happily together.

'It was just teenage puppy love,' Iris says. 'It was never going to work. I simply speeded things up a bit.'

'It was real!' I shout. 'I know we were young, but Jacob and I really loved one another. We never stopped.'

It's like I'm not here, like I'm watching this happen to someone else. Even my own voice sounds far away. 'What we had was good and pure,' I say.

Iris scoffs. 'There's never been anything good or pure about you, Eva Walsh. You came from a broken home and then you tried to break mine up too. You took advantage of our kind nature. I made you part of my family and how did you repay me? You destroyed my marriage and tried to take away my boy!'

I didn't. It's not true. I was a child with a dead mum and no other relatives. Jacob made me feel safe, Charlie was my only friend, and Michael and Iris were kind. Everything was perfect until that rumour. Yet now Iris is telling me Jacob didn't break up with me because he believed Bianca. We split up because of *Iris*.

'What did you do?' I hiss through my teeth, my left hand curled into a fist, my other hand wrapped around it, protecting my ring – my last connection to something that could have lasted forever.

'I don't know why you're so angry,' she says. 'You left him first.'

'You threw me out!' I cry. 'I went to university in London and Jacob was meant to follow. We were in love. What did you do, Iris?'

She rolls her eyes and gives me a pitying shake of the head.

'Jacob was very ill after you left. He was distraught about his father cheating on me and then you left him in his hour of need, so he took to his bed and refused to leave. He was ever so poorly, the little lamb. But I was there for him, like always.'

'Why was he really sick, Iris? Tell the truth.'

'He was too poorly to answer your calls,' she continues, as if I never said anything. 'So I took his phone away. When you texted, I answered for him. I eventually texted you saying it was over and took you off all his social media. It was better that way.'

Every word she says is like a punch to the stomach. The

week after I left Cragstone I called and called Jacob's mobile, but he never answered. When I rang the home phone Iris would hang up on me, but more often than not the home phone was engaged – probably unplugged. It wasn't Jacob who called me names and told me I'd broken his heart, then dumped me. It was his evil mother.

Tears are streaming down my face, but I don't bother to wipe them away this time. 'What about the letters I wrote Jacob?'

She laughs. The monster actually laughs.

'Oh, I didn't even read those. Tore them straight up. My boy didn't need that kind of stress in his life. By the time I nursed him back to health he was free of all the things that were worrying him – no more girlfriend, no more studies, no annoying father or sister telling him lies about me, just a nice calm life at home with his mama. Don't worry, he was initially sad when I told him you'd called to say it was over, but when I told him you'd met someone else in a matter of weeks, he was too angry to love you anymore. He saw you for what you were.'

I want to slap her, but all I can do is sob hysterically. I didn't date anyone for years after Jacob finished with me. It's all lies. How could she have done this to her son? To *us*?

'Jacob had a whole life ahead of him that he never got to live because of you!' I shout.

Iris makes a face, like *I'm* the mad person. 'Oh, he lived a life, Eva. He lived a beautiful life in a town surrounded by people who loved him, in a home that was safe, with a mother who doted on him. He wasn't well enough to go out in the real world and deal with all that commotion and heartbreak. I kept him safe.'

'Is that why you turned him away from his own father, his sister, other girls he dated?'

'None of them really cared about him. They would have all hurt him in the end.'

'No, they wouldn't. You made him a prisoner!' I scream. 'What you did was wrong. It was immoral and cruel, and he deserved better than you. He died because of you, Iris. Escaping *you!*'

Out of nowhere she pushes me so hard my head hits the wall behind me with a crack, sending a shot of pain from the top of my neck to between my eyes. I hold the back of my head with both hands, my ears ringing with a high-pitched whine. If she did all of this to her son back then, how much more has she done since? Is she the one behind the text and postcards and creepy emails?

'I'm leaving,' I say.

I shove past her and run upstairs to Jacob's room, where my rucksack is already packed. I slam the door behind me and lean against it, surveying his whole world. The narrow single bed where he used to hold me and tell me everything was going to be OK. His desk where he worked a job he probably hated, scribbling frantic messages to himself about how hopeless he felt. His wardrobe full of the same clothes he'd had since he was a teenager because he never went shopping and never had anywhere new to go. I bat away the tears on my cheeks, my head pounding from Iris's assault. I need to get to Ryan. I was wrong to pity Iris... She's dangerous. I tidy my face up in the bathroom, looking over my shoulder, half expecting her to plunge at me with a bread knife *Psycho* style. But all is eerily quiet downstairs, which is more worrying.

I wait until I can breathe normally again before descending the stairs with my rucksack and putting on my shoes and coat as quietly as I can. I can't hear Iris.

I try the front door. It's locked. There are normally keys in a bowl by the door, but they're gone.

'Iris?' I call out. 'Open the door.'

Silence. *Has she gone out and locked me in?*

I leave my bag in the hallway and march to the back of the

house. The kitchen is empty, so is the living room. *Where the hell is she?*

'Iris!' I shout.

I try the back door in the kitchen, but that's also shut. Is this what she used to do to Jacob? Imprison him?

I run upstairs but her bedroom is empty. So is the bathroom. I'm about to go back downstairs when I hear a muffled sound coming from her room. I step inside, open the wardrobe door, and there she is, squeezed into the small space beneath all her clothes, beside the gifts her daughter and grandson will never get to open.

'Let me out of the house,' I say.

'No.'

Iris is sitting on her right hand. She must be clutching her door keys. This is ridiculous.

'I'm not staying in this house another second,' I say. 'Don't make me go downstairs and call the police.'

Iris smiles and holds something out with her left hand. It's the landline receiver, a curly severed cord hanging from one end. She's cut the receiver from the phone. What am I meant to do now? Wrestle her for the door keys?

'Give me my mobile phone back,' I say as calmly as I can.

'I don't have it.'

'There's no point pretending anymore, Iris. We've gone beyond that. Give me back my phone and unlock the door, and I will stay out of your life forever. I think that will make us both happy.'

She shakes her head. 'You're not going anywhere,' she says. 'Michael left me, so did Charlie, and now Jacob. I'm not letting you leave me too.'

THIRTY

I can't believe what I'm hearing. Does Iris seriously think I'm going to stay in this house and play happy families with her? Replace the children she drove away? I'm not staying, nor am I physically fighting her for the front door keys because I'm not sure I'd win. I may be younger than her but she's stronger than she looks.

I imagine how scenarios like this with Jacob would have played out. How many times did he try to go out to see Bianca or his friends, and his mother stopped him? How many times did he think he was going to escape, study in Scotland or try to visit his sister in France only for his mother to physically stop him or for him to fall mysteriously ill? He would have been too weak to put up a fight; his mother would have made sure of that.

I walk out of Iris's bedroom, leaving her curled up in her wardrobe, and head downstairs. Charlie's suspicions were right – Iris must have been drugging Jacob via his food and drink. I pass the living room, where strips of wrapping paper are still scattered all over the floor, and enter the kitchen, where the breakfast food is still on the table.

I sniff each item, but nothing smells strange. I search every cupboard and the fridge, but they're just full of Christmas fare: Bisto gravy, fancy chocolate biscuits in unopened tins and enough cheese and bacon to sink a ship. The only thing that doesn't sit right with me is the quantity of dried fruits and nuts she has. No one needs that many almonds. Iris even has sandwich bags full of almond flour that she's ground herself. But then she did say Jacob loved to eat his mother's cookies and cakes, so maybe she used them for that.

This is getting me nowhere. I'm wasting time. The longer I stay in this house, the higher the chance of Iris doing something even more crazy or dangerous.

I glance out of the window, where, through the swirling snow, I can just make out the bus stop across the road. It has an electronic display board showing when the next bus is due. It's Christmas Day so there aren't any buses running, but the time is there in glowing orange numbers. It's nearly two o'clock already. What did Orla say about Mario arriving? She said he would be here by early evening. I've been dreading my ex coming to Cragstone, but now I wish he were getting here sooner. What am I meant to do now, just spend the entire day waiting for the last man I want to see to rescue me? No. I need to get to Ryan. He's the only one who understands what's happening.

There has to be a way out of here. I'll smash my way out if I have to. I just need to put as much distance between me and this house as possible.

I do up my coat, shrug on my rucksack and go back into the living room. Iris's pitiful pile of gifts is still on the sofa. What a sad little life she ended up with.

My plan is to try the windows and see if they open wide enough to climb out of, but as soon as I step into the room, I realise my first mistake. The windows are different to the draughty old sash ones the Donnellys used to have. These are double-glazed with locks and totally unbreakable.

'There's no way out,' Iris says from the hallway.

She's sitting on the stairs, poking her face between the banisters like a child, grinning. Her eyes are puffy and red, but she's put on fresh lipstick that cuts like a jagged crimson slash across her face.

'Jacob once tried to climb out of the front window and he hurt himself. We couldn't have that, so I got double-glazing. It took quite a chunk out of my savings, but it was worth it to keep my boy safe.' She claps her hands twice and hauls herself up. 'Now then... the day is running away with us, Eva. We really should clear up the breakfast things and get the potatoes on.'

Before she's fully on her feet I tighten the straps of my rucksack and run to the kitchen.

'There's a good girl,' she cries out as I run past her. 'Start peeling the veg.'

I slam the kitchen door behind me, jamming one of the chairs beneath the handle and pushing the heavy wooden table to bar her entrance. The handle turns but the door doesn't budge.

'Eva!' Iris shouts out. 'You can't leave!'

I try the back door again even though I know it's locked. The door has a large, frosted window in the centre, but unlike the windows at the front of the house this one isn't double-glazed. I look wildly around me as Iris bangs on the kitchen door, wailing about being let in. I contemplate grabbing a chair when I notice a heavy stone pestle and mortar on the counter. It looks like it's been used recently to grind something up: a fine dusting of something resembling coarse flour or brown sugar coats the sides. I wrap tea towels around my hands and grab both heavy pieces, using them to smash at the back door window, turning away as slivers of glass fly through the air.

'Eva!' Iris screams from the hallway. 'What's that noise? Are you OK? You're going to hurt yourself!'

A gust of icy air blows through the hole in the door and blasts me in the face as I use both pieces of the pestle and mortar to chip away at the doorframe until it's free of sharp glass. I ignore the banging at the kitchen door and Iris's shouting as I stick my head out of the hole and survey the icy garden beyond. I hadn't noticed it before, but it looks nothing like it did when I lived here. Instead of the manicured lawn that Michael was so proud of, with its pretty garden furniture and beds of lavender, all I can see now is tall grass and tangled bushes covered in snow. I drop the tea towels and pestle and mortar, take off my rucksack and throw it through the smashed window before climbing out on to the patio. Once I'm standing in Iris's dishevelled garden, grass up to my knees, I can see that the only way out to the street is through the door at the back of the garden. I run to it and try to yank it open, but it's locked.

There's a loud crash behind me and I glance over my shoulder. Iris has managed to push the kitchen door open wide enough that her arm is sticking through the gap and she's waving it around frantically like a scene from *The Shining*.

I run along the perimeter of the garden, my feet slipping on the patches of icy mud and settled snow, until I find a gap in the fence. It's not very big but the wooden slat beside it is sufficiently loose that I can pull at it until it slides to the side, leaving me with a hole large enough to squeeze myself and my bag through.

The neighbour's garden is completely different to Iris's. The grass is short, the path is new, and I can see where flowers probably bloom along the edges in the summertime. Someone is in the kitchen, washing up at the sink. It's Christmas Day – no one can say no to a neighbour in need on Christmas Day. It's a man and he's staring at me. Oh no. A cannonball drops to the pit of my stomach. It's Harry, and this is Vicky's house.

Shit. He's seen me.

'Eva! What on earth are you doing in my parents' garden?' he says, opening the door with a bemused grin on his face. He's wearing a woolly jumper with a picture of a snowman on it, and a silver paper crown is perched on his head.

I don't realise I'm shaking, my breaths coming in sharp pulls, until Harry has his arm around me. He takes my heavy bag off my shoulder.

'Come inside, it's snowing,' he says. 'Oh my goodness, your hand is bleeding. You're hurt!'

'It's nothing,' I say, sucking on the graze to show it's not serious. 'I cut myself carving the turkey.'

I don't have time for small talk; I need to get to Ryan's house. I think back to last night and Harry trying to kiss me, his sticky Santa beard in my mouth, the way his hands clasped around me and wouldn't let go. He likes me, and he repulses me, but he may also be useful.

'I wanted to see you,' I lie. 'I couldn't come around the front as Iris's door is locked and she's asleep. I didn't want to wake her for the key, so I came via the garden. I hope you don't mind.'

'Not at all!' he says, beckoning me towards the house. 'Come in. Say hello to my mum and dad.'

No, thank you. I'm sure I'm the last person Vicky wants in her house. And I don't want to go from being trapped inside one house to being trapped next door with pervy Harry and his vicious mother.

'I tell you what,' I say, running my finger up his arm. His eyebrows shoot up in surprise and his smile widens. 'Why don't we go for a walk?'

'In the snow?'

'It will be romantic.'

'Well, you should at least leave your bag here. It weighs a tonne.'

'No! No... I'm getting a lift back to London from my friend in an hour, they're picking me up at the hotel. I thought you and I could have some time together first. Alone.'

His face lights up.

'That sounds magical! Let me grab my coat and shoes.'

I glance at his feet. He's wearing giant squishy slippers in the shape of reindeer. He wiggles a foot in the air, making the bell around Rudolph's neck jingle. *Jesus.* I lower my voice into a whisper.

'Your mum isn't my biggest fan so let's do this top secret,' I say with a wink. 'You let me out the garden door, and I'll meet you outside the chemist on the high road in five minutes where no one will see us. Tell her you need some fresh air. Then we'll be left totally alone for a whole hour.'

Harry steps closer to me, tucking a stray hair behind my ear and tilting my chin up in a way he's probably seen in countless romcoms. He brushes his lips against mine; I taste Baileys and Brussels sprouts. 'We can do a lot in an hour,' he says.

I want to wretch but instead I force myself to smile and nod along. He rushes to the garden door, pulls at the lock, which I could have done myself, and ushers me through.

'See you soon, you little minx.'

I keep nodding and smiling, then as soon as he turns his back I shut the door behind me, wipe my mouth and run in the opposite direction from the high street. As I pass Iris's back door, I'm sure I can hear her screaming out my name.

THIRTY-ONE

The snow is falling faster now, and I can no longer feel my feet, but I can't slow down. Not until I get to Ryan's house. The clifftops are about twenty minutes from here. I know I'm going in the right direction because with every step the wind gets sharper and brinier. I'm cold and hungry but all I care about right now is widening the gap between me and Iris. And Harry. He really believes he's a nice guy, one of the good ones, when he's done nothing but hound me and push himself on to me since I got here. I shouldn't have led him on like that and used him, but he'd already seen me, so I had no choice but to lie. He's going to really hate me now. Men like him go from adoration to violent hatred in the few minutes it takes for a woman to laugh at them.

I may not have gotten my phone back but at least I have all my belongings in my rucksack along with the evidence I gathered, plus Ryan's telephone number in my jeans pocket. I trust him; I know he'll help me. I have to go with my gut because I don't have much else left. I've been walking for about ten minutes, but I've not seen a phone box yet. Do they even exist anymore? Worst-case scenario I go straight to his house.

The thought of being inside his warm home, safe and protected, spurs me on. As does the rage I'm feeling about what Iris told me. I swallow down the pain in my throat and dig my hands deeper into my flimsy coat, wishing I'd remembered my gloves and taken Michael's old scarf before running out of the house. Inside my pocket I fiddle with the ring Jacob gave me, twisting it around and around with my thumb. It feels right on my ring finger in a way my last engagement ring never did. I rub my nose with the back of my icy hand. The thought of Jacob driving to London, to me, along this same road makes me want to cry. He really did think I was waiting for him and that we were about to have a beautiful future together. I can't imagine how any of this would have panned out had he not died.

It's mid-afternoon and the sky is beginning to darken, the thick clouds heavy with impending snow growing blue and grey like fresh bruises. I cross my arms tighter around my chest, pushing my damp hair from my face and calculating how much further I have to go. There's only one road in and out of Cragstone and I'm walking along it. With each car that passes, and so far there have only been three, I flinch and turn my head, fearing one of them might be Iris or Harry. Or Mario. I'm not sure which one of them would be worse right now.

My eyes are streaming from the bitter wind, flakes of snow catching on my eyelashes and my lips turning numb. I pass a wine bar, which must be the one Ryan wanted to take me to, but it's locked up and dark inside.

Out of the gloom a cluster of houses begins to materialise, next to them a squat white building with blue and white awning and a giant ice cream outside. I'm here.

I quicken my step, stamping my feet to get some feeling back into my toes, my shoulders aching from the pull of my rucksack. One hot solitary tear escapes my watery eyes, scalding my frozen cheeks. Everything is going to be OK. Between the stalker evidence in my bag and Charlie corroborating about her mother poisoning her and her brother, Ryan will be able to take this further up the police chain. I can't bring Jacob back, but I can avenge his death.

There are three houses next to the ice cream shop, but none of them have their lights on. Which one is Ryan's? One has a small trampoline and a child's bike propped up against the wall, so it's not that one, and the other has a mobility scooter parked outside so I doubt that's his either. I try the third house and spot a name above the doorbell: R Clarke. I'm at the right place.

I ring the doorbell and wait. The snow is falling so fast I can no longer see the road. All is silent save for the wind howling through the trees and waves crashing to my right. This is a beautiful spot in the summer. A few steps away there's a flight of stairs leading down to a pebbly beach. Cars park along the main road and kids run up and down the stairs for their ice creams and to buy buckets and spades. Jacob and I used to walk along here hand in hand. He'd pick up pretty stones, kiss them and place them in my pocket. We would talk about our past and our future and how we'd make everything yet to come better than it had been before. We always said how nice these houses were, how lucky the people in them were to have this view.

We scattered my mother's ashes along this coast too.

'Let's throw them somewhere I don't like,' I said to Jacob at the time. 'Not here. Not over a pretty beach. It's not her I want to think about when I'm here with you.'

We ended up scattering them over some rocks where nobody goes. It's strange how little I've thought about my mother since returning to Cragstone. Jacob is the one who haunts me now.

I ring Ryan's doorbell again, but there's still no answer. I shrug my bag off my back, prop it up against his front door and roll my shoulders. I press my head against the window, my hands on either side of my face, and peer inside. Through the glass I can see Ryan's living room is modern and clean, everything immaculate and in its place. I bet it smells good too. There's a Christmas tree in the corner, all the presents gone, probably being enjoyed by his family already.

'Crap,' I say out loud.

It's Christmas Day – of course he's not in. Ryan loves his family. He's probably with his mum and sister at Steve and Orla's house, playing with his nephews. I try opening the door in the vain hope a policeman would have left his door unlocked. He didn't. Then I walk around the property and try the back door. Also locked. What did I expect?

I don't know what to do now – this was my one and only plan. How long do people spend with family on Christmas Day? Maybe he'll be leaving soon now that it's nearly dark, anticipating the weather worsening, or maybe he'll be there late, waiting for the kids to go to bed so they can all have a drink and play board games in peace. Oh God, what if he's staying the night so as not to drink and drive?

I knock on the doors of both houses on either side of his, but no one is home there either. I'll just have to wait and hope someone is back soon, even if it's one of his neighbours who may let me use their phone to call Ryan's mobile. Alternatively, I could walk back into town, but that will take another thirty minutes. There's no point me sitting in the hotel lobby, the only place that's probably open, because that's where I said I was meeting a friend. If Iris and Harry are searching for me, the hotel off the high street is the first place they'll look.

I leave my heavy rucksack under Ryan's porch and decide to walk around a bit to stay warm. I head away from Cragstone, stomping my feet every few steps. If I go a little further, I'll come to a second bay, a more secluded patch of sand with no access, just a steep drop and jagged rocks. The cliff where Jacob died.

I keep my chin tucked into my collar and walk along the empty road, trees and fields to my left and the sea to my right.

The air is heavy with the scent of seaweed and snow, and I can still hear the waves crashing ferociously against the rocks. With each step I take they grow louder. Angrier. Like they want more blood. I imagine what it must have been like for Jacob driving along here nearly a month ago, drunk and heady with rage and hope. The road isn't properly lit, and even with the moon shining off the settled snow I still can't see very clearly. I reach the part of the road where the barrier stops and the cliff gets closer to the road, stumbling as the hard grassy verge beneath my feet becomes undulated. Tyre marks, belonging to Jacob's car, now deep, frozen puddles. This must be the exact spot where he lost control and disappeared off the edge.

A gnarly lump forms in my chest and I struggle to breathe as I follow the ruts in the rock-hard mud leading to the edge of the cliff. A few bunches of flowers and a wreath have been left by the side of the road, all now dead a month later, hanging wet and limp in the snow.

I can't believe all of this happened on Ryan's doorstep. How must he have felt spending the day picking up my ex-boyfriend's teeth from a rockpool then going to sleep barely a hundred metres away?

All is silent against the distant cries of seagulls carried on the wind and the roar of the sea slamming against the cliff. I lean over the edge and shudder. This is where Jacob's car fell, where his body was thrown on to the jagged rocks below, where his blood stained the pretty stones and his clothes got tangled up with seaweed and foam. This is also where my gift was found. I twirl the engagement ring around my finger and close my eyes like I'm making a wish. Maybe if I twist it around enough times, I can turn back time.

I jump at the rumble of a car in the distance, faint lights glowing through the misty darkness. The sound stops, and the lights go off, and I wonder whether one of the neighbours is home. I should head back to Ryan's house. It's too dangerous here so close to the edge, hidden by snow and darkness.

I head back to the road and solid ground again, turning in the direction of town. Through the flurry of white I can just make out the dark shadow of a car parked on the side of the road, but I don't know if it's the one I thought I heard or if it has been there all along. What if it's Mario? My stomach flips and I realise that I was wrong: seeing him right now might not be the worst thing in the world. I don't want to go back to my old life but we could sit in the warmth of his car. I'd explain about Jacob's mother and how my ex thought we were in touch but weren't, then I could use Mario's phone to call Ryan. He'd understand. I start to quicken my pace in the direction of the parked car, my trainers making the hard ground crack beneath my feet, the sound ringing out in the snow-muffled silence. I can't see anyone nearby. No people, no other cars on the road, I'm the only sign of life.

The ice cream shop comes into view, and I break into a run. Then I hear footsteps that are not my own. I stop, and so does the sound. I turn around but all I see are trees on my right and the cliffs in the distance falling down into churning waters. I hunch my shoulders against the cold and quicken my stride, unable to shake the feeling that someone is watching me. I don't think that's Mario's car after all. I need to get my bag and get out of here. I break into a run again, taking my frozen hands out of my pockets, my breaths so loud that all I can hear is my heavy panting and my feet hitting the frozen ground. I don't hear the man running behind me, or register how close he is, until he wraps his arms around my middle.

The breath is knocked out of me, and it takes me a moment to realise what's happening. I go to cry out, but he clamps his strong hand over my mouth. I take deep breaths through my nose, the icy air burning my nostrils and the back of my throat, my arms trapped by my sides as his hard chest presses against my back.

'Shh,' he's saying in my ear.

My heart is beating so loudly I can feel its vibrations in my head, my ears ringing with the rush of wind and sea and blind hot panic. I try to shake him off but he's holding me so tightly my feet are an inch off the ground. I twist my head to the side, hoping to see who it is, but my cheek just rubs across a damp, black puffer jacket. I'm wracking my brain, trying to think of who I know who owns a coat like that. It could be anyone. I don't think I've ever seen Harry wearing anything that isn't a uniform or a silly costume. This man is tall. Harry isn't tall, but Mario is.

'It's OK,' the man says softly in my ear.

I know that voice. I stop struggling and close my eyes. I need to be calm if I want to think straight. I need to place that voice. I take a deep breath and I'm hit with that smell I know so well. Black pepper and cedarwood.

The man's hand slowly peels away from my mouth, and I take in an icy lungful of air. His hands remain on either side of my trembling arms, pinning me in place. My legs are threatening to give way beneath me; I couldn't run right now if I tried. I'm too scared, too cold, and I have nowhere to go where this person wouldn't be able to chase me and bring me down.

'Please don't scream,' he says as he turns me around.

My view changes from beach and blizzard to a close-up of a black coat. I look up into his face, taking a few beats to register what I'm seeing. Who is this man in a woollen beanie, with thick stubble and large brown eyes? Then it hits me, and I feel myself falling.

'Jacob?' I whisper, and then everything turns to black.

THIRTY-TWO

I must have fainted because when I wake up I'm warm and in the passenger seat of a car, and Jacob, *my* Jacob, is sitting beside me driving. I try to speak but nothing comes out. He passes me something. A bottle of water.

'For your throat,' he says. 'Your mouth must be dry.'

It is. I take a slow sip, my eyes fixed on him the entire time. His silhouette is the same, the straight nose and Cupid's bow lips and deep brown eyes. He's taken his hat and coat off; his hair is thicker and longer than in the photo on his coffin and his shoulders more muscular than I remember. Did I fall and bang my head and I'm dreaming? Did I die and Jacob is taking me to heaven in a Volvo?

'You're probably a bit shocked right now,' he says.

I'm going to vomit.

'Stop the car!' I shout. 'I'm going to be sick.'

He doesn't slow down; instead he hands me a plastic bag and a packet of tissues.

'I came prepared,' he says. 'I can't stop the car, cookie. I can't let anyone see me.'

Cookie. I forgot he used to call me cookie. It was our thing, an in-joke we had about his sweet tooth and addiction to biscuits. He said I was his biggest addiction. I dry heave, the bag clamped to my mouth, my eyes still trained on this new, grown-up Jacob beside me. I manage not to throw up, and after a few sips of water I stop shaking.

'I have some blankets in the back if you're cold,' he says.

I shake my head. The car seat is heated, and I'm sweating. I struggle out of my coat, placing it on my lap.

Jacob does a double take. 'Is that my jumper you're wearing? And my jeans?'

My voice comes out in a low croak. 'Yes.'

'I like that.'

Outside everything which should be white is a dull grey in the dark. Grey tarmac, grey fields, black sky. We aren't on the main road where he found me, the one that leads to the motorway; this one is heading inland. We pass a small lake with a little house squatting beside it, every window glowing. I can't tell in this light, but I think the house is yellow. In the daylight, surrounded by this much snow, I bet it looks like an egg yolk.

'What's going on, Jacob?'

'I'm not really dead.'

'I figured that part out already.'

He laughs, making a ball of fire glow in the pit of my stomach. It's been ten years since I heard that sound. I'd forgotten the timbre of his laugh and the way he smiles with his mouth open, showing every one of his perfect teeth.

'When... How... What's going on?' I stammer.

'I'll tell you everything shortly.'

'Where's my bag?' I ask.

'What bag?'

How on earth am I going to explain this to Ryan and Bianca and everyone else in Cragstone? Does Iris or the rest of Jacob's family know? I doubt it. I think I'm actually going to be sick this time. I stick my head inside the plastic bag, but the nausea passes.

'Who knows you're still alive?' I ask.

'No one. Just you.'

I have a million questions, but I don't know where to start. I can't even work out *when* all of this started. How far back should I go? When I got the text message about his funeral, or when he had the accident, or when he started emailing me believing that we were in a relationship?

'I made this for you,' he says, digging inside his pocket and handing me a smooth white stone.

I take it and study it closely. It fits perfectly in the palm of my hand and is covered in an intricate pattern of hearts drawn with black permanent marker. On the back it says, 'Forever.'

'It's from our favourite beach, the one near the ice cream shop,' he adds. 'It's the foundation stone for the future we're going to build together.'

This is too much. My head is both too full yet empty and stuffed with cotton wool, like I'm floating somewhere above my body. I put the stone in my pocket, but its weight does nothing to pin me down. I'm not really here.

Jacob turns right, the empty fields and the house by the lake disappearing in his rear-view mirror until we're weaving through unlit country lanes, hedgerows on both sides, no houses or cars. After a few minutes he turns left into a tiny slip road that looks like the entrance to a house, except it's a narrow tunnel of dense trees with no end in sight. The windscreen wipers are batting from side to side, clearing the snow from the glass, their rhythm as fast as my heartbeat. There's nothing down this road. We're in the middle of a forest in the middle of nowhere.

'Where are you taking me?'

Jacob places his hand on my knee and squeezes.

'Home.'

THIRTY-THREE

It's a relief to open the car door and feel the sharp bite of winter on my face. I gulp down air as if it's clear spring water but when I try to stand my legs are still wobbly. Jacob is by my side in a flash.

'Take it easy,' he says. 'You're still in shock. Are you hurt? You fainted earlier and I caught you, but I don't know if maybe you pulled a muscle or hurt your knees as you fell. Lean on me, come on. Up you get.'

I'm struggling to process what's happening right now. This man with his arm around me, locking the car door with his other hand and leading me down a dark path towards a wooden cabin glowing with warm light... Is this really the man whose funeral I attended four days ago?

'Why do you smell like Michael?' I ask.

'I'm wearing his aftershave. He left it behind.'

So the scarf I've been wearing was Jacob's, not his father's.

'I'm happy to answer any questions you may have,' he says as he opens the door to the cabin. 'Anything you'd like to ask me?'

Anything I'd like to ask him? Is he serious?

I let him lead me into the little house, where he gently guides me to a couch covered in throws and blankets. The house is just one room but it's cute and cosy, with a double bed on one side and a woodfire stove in the other corner. There's a pot of something on the hob, a desk with a laptop and notebook, and a pile of firewood beside a hearth that has the remnants of charred wood in it. There's even a small Christmas tree next to the bed decorated with tiny fairy lights. Jacob shuts the door. The sound of the howling wind and rustling trees outside stops, and I'm instantly cocooned in silence. He lights the fire then remains by the fireplace watching me, as you would a wild animal you've brought into your home.

I shakily get to my feet then run at him, throwing my arms around his neck.

'Jacob?' I say into his neck. 'It's really you, isn't it? You're really alive.'

His body sags in relief and he hugs me back, his long arms wrapping all the way around me, my head fitting perfectly on his chest as it always did.

'Eva.' He says my name like a silent prayer, like no time has passed at all. I'm seventeen again and back in his room, and I'm curled up on his bed, and he's telling me everything is going to be OK.

I start to cry, and he holds me tighter, leading us back to the couch and sitting beside me. I don't let go. I can't. All I can do is cry and hold on to him, scared that if I sit up and open my eyes, he will disappear all over again.

'Tell me everything,' I say into his chest, wiping away my tears and letting out a hiccup. I've been a nervous wreck since I received the text about his funeral, but now I'm in his arms, the one place I've longed to be since I sat before his coffin in the church, every ounce of strength has left my body. Jacob laughs gently as he holds me tight like we're lovers who have been parted for a few weeks. Not like a man who has returned from the dead.

'I've already told you most of it,' he replies.

When? Ah yes, of course, the emails he sent to pretend-me. To him we *are* lovers who have finally been reunited, not virtual strangers who haven't been in contact since they were teenagers.

My eyelids start to droop as he plays with my hair, the way he used to do all those years ago when I couldn't sleep. 'Tell me everything from the beginning anyway,' I say, exhaustion settling into my melting bones. 'I want to understand the full picture. Everything that has happened since I left, what your mother did and the car accident.'

Jacob takes a deep breath, my head rising along with his chest.

'For a long time, I didn't realise I was trapped,' he begins. 'Sometimes imprisonment feels like love. It started with that rumour about you and Dad, which I never believed by the way. When Mum threw you out, Charlie and I were furious. Dad had already confessed everything by then, but it made no difference. We refused to speak to Mum and bought tickets for London for the next day, but she found them and ripped them up. I didn't want to be in Cragstone without you. I couldn't wait to start my new life in Oxford, to visit you on weekends and see what we could become. Finally, just you and me.'

'I wish you'd followed me,' I say quietly.

'I tried.'

I snuggle closer to him, staring at the flames licking at the logs in the hearth. I can't believe this is real, and part of me doesn't even care if it isn't. I can't move and I don't want to – it's not until now that I realise this is all I've ever wanted. Jacob, beside me, just us.

'Then I got ill,' he continues. 'I told you all this in the emails, but I didn't go into too much detail because I was scared of my mum finding our conversations. She used to insist on my leaving my laptop downstairs at night and sometimes I was so ill I'd be stuck in bed for days. I knew she was checking my emails, so I would print out my favourites to read in bed at night before deleting all our conversations from my Gmail.'

'Tell me what happened before you were meant to leave for uni,' I ask.

Jacob rubs his face with two hands, as if the memory is too hard to drag back up. 'For years I was convinced I had a rare illness; I'd get stomach aches and dizziness and some days I could hardly breathe or walk. Mum fussed over me and took me to every doctor and specialist, but no one could work out what it was. When it first happened, the week you left, it was so bad I thought I was going to die. I have no idea how long I was in bed for. Once I was able to walk and talk again Mum told me that you'd dumped me and found someone else. Oxford had already deferred my studies for a year so I could stay in Cragstone with you, and they said they couldn't keep my place open indefinitely. I missed the deadline date to reapply, although at that point I was past caring. All I could think about was getting back to being my old self again and getting back to you. But I was too late... You'd moved on. I was sad and angry, but I didn't blame you for breaking up with me. You had every right to start again after what my family put you through. My heart was broken forever, though.'

'I didn't dump you,' I say, sitting up. 'I never left you for anyone else.'

Jacob turns to me so we're face to face. 'Yes, you did. You started dating that guy who played rugby for the county.'

'I've never dated a rugby player. Who told you that? Your mother? She lied to you, Jacob. She lied to us both. She admitted everything to me this afternoon. She told me that after I left Cragstone she texted me pretending to be you and broke up with me, then lied to you about me leaving you. I even wrote you letters, but she destroyed everything.'

Jacob looks into the distance, like he's trying to work out a complicated maths equation. His brow furrows and his eyes dart from side to side.

'So you never left me?'

'No! I got to London expecting you to follow as planned. I messaged you and tried to call but your mother intercepted. I thought *you'd* finished with *me*. I never would have walked away from what we had, Jacob. You were my world.'

He makes a small jerking movement with his head, his face twitching as he processes this new information and how different life could have been. He's re-writing history, his story, like I just had to do.

'Why are you only telling me now?' he cries.

He's talking about the emails. What has the person pretending to be me been telling him? I really need to explain everything, but it's too much right now. I don't know where to start. I have too many questions of my own I need answering.

'There's so much we need to talk about,' I say. 'But finish your story first.'

He looks around the room as if he's lost his thread and can't find it again. After a few seconds his body slumps, he rubs his face again, then takes a deep breath.

'As I said, I was heartbroken when we broke up, and I no longer cared about anything. I was too ill for school, Charlie went to France and my dad moved miles away with Amelie, and I genuinely believed the only person left in my life who loved me was my mum.'

Just as Iris had planned. The rage I feel prickles beneath my skin like growing thorns. Jacob is staring at me with concern. He thinks he's said something wrong. I cup his beautiful face in my hands. He's a man now yet when I look into those brown eyes framed with thick lashes, all I see is the eager-to-please nineteen-year-old I fell in love with. He never stood a chance with that psycho for a mother. Poor boy. My poor, kind, gullible boy.

'Charlie thinks you were being poisoned,' I say quietly. 'By Iris.'

He leans into my touch as I stroke the rough stubble on his cheeks, closing his eyes and letting out a long sigh.

'How is my sister?'

'Bereft. As is your father. They think you're dead, Jacob. I don't think you realise how much they love you.'

A tear escapes his left eye and lands on my finger.

'I've done a terrible thing, but I couldn't think of any other way out. My mother threatened to kill herself if I ever spoke to my dad and Charlie again; she told me they were brainwashing me into leaving her. And I believed it for such a long time.' He rubs his eyes and kisses the tips of my fingers. 'I should have listened to my sister because our mother *was* making me sick.'

'With what?' I ask.

'Cyanide.'

I gasp and let go of his face. So Charlie was right. I'm certain now that Iris was making me ill too, but I never found anything in the house that resembled poison.

'Where on earth did Iris get cyanide from?'

'Online,' Jacob replies. 'Health food shops. Even the local supermarket sells it.'

I make a face and he lets out a sad chuckle. 'You've been in my mum's house for a few days, right?'

I nod. How does he know that?

'Did you find anything strange in her kitchen cupboards?'

I shake my head. 'I saw quite a lot of nut powder, and dried fruits and almonds, but I figured it was because she likes baking.'

'They aren't almonds,' Jacob says. 'They're apricot kernels.'

'Kernels? Why would she have them?'

'They sell them everywhere to grind up and use in exfoliators, or people eat them like nuts in very small doses. Some people say apricot kernels can even heal cancer. But I don't know why they sell them untreated because if you eat more than three or four you can get cyanide poisoning. I finally worked out that my mother had been grinding them down into powder and adding it to my drink and food for years, way above the recommended dose. I had no idea.'

Oh my God. I place my hand on his chest, and he covers my hand with his. His eyes are filling with tears again, his shoulders slumped forward. I wish I could take away his pain and pass it on to his murderous mother.

'Why didn't you call the police?' I ask.

He looks at me with surprise. 'You told me not to, remember? You said we had to stick to the original plan because pressing charges would slow us down and make my mum even angrier.'

He's talking about the emails again. Whoever was pretending to be me knows everything now. I have to say something, but Jacob is still talking, his words tumbling over one another. This is probably the first time he's ever uttered all of this aloud and I need to hear what he has to say.

'At that point I just wanted to get away from her,' he continues. 'You don't understand how relentless she was, Eva. She's a lot more tech savvy than you'd think, and she had plenty of spare time after selling the business. She kept stealing my things, monitoring my laptop and phone, even sewing tracking devices into my clothes and bags so she could follow me when I went out. Then if I saw friends, she'd punish me, making sure I got ill the next day so she could prove that leaving the house was making me worse. She ruined any chance of me having an education, a social life or a relationship.'

'I heard about you and Bianca.'

'Sorry.' He looks down and has the decency to look embarrassed. 'I thought you hated me, Eva, and that I would never see you again. I was still angry with you. At first, dating her was a bit of a "fuck you". It was mean of me, and petty, until I realised Bianca is just as broken as the rest of us. She was kind, and caring, and so were her family. They were there for me at a time when nobody else was.'

It should have been me. I should have been there for him.

'But then your mother ruined that too,' I say.

He nods. 'It wasn't until I got back in touch with you that I started to question my life and consider whether maybe Charlie was right about our mother making me ill. Maybe my dad and sister hadn't turned against me, they were just trying to protect me. I started to avoid any food and drink Mum made me, insisting I did the shopping and cooking, and only pretending to eat her desserts, and that's when I noticed how much better I felt. Of course I continued to pretend I was ill so she wouldn't realise what I was doing, but I was secretly plotting my escape. At that point I was completely alone. All I had left was you, cookie.'

Except he didn't have me. He *was* totally alone, and not just being manipulated by his mother but by someone online. Someone out to hurt him. Well, it backfired because Jacob got away and I'm here now, with him, exactly as he had planned. Except this isn't a happy ending... because everyone thinks he's dead.

I need to tell him the truth about the emails and the photos of me, but the way he's looking at me right now is pulling at something deep inside of me. Jacob isn't dead. Jacob didn't leave me. Jacob never stopped loving me.

'You still have me,' I say. 'I'm not going anywhere.'

And in that moment, everything else slips away: the pain of the last week, of losing Mario and my home and my job, all the emotions I've been feeling since returning to Cragstone. All I'm left with is all I've ever wanted. Jacob. His soft gaze has hardened, his deep brown eyes now black with longing. I lean forward and brush my mouth against his. His eyes widen a little then he smiles because he can feel it too, this thread between us that not even death could sever. Our kisses are slow at first, his lips parting with a sigh, his fingers stroking the back of my neck, then all at once it turns into something urgent. I pull at his shirt, Jacob pushes me back on the sofa, and his beautiful, handsome face is all I see. I'm lost. I'm his. I'm not going anywhere.

THIRTY-FOUR

I remember now. This. I don't have a word for what Jacob and I have always had, but it's more than a connection or love. Those words are too rudimentary, too pedestrian. It's bigger than all of that, yet also small and quiet and only ours.

We're curled up together beneath three layers of fluffy blankets. My legs are perfectly flush with his, my back pressed up against his chest, his shallow breaths warming the crook of my neck. He's wearing a watch, and I can see it's nearing midnight.

'I love you,' he whispers into my hair.

I turn my head to the side, his lips finding mine before I can speak.

'I... a little bit... hate you,' I say.

Jacob laughs. 'What?'

We've not left the bed all evening and I allowed myself to pretend everything was fine. But now we need to talk, and we need to work out what the hell happens next.

'For nearly a week I thought you were dead,' I say. 'What the hell, Jacob!'

I turn over so we're nose to nose, and once again he has the decency to look contrite. I blink back tears as I think back to his funeral, the coffin covered in flowers he would have hated, and the way his sister was sobbing on their father's shoulder. You don't do that to people who love you.

'I'm sorry,' he says. 'There was no other way of escaping where my mother wouldn't follow. I knew the only way I could stop the hold she had over me was if one of us was dead. So it had to be me.'

Maybe he's right. I don't know. It's all too much to take in.

'How did you do it?' I ask. 'How did you fool everyone into thinking you were dead?'

Jacob stares over my shoulder at the fire still crackling in the hearth. His jaw tenses and twitches as he works out where to start.

'First, I saved up money. A lot of money. I bought a cheap car and rented this cabin using fake ID I found online. It's easier than you think. Then, whenever Mum went to the hospital for whatever ailment she decided to have that week, I drove out here and started to get the house ready, hiding my car in a lane you can't see from the road. When the time was right, I placed a half-drunk bottle of whisky and another empty one in the car, along with a bag of clothes as if I was running away. I waited until late at night, once Mum was asleep, then drove my car as fast as I could towards the cliff before stopping right on the edge, getting out and pushing it over. I had to dig out the skid marks a bit, make it look like I hadn't stopped the car, but there was so much rain that night it was hard to tell anyway. The beauty of it was that I knew no one would find the car until the morning, and that it would be hard to get down there in such terrible weather. I knew a lot of the evidence would get washed away and it would be impossible to confirm what was there and what wasn't. Including my body. The houses on the cliff were too far away to see or hear anything, and this time of year the waves are so loud they overpower any sound anyway. I had plenty of time to walk to my new car, drive to the cabin and wait.'

Clever Jacob, making it all sound so easy.

'But your teeth,' I say.

He gives me a wry smile and pulls his lips back. I've kissed him a million times in the last few hours yet didn't notice he has two molars missing.

'I pulled them out. I also extracted enough blood from myself a few weeks before the accident to soak the car seat with and I chucked some over the rocks for extra measure.'

Jacob was planning to study medicine – he knows how to take blood and pull teeth. How desperate he must have been to put himself through that. After ten years of him stuck at home, everyone had clearly forgotten how smart and strategic Jacob 'Star Boy' Donnelly was.

'What about my gift?' I ask.

His eyes cloud over as he takes my left hand, studying the engagement ring on my finger. 'I told myself that if this ring found its way to you, then it was meant to be.' He kisses my hand. 'I've been watching you, Eva. I watched you go to the funeral, and to the pub with my friends, and get drunk with that dickhead, Harry. I saw you going into my house, turning out my bedroom light at night, wearing my pyjamas. And this evening, when I saw you twisting this ring around your finger while staring out over the cliffs where I died, I knew it was time to tell you the truth. And I was right.'

I'm suddenly wide awake and freezing cold. I edge back along the mattress a little. Jacob was the man in the shadows, the hooded figure I ran away from.

'You've been watching me?'

'Of course. I had to.'

'Why would you scare me like that?' I cry, rearing up at him. 'I've been terrified all week thinking someone was trying to hurt me. What else did you do? Did you send me things? Jacob, what have you done?'

Jacob visibly flinches at me raising my voice and sits up too. He tries to reach out for me, but I pull away. 'Oh, cookie. I didn't mean to scare you. I was protecting you, keeping you safe, waiting until the right time to tell you everything.'

I think back to all those terrifying moments when I thought I was imagining things – the man watching me from the shadows, the footsteps – but it was just Jacob. I remind myself that in his mind he was protecting me. And maybe he was – but what about the postcards and photos? Who was protecting him?

'Are you hungry?' he asks.

'Yes.'

He gets up and pulls on his boxer shorts, throwing me his t-shirt to wear. The cabin is warm from the fire, the room cast in black and amber shadows like something from a romance movie where two people are snowed in during Christmas. I can't decide if this is romantic or absolutely crazy. Perhaps a little of both. I don't know what's real anymore.

'I forgot to say that if you need the bathroom, it's through there,' he says, pointing at a door I didn't notice before. 'There's a shower and hot water, although the toilet isn't great. There's one outside that works a lot better... you know, if you need more privacy.'

He gives a little laugh as he stirs the soup on the hob. I go to the bathroom and splash my face with cold water. The cabin is old but looks recently renovated with a power shower and new taps. My reflection makes me flinch; I thought I would look tired and pale, but I look happier than I have in a long time. My eyes are shining, my cheeks flushed, and I realise I'm smiling. I tidy myself up then join Jacob in the kitchen area, where I help him cut and butter thick slices of bread. This is all very idyllic. I don't like it.

'Sit down,' he says, pointing to the candle-lit table and placing a steaming bowl before me.

'Did you make this?' I ask as I take a sip of the vegetable broth. 'It's delicious.'

'Yes. I've been planning this moment for a long time,' he replies, his face beaming with pride. 'Dumping Mario was perfect timing. I told you he was untrustworthy.'

I splutter, the soup scalding the back of my throat. He told me? What else has he been telling 'me'?

'You saw those emails he was getting,' he adds.

I did see them, but Jacob didn't.

'I told you about the emails I saw from his assistant?' I ask him.

'Of course you did,' he replies.

I open my mouth to say something then shut it again. What is Jacob talking about? How did the person pretending to be me know that I found emails on Mario's phone? I never told anyone about them except Amanda. To everyone else I was vague and said he simply cheated on me. Jacob dips his bread in his soup, takes a bite and gives me a wide grin. I can't get all of this information to align, yet Jacob continues to eat his food completely unperturbed.

'Full up already?' he asks.

I shake my head and take another sip of the soup, but it's lost all its flavour.

'Once I saw you'd broken up with him I could finally put my plan in motion,' he continues. 'I crashed the car and waited for them to pronounce me dead. It took longer than I'd hoped, but you can't calculate every detail. Then I sent you the text.'

'Text?'

I drop my spoon and it clatters to the floor. He picks it up and pats my hand. 'For the funeral. I pretended to be Charlie – thought I'd keep it realistic. When I saw you arrive at the station, I was so relieved. I knew then that everything you'd written in the emails was true, you really did love me.' He chuckles to himself. 'You have no idea how hard it was to stop emailing you after I was supposedly dead.'

His voice is floating away, like my head is under water. I don't understand. *Jacob* texted me about his own funeral.

'It was you?' I shout.

He flinches again. I notice he does that when I get angry. Did Iris get angry a lot? Did she shout at him?

'I'm sorry,' he says. 'I presumed you'd worked it all out. It's why I put bottles of whisky in the car because you know I hate whisky, so I figured you'd know something was off about the accident. I also sent you little notes and chocolates, clues that I was alive and coming back for you. It was all going so well until I realised my mother hadn't given you my gift. That was the last step of my plan, and she was about to ruin it for me. So I had to take action.'

I can't move. My hands are sweating, and my tongue feels like it's made from old carpet. *What action?*

'What... what did you do?' I manage to stutter.

'Are you OK, cookie? You look pale. Let me get you some brandy. It's your favourite one, that nice Gran Duque D'Alba XO Dad bought for the Christmas we were all together. You said you liked it, so I got it in just for you. Actually, I've bought a lot of things for us to enjoy together. It's Christmas, after all.' He passes me a small glass and I drink it in one gulp.

'Keep going with your story,' I say, trying not to choke.

'I looked through the window of my mum's house one night and saw that my gift to you wasn't under the tree, so on Christmas Eve I let myself in, took it out of my mother's usual hiding place and put it where I knew you'd find it Christmas morning,' he continues. 'I also cleared up a bit because Mum always left the tidying to me. Anyway, all's well that ends well. Here you are, wearing the ring I bought you on the correct finger – that's all the proof I need that this is it. It's all been worth it. This is the beginning of our forever.'

Jacob gets up and drops to one knee beside me. He takes my hand in his, running his thumb over the sparkling green gem of my ring, and clears his throat.

'Eva, will you do me the honour of being my wife?'

The buzzing in my ears grows louder and my entire body becomes weightless. No one was after me in Cragstone; it was Jacob all along. He faked his death, he lured me back, he sent me the postcards and chocolates, all the while lurking in the shadows. He even let himself into his mother's house while I was upstairs. Was it him I thought I saw at the bedroom door? Was he watching me sleep?

And now this man, this delusional liar, is on one knee waiting for an answer.

I love Jacob. I really do. Don't I?

I study his face, the way his eyes look up at me like Bambi, his thick lashes that make him look so young and innocent contrasting wildly with his thick stubble and wide shoulders. His hand grasps mine tightly, like he's scared I'm going to run away. I won't. I love him. I think.

It felt like love a few hours ago when our bodies were entwined. It felt like love at the very beginning, when we were still children, and after when I thought I'd lost him for good, but I don't know this man at my feet. And he doesn't know me, not the real me; he only knows the person who has been pretending to be me. Will he still want to marry me when he realises that for the last year he's been conversing with a stranger?

'Is that a yes?' he asks, the expression on his face so open and hopeful it makes me want to weep.

When I first saw the ring, I imagined what Jacob proposing to me would look like, telling myself that I'd have said yes. I guess it's a lot easier to fantasise about loving a man when he's dead.

Whatever I do next, I have to be smart.

'Yes?' I say hesitantly. Jacob jumps up and goes to hug me, but I stop him. 'But we have to take things slow. It's all very messy right now – no one even knows you're alive. What you've done is illegal, and we can't marry if you are officially dead, so let's not rush into anything, OK? We have a lot to talk about.'

Jacob nods like a little boy listening to a grown-up. He closes the gap between us and although I know this is a mistake, my heart still skips a beat as he leans in and kisses me softly.

'I love you, Eva Walsh,' he says. 'I promise everything is going to be OK.'

Against my better judgement, I believe him.

THIRTY-FIVE
26 DECEMBER

I fell asleep in Jacob's arms last night and when we woke up it was light outside, the day a harsh white amplified by the fallen snow.

'This is the first day of the rest of our lives,' he said. But it wasn't joy I was feeling unfurling in my chest; it was something akin to apprehension. And it hasn't lifted all morning.

Jacob has spent the last hour making us an elaborate breakfast while telling me his long-term plans and I'm too stunned to say anything in response. He really has thought of everything. The cabin is stocked with food and drink; there's even an outfit laid out on the sofa for me in my size. He says we can stay for as long as we want in this little house in the middle of nowhere, because now that I have no job and he no longer exists, we are completely free. He's been so busy cooking for me he's still in his pyjamas and dressing gown. The Jacob I knew was stoic, solid, controlled, yet this one is flapping his arms around wildly as he describes our future together in great detail.

'We can take a boat to Spain,' he says. 'I have a fake passport and enough money to last us until we find work. Or France. Or maybe Italy. I haven't forgotten all the languages I learned at school!'

He doesn't intend on telling anyone he's alive; he says he'll simply become the person on his fake ID. That's how he plans for us to get married. This isn't the man I used to know – this is a tiger who has finally been let out of his cage. A tiger who has suffered at the hands of another and isn't coping very well.

The whole time Jacob is talking I keep thinking about the email exchange between him and the person impersonating me. I don't know how to burst his happy bubble and tell him it was never me, and I don't know if it even matters anymore. I've already said yes to marrying him, he wasn't conned out of his savings, and those emails helped him find the confidence to escape his mad mother.

'What do you think, cookie?' Jacob says, pulling me on to the couch and wrapping me in his long arms. 'France or Spain? Spain has better weather but I'm fluent in French. Well, I speak Spanish well too, but I prefer speaking French. And the food is good too. Actually, the food is better in Italy.'

He's talking fast, like he's on drugs, his eyes wide and gestures erratic. I need to speak to Ryan. He'll know what to do. Has he seen my bag yet and looked inside? He must be wondering where I am. I hope he isn't too worried.

Jacob starts to cough, and I rub his back.

'What's the matter?' I ask. 'Are you ill again?'

He shakes his head. 'It's my lungs,' he says, gasping through shaky breaths. 'Long-term side effects of the cyanide.'

He needs medical help in more ways than one. I fetch him a glass of water and he sips it, catching his breath. I've hardly said a word since he proposed but he doesn't seem to notice or care.

'I'm fine. I'm fine. I've had a few seizures over the last month or so,' he says with a nervous laugh. 'But don't worry, it's all under control. I don't think it's permanent. Just the toxins working their way out of my system.'

'We can't let your mother get away with this,' I say.

'Well, I can hardly go to the police now.'

Maybe he could. Ryan would understand. Could Jacob testify against his own mother without getting into trouble himself? Probably not. Whatever happens I'm not leaving the country with a mentally unstable, physically sick man. Maybe I could love Jacob properly one day, if he got help, but none of what is happening in this cabin right now is right.

It's started to snow again, the windows becoming furry with freshly fallen flakes. I didn't notice when we arrived, probably because it was dark, but all the windows have metal grilles nailed over them. Surely there are no wild animals out here, or burglars. It's probably to protect the glass from falling branches. I peer beyond the metal but all I see is white: trees and shrubs and a path covered in so much snow it has muted the world. We could be anywhere. I don't even know for how long Jacob had been driving, or how far, before I woke up in his car.

'Where are we?' I ask.

He leads me to the breakfast table in the centre of the room, wraps his arms around my waist and kisses the back of my neck. 'Don't you worry about that. Just relax, enjoy our Christmas together, and when the weather is better we can finally begin our sunny life abroad, just the two of us.'

I sit down and he serves me the food he's made, pancakes and bacon and all the same dishes his mother prepared for me yesterday morning. Although I don't fear being poisoned this time, I still have no appetite.

'Is it not nice?' he asks.

'It looks great, but I don't normally eat this early.'

'It's not early. It's nine thirty. Come on, you need your energy.'

'I feel a bit sick,' I say.

Jacob's face lights up. 'Imagine if you were pregnant! I know these things don't happen straight away, but wouldn't it be wonderful? Remember how we were both talking about wanting twins? And you don't use contraception... so you never know.'

I've never said any of those things to him. Is that another lie he was told by the person pretending to be me? I don't want twins, and I've had a contraceptive implant fitted since I was twenty-one. The only person I've ever talked about having children with is Mario. My shoulders slump as I realise Mario is probably in Cragstone right now. Did he give up on me when he saw I wasn't there and go back to London or Italy? Or is he driving around with Iris, Harry and Ryan looking for me? I feel even worse now.

'Sorry, I need to lie down,' I say to Jacob. 'I'll help with the dishes later.'

He waves his hands at me as if I don't need to worry about a thing and leads me to the bed, tucking me in like he's practising to be the perfect father. He kisses my forehead and strokes my hair.

'Get some rest,' he says. 'I'll clear this up then I'll go outside and cut up some firewood. I have a shed full of tools next to the outside loo. This place is fully equipped for any eventuality.'

He's so proud of his little hut and all he's done to provide for me and our fantasy future. Planning this has probably kept him going for the last year. I close my eyes and feign sleep, listening to the sound of him washing up and putting away the plates, whistling as he works. After a while he walks past me, and I feel a rush of cold air seep into the house as he opens the front door. I wait for him to shut it behind him before I sit up, cocking my head to one side at the sound of metal against metal. Is Jacob locking the door? I jump out of bed and test the handle, but it doesn't budge. He did! Why would he lock the front door behind him when I'm still inside?

I hide behind the curtains and watch him through the grates on the window. His silhouette looks dark and foreboding against the white landscape. He's got his thick coat over his dressing gown, his hood up, and he's wearing heavy boots. As he walks past the car, he places his phone in his dressing gown pocket before picking up an axe, but he doesn't head towards the pile of logs – he walks right past it. Where's he going with the axe if he's not chopping wood? He weaves past a few trees, his hair and shoulders now speckled with snowflakes, and as he reaches a small hut to the side of the building, he drops the axe and goes inside. Oh. My entire body turns liquid with relief. He's going to the outside bathroom. Jacob was pretending he had to chop wood so he could use the toilet far away from me. OK, that's understandable. It's also very convenient because it buys me some time. I need to find his laptop.

I look around the cosy little hut, now immaculate again, and run over to the desk in the corner. It's piled high with paperwork, including a notebook scribbled with Jacob's spiky writing, and a laptop. I glance over my shoulder before opening the Mac, wincing when it lets out three jolly notes as it sparks to life. It's asking for a password.

Think, Eva. Think! What is Jacob obsessed with?

I try 'Eva'. Nothing. I try 'Eva Walsh'. Not that either. Hoping laptops aren't like ATMs and I get more than three attempts, I try 'Cookie' and the screen fills with colour. Yes! I'm in. Then I recoil. Jacob's desktop picture is a giant photo of my face. I don't recognise it. Where did he get that from? The necklace I'm wearing is the one Mario bought me for my birthday last year, so it must be a recent photo. I think it was taken at Mario's parents' anniversary party. How far down the Facebook rabbit hole did Jacob have to go to find this? Then how long did he spend editing and cropping the picture so everyone but me was cut out of the image?

I scan the screen. I don't know what I'm looking for – emails, perhaps, or some kind of catfishing evidence. A few tabs are open, so I try them first. One is a guide to Spain; another is a medical website explaining cyanide poisoning. I go to check his Gmail when a loud beeping sound makes me jump. I spin around but the door is shut. I'm still alone. It sounded like a message alert, but didn't Jacob take his phone with him to the toilet? Something beeps again, this time accompanied by a vibrating sound.

I scrabble through the papers on his desk then check the drawer. Beneath two more notebooks and some postcards of Cragstone is a phone. My mobile phone.

What is my mobile phone doing in Jacob's desk in the middle of the woods?

THIRTY-SIX

I look behind me again, check Jacob is still outside, then study the phone in my hand. It's definitely mine. The only way you can access it is via my thumbprint or a six-digit code, so I doubt he's been able to look at it. I gain access and see eight missed calls from Amanda and lots of text messages.

Hey, let me know when you're arriving for Christmas 😊

Eva, are you OK? Text me.

What the hell is going on? You're freaking me out.

Mario called me looking for you. Then called again to say the hotel receptionist said you lost your phone. Have you found it yet? Why haven't you messaged me some other way?

Mario went to pick you up and told me a crazy woman was having a fit, saying you smashed her kitchen window. WTF is going on? I'm worried about you!

I press on Amanda's name, but it won't connect. I check the bars on the phone: there's hardly any reception. Where are we that I can't even make a phone call? The phone has 73% battery though, which means Jacob has been charging it. And although he can't access the phone, he can still see the messages I receive when they flash up on my screen.

I text Amanda, hoping it connects even though there's no reception.

> *I'm fine. Long story. Got my phone back but can't call. Tell Mario to go home.*

I want to say more but I can't, not yet. Not until I know what the hell I'm going to do about Jacob. He thinks we're two romantic heroes escaping to the Med, but I can't go anywhere with him. He needs professional help. Plus I can't stop thinking about my bag at Ryan's house. No doubt Iris has told the police I smashed her window, then Harry will tell them I lied to him and ran off, and Ryan will confirm everything I told him and show his superiors all the evidence. Am I a victim in their minds... or a criminal?

Out of the corner of my eye I see something flash up on Jacob's laptop screen. I'm wearing nothing but knickers and his old t-shirt, I have nowhere to hide the phone so I stuff it down the side of a sofa cushion then click on the 'New Message' alert on his desktop. It's an email from a company called IBYG telling Jacob that Eva Walsh is still waiting to hear from him.

Eva Walsh? Why am I waiting to hear from him? I look behind me, checking Jacob is still outside, scared I won't be able to hear him come in over the thundering in my chest. I wipe my shaky, clammy hands on my t-shirt and move my fingers over the touchpad, clicking on the link. It takes me to a website. A site called I'll Be Your Girlfriend.

My fingers tremble as I scan the page, bile burning the back of my throat as my name and face appear everywhere. I feel like I'm drowning, struggling to see and breathe properly, a buzzing sound in my ears. I click on Jacob's profile on the top right then scroll down to 'My Girlfriend'. It's me. Jacob has inputted data and it's all about me – my likes and dislikes, my past, our shared memories. Has he been building an online profile about me? I click on 'Conversations' and there are all our email exchanges. Except it's not me he's been talking to, and it's not another person, it's a *computer program*. Jacob has been talking to himself.

My hands are shaking, and my head has grown light like it did when I first saw Jacob on the clifftop. I should have eaten something. I can't faint again; I need to know more. I hold on to the desk to steady myself, willing my eyes to focus so I can look at this creepy site in more detail. I click on 'Photos' and there I am, except it's not me. He's uploaded pictures of himself along with a handful of photos of me that he must have found on LinkedIn and other public pages, then chosen from a selection of templates of other couples whose faces you can replace. There we are kissing on a park bench, and again hand in hand in a field. There are even photos he's made of me in sexy outfits and lingerie.

I scroll through them all, swallowing down the saliva filling my mouth, willing myself not to be sick. The conversations and photos go back nearly two years, since Mario and I got together. Did this start as some kind of mental escape and then escalated? Was Jacob originally trying to impress Harry? Or, the more terrifying option, did he begin to enjoy what he was reading so much he crossed over from fantasy to self-delusion and now believes his own lies?

I hear the grind of metal on metal and slam the laptop shut, throwing myself on the sofa as Jacob opens the door, his arms full of chopped firewood. I can't move or speak; I just stare at him. This stranger. This dangerous man.

'Give us a hand, Eva,' he says, followed by that beautiful smile of his.

I snap back to the present, jumping to my feet and running over to help. I have to act normal. He can't know that I know about my phone or the website, not yet.

Between us we carry the firewood to the hearth as he chats away about the weather and how long it will take for the roads to clear. 'It's a blizzard out there,' he says, taking off his coat but keeping his dressing gown and boots on as we crouch by the fire. 'Good job we have all we need here because there won't be any access into the forest for a while. But that's OK, right? We can keep ourselves busy.'

He gives me a wink that years ago, maybe even just yesterday, would have sent my stomach into a spasm of butterflies, but now it fills me with cold, dark fear. I'm trapped in a cabin, in the snow, with a madman. A man who has been stalking me, watching me, lying about me.

'Are you OK?' he asks.

I stand up, pulling at his baggy t-shirt I'm wearing, suddenly very conscious that I'm practically naked.

'Why did you never look for me on social media?' I ask him.

He looks up, confusion criss-crossing his handsome face. 'We've had this conversation before.'

No, we haven't. 'I can't remember,' I say.

'I told you. I stopped using social media when I realised my mum was hacking into my accounts and messaging my friends as me every time I got ill. It wasn't worth the hassle. Also, it was hard to find you. I looked for years until one day you popped up on LinkedIn. I nearly created an account so I could message you, but I was scared my mum would see – she used to be on there a lot for work, so I had to be smart. That's when I found your email address, and now look at us. It all worked out.'

Is he lying to me, or to himself?

'I should get dressed,' I say.

He grins, signalling to a pile of clothes. He really thinks this is romantic. The computer program would have told him whatever he needed to hear. Whatever would fuel his fantasies about me. About us.

I look at the clothes he's bought me – a vest, a jumper and a pair of jeans. They still have the price tags on. None of it was cheap.

'Underwear is in the top drawer,' he says, watching my every move. 'I didn't buy you a bra as I wasn't sure of your size.'

I open the drawer and pull out a tiny lacy thong.

'Go on,' he says, eyebrows raised. 'Get dressed. Although it's all coming off soon anyway.'

No, it's not. I'm getting dressed and I'm getting the hell out of here.

I rip off his t-shirt and pull on my jumper in the least alluring way possible, tripping over as I try to climb into the ridiculous underwear and tight jeans.

'I'll put the other jeans in the wash,' he says.

'No!' I cry out.

Ryan's telephone number is in the pocket. I can't lose that.

Jacob looks concerned so I have to think fast. I run over to him and throw my arms around his neck. 'You're so kind, always doing everything for me.'

'And how are you going to thank me?' he replies, kissing me back. His lips on mine feel good, us being together feels right, but I have to keep telling myself that this isn't the real Jacob. This isn't the man I once knew and trusted. His hand slips beneath the waistband of my new jeans and I pull it out. I don't want him anywhere near me.

'Later,' I say. 'Let's watch a movie first.'

I think he's going to keep pressing for something more, but he doesn't. He likes the idea of a movie and runs to the kitchen area, from where he produces a bowl of popcorn and a bag of M&Ms.

'I told you I was prepared for everything!' he says, grabbing a blanket and snuggling beneath it with me. 'Phone reception is terrible here, but luckily the WiFi is good. What should we watch?'

WiFi? Dammit! I should have called Amanda on WhatsApp. But what would I have said? I don't even know where I am. I make a mental note to take Ryan's number out of the jeans pocket and hide it somewhere. As soon as I have a chance to text him, I will. I need his help; I can't deal with Jacob by myself.

'You choose,' I say to Jacob, handing him the remote control.

'I've already added all your favourites to my list on Netflix.'

Of course he has.

I take a handful of popcorn and force myself to swallow it down. I'm going to need as much energy as I can muster if I'm going to get out of this. The popcorn is like chewing on polystyrene. I eat some chocolate with it and try not to gag, all the while nodding away and humming in agreement at Jacob's film choices that I couldn't care less about.

'This one's fun,' he says, burrowing under the blanket and leaning his head on my shoulder. He's so big and heavy. His broad shoulders and sculpted arms have always been attractive to me, manly, desirable... until now that I'm working out how easy it will be to get away from him.

A buzzing sound escapes from beneath the sofa seat. *Shit!* My phone is squeezed between the two sofa cushions I'm sitting on. Why didn't I put it on silent? I push against it, trying to muffle the sound, but it buzzes again.

'What was that?' Jacob asks.

'What?'

He whips the blanket back.

'I thought I heard my phone.'

He takes his own mobile from his dressing gown pocket and frowns at it. 'Not mine,' he says.

The phone beeps, and this time Jacob runs to the drawer in the desk, rifling through all the paperwork.

'Have you been looking in my drawer?' he shouts over his shoulder.

'No.'

'Your phone was in here. Did you find it? I wanted to give it back to you.'

'I don't know what you're talking about.'

He urges me to stand up. There's no way I can say no without looking suspicious. I get up and he fishes between the cushions until he finds it.

'Ah! There it is. How did it get on the sofa?' He frowns at the display. I wrack my brain as to what I said to Amanda. It was nothing incriminating.

Jacob is smiling. '"You're so selfish, Eva,"' he says, reading what Amanda must have replied. '"You're telling me you couldn't have messaged me any other way? I've been worried out of my mind. Deal with Mario yourself. I'm done with running around after you." What a nice friend you have,' Jacob says, putting my phone in his dressing gown pocket without taking his eyes off me. 'Now tell me why you lied to me, Eva.'

THIRTY-SEVEN

Amanda hates me. She's the only friend I have left, and she wants nothing more to do with me. I swallow down the pain in my throat and try to calm my breathing. Jacob looks angry, as if I'm the one who owes *him* an explanation. Well, I'm not answering his questions until he answers mine. The best offence is a good defence.

'What were you doing with my phone?'

He gives me a pitying stare, shaking his head from side to side. He looks just like his mother when he does that.

'You shouldn't lie to me, cookie. You know everything I do is for you.'

'Answer my question! What was my phone doing in your desk?'

He rolls his eyes, like I'm being a silly little girl. 'You dropped it when you were running through town in the rain a few days ago. You'd been to the supermarket and fell over on your way back to Mum's. I wanted to help you, but you weren't ready to know the truth about me yet. I found your phone under a hedge.'

My entire body is trembling so hard even my teeth are aching. That was the evening I'd spoken to Bianca in the supermarket and I'd seen a man watching me from the shadows. I was terrified. I remember running down the high street, slipping on the wet pavement, the pain of falling on my knees, which are still bruised and sore. And all along it was Jacob I was running from.

'You scared me!' I shout at him. 'How could you?'

He winces at the volume of my voice. 'It was all part of the plan. You need to trust me, Eva. Marriage is built on a foundation of trust.'

I laugh. I can't help myself. Is he serious? He really thinks I'm going to marry him after all this?

'Trust?' I shout, stepping closer to him. He edges away. 'That's rich coming from you! You haven't stopped lying to me since you sent me a text message about your own funeral.'

'That was simply a means to an end.'

'It's all lies,' I say, stomping over to his desk and picking up his laptop. 'I had a look. You know full well we haven't been having a long-distance relationship for the last two years. It's all in your head. It's make-believe.'

Jacob looks visibly hurt and confused. 'What are you talking about?'

'I'll Be Your Girlfriend dot com?' I spit. 'Seriously? Did you have fun getting messages from a fake me, and getting to live out all your sordid little fantasies?'

'It's real!' he says. 'You love me. I know you do because you came back to me.'

'Because you forced me to! You know how much I hate Cragstone, yet you tricked me into returning. Then it started up again, the rumours and the whispers, this time everyone saying you and I had been secretly seeing one another. They accused me of causing your death because you were on your way to visit me. Did you know that? That I've spent the last five days defending myself, surrounded by people who hate me? Yet *you* started those rumours, didn't you?'

Jacob blanches, his face pale and his lips pinched. 'All I did was tell Mum and a few others that we were in touch. It's not a big deal. You said we had to keep our love a secret, but I couldn't help myself. Harry is such a slimeball, telling me how he planned to message you on Facebook, so I showed him the pictures you sent me.'

'I never told you anything because you've been talking to a bloody computer all this time.' I run both my hands through my hair. I could scream right now. Maybe I should – it might shock some sense into him. 'I never sent you those photos, Jacob. You made them, on your creepy little website, along with two years' worth of conversations with an algorithm you programmed with my data. You don't know me! Yesterday was the first time I've had any contact with you in ten years.'

'No,' he says, snatching the laptop out of my hands. 'How could you say that? Our love is real!'

'Did you interfere with my relationship with Mario?'

He swings around to face me, his deep brown eyes like two hollows in a skull. 'You told me you didn't love him the way you love me. That your engagement was just a ruse. A misdirection.'

What twisted version of reality has he been telling himself?

'What did you do, Jacob?'

'I gave you a plausible excuse to finish with him. I sent him those emails.'

'The emails pretending to be my assistant? Knowing I'd see them?'

'Of course. It was a means to an end,' he says again. 'It was our plan all along.'

Now I understand why he knew about the emails... because he sent them. *Bastard.*

'Then once I left him, you contacted Mario and told him you and I had been having an affair all along, didn't you?'

'Just before the accident, yes, so he wouldn't beg you to come back. I was helping you. Helping *us*. It was all part of the bigger strategy.'

'You ruined my life,' I say quietly, tears gathering in my eyes. 'You're ill, Jacob. You're an unwell man.'

'No, I'm not!' he screams, throwing the laptop to the ground. He's still wearing his heavy boots and he stamps on the Mac, once, twice, three times, accentuating each word with each crush of the laptop. 'My mother always said that – "You're ill, son," and, "You need help, son." But I didn't. I was fine. S*he* made me ill and now *you* are making me feel ill too.'

He keeps jumping on the laptop, pieces of plastic and keyboard keys skittering along the wooden floor. He's pulling at his hair, his beautiful face now a red, grotesque mask of wild frustration. I run to the sofa and curl up into a ball in the corner, my knees raised up to my chest. I'm trapped in a cabin in the middle of nowhere with a madman I don't really know, and now he's destroyed all the evidence of what he's done to me. Would the police be able to access the messages he's been sending and the photos of me on that creepy website without his password?

'This isn't going to work,' I say to him. 'You and me. This is a bad idea.'

'It *will* work, of course it will, we're soulmates. You don't understand. I have a plan.'

'I don't want to be part of your plan,' I say, pulling the engagement ring off my finger. 'You're scaring me.'

'No,' he says, hurrying over to me. He crouches down beside me, so we're eye to eye, and strokes the hair out of my face. 'I'm not scaring you; I'm *protecting* you.'

'Protecting me from what? Aggressive, creepy men who are out to get me?'

He nods, not understanding the irony of my words. I hand him back the ring, but he refuses to take it. His eyes are swimming with tears, making something in my chest tear like tissue paper. How did we get here? How did the boy who saved my life turn into a man who has single-handedly destroyed it?

I get up, place the ring on the table, grab my coat and push on my trainers. My coat is heavy on one side, and I remember Jacob's gift to me: the stone from our favourite beach. I won't be keeping this one. Jacob watches on silently without trying to stop me. I go to open the door, but it's locked. Did he learn this from his mother?

'Let me out,' I say wearily, all my energy suddenly depleted.

Jacob shakes his head, picking up the ring and inspecting it. 'We're twenty-six miles from Cragstone and there's a blizzard. It's too dangerous out there.'

'It's too dangerous *in here*. I'm going home.'

'You have no home,' he says, stepping closer to me. 'Remember? No fiancé, no job, no friends, no money... just me. You need me, Eva. You always have done. I can save you again.'

'Unlock the door,' I whisper.

He's looming over me now, his mouth so close to mine I can feel his breath on my lips. 'We can't leave. We have to wait.'

'Please.' I start to cry, huge heaving sobs that make my entire body convulse. My back is against the wall and Jacob is blocking my way. He reaches out for me, but I push him back, my cries becoming gulping wails. Why is he doing this to me? All I wanted was to leave Cragstone and the horrors of my childhood behind and start afresh. And I managed to, eventually. Maybe Mario and I could have made it work had Jacob not got involved. I'll never know. I can't go back to who I was... or become who he needs me to be.

'Cookie,' he says, stroking the tears off my cheek. 'Let me look after you.'

He pulls me into him and this time I let him, resting my head on his hard chest as he holds me tight, telling me everything is going to be OK. I keep crying, my mind so crowded I no longer know what's real, who to trust, how I can get out of this mess. He's holding me tight, rocking me like he did the night my mother died. It used to make me feel so safe, back when it wasn't him that I feared.

He slips the ring back on to my finger. 'I love you,' he says. 'Forget everything from before. We've found one another and that's all that matters.'

How can I forget the things he's done? I'm trapped. I have nothing and no one, and there's no way out. What was it Bianca called me? *A calculating bitch who manipulates everyone around her to get what she wants.*

I stop crying and take a shuddery breath. Maybe Bianca wasn't wrong about me. Maybe there's more than one way out of this mess.

THIRTY-EIGHT

I kiss him.

I can't think of an easier way to defuse the situation, so I kiss Jacob, and he kisses me back, and I push away every ounce of guilt I feel about tricking the man who's keeping me prisoner.

'I'm sorry I shouted,' I say. 'I'm really tired. This week has been tough.'

'I understand, cookie.'

I used to think that nickname was cute, but I hate it now. I hate it with every ounce of my being.

He pulls me to him again, playing with a strand of my hair. 'I love you and I'm going to do all I can to make you the happiest woman in the world.'

Then let me out of here, I want to scream.

'Right!' I plaster a smile on my face although my cheeks are still damp with tears. 'Enough of all this drama. Let's enjoy our time together in this pretty little cabin before we start our new life in the sun.'

Jacob's grin makes my heart hurt. He believes me, and why wouldn't he? After all, I'm playing along with his make-believe game. I'm being the woman he programmed into his computer, spoke to every day, dreamed of marrying and starting a family with. That woman has no say in how she lives her life and that's what Jacob wants.

'Put that movie on and I'll make us a nice lunch for later,' I say, heading towards the kitchen area.

Jacob follows me. 'I'll help. We can cook together.'

Getting away from him is going to be harder than I thought. I kiss him again and feel him relax beneath my touch.

'Do you trust me?' I ask.

He nods. 'With my life.'

'Then let me do this for you. You have already done so much for me, it's my turn to show you how much I love you.'

Satisfied with my answer, he goes back to his popcorn and romcom, calling out parts of the plot to me as I pretend to watch the film even though my back is to the screen and I'm trying to figure out my next step. I need to get my phone and the door keys off Jacob, retrieve Ryan's telephone number from the jeans on the floor and escape this place. I wish I could drive; if I could, then all I'd have to do is steal Jacob's car. He would never be able to follow me if I was driving, but on foot I'm going to need more time. Which means I need to slow him down. But how am I going to do that? I don't want to hurt him; I just need to debilitate him. Oh God, is that what Iris told herself while poisoning her own son? This is awful. I can't do it.

I make myself look busy, starting by sweeping up the smashed-up pieces of laptop. It's unsalvageable, but I'll never forget the name of the website so I'm sure the police can look into that. I then put on a wash load, ensuring he's not looking while I transfer Ryan's telephone number from Jacob's old jeans that I was wearing earlier to the new ones I have on now.

'Do you have any dirty washing?' I call out.

Jacob pauses the movie and looks over at me. The expression on his face is pure joy. He looks like the boy I fell in love with. *No.* I close my eyes and take two deep breaths. This isn't the same Jacob. This man is violent, delusional and possessive. I'm not safe.

'There are a few things in the laundry basket,' he calls out.

He's sitting on the couch with two phones in his dressing gown pocket and I need mine back. I need to get his clothes off him, which means playing the good little housewife. I fetch the rest of the laundry, switch the machine on and join him on the sofa. He opens his arms wide, wanting me to cuddle up to him. I go along with it.

'What would you like for lunch?' I ask.

'We only had breakfast a few hours ago,' he replies.

I kiss the crook of his neck and he gives a contended sigh. He really must think everything he did has worked – that pretending to be dead, luring the woman you love to your funeral, stalking her, stealing from her and kidnapping her is the ideal romantic start to married life.

'I know, but I hardly ate anything. I want to cook you something special. What is there to eat?'

'Eva, you are so perfect,' he replies, tangling his fingers in my hair. 'There's rice, pasta, tins of beans in the cupboards, plus meat, cheese and vegetables in the fridge. I know you'll work your magic.'

'How about you have a shower and get dressed while I cook?' I suggest.

He smirks. 'Want to join me?'

I can't think of anything worse. I just want my phone back.

'Maybe. Let me get started with prep and I'll think about it.'

He kisses me long and slow then strips out of his nightclothes, leaving everything on the bed before heading for the bathroom, the only other room in this tiny cabin. I wait until I can hear the water running before racing over to his dressing gown and picking my phone out of the pocket, putting it on silent and punching in Ryan's telephone number. It's midday on Boxing Day – surely he'll answer.

I keep my back to the bathroom door, chopping up an onion and some garlic while I wait for the phone to connect. There's a noise at the other end.

'Hello? Ryan? It's Eva. Can you hear me?' I whisper.

Ryan's voice is a series of crackles and staccato words. Reception is too weak. *Dammit!* I hang up and call him again on WhatsApp because Jacob said the WiFi was better.

Ryan picks up again immediately. 'Hello?'

A surge of relief floods through me at the sound of his voice.

'Can you hear me?' I say quietly.

'Who's this?'

'Did you say something, Eva?' Jacob calls out from the bathroom. *Shit!* Jacob can hear me. This isn't going to work. I hang up and walk over to the bathroom door.

'Is risotto OK for lunch?' I say to Jacob.

'Lovely,' he replies. 'I won't be long. Love you!'

'You too,' I trill.

I type a message to Ryan on WhatsApp.

It's Eva. Jacob is alive and I'm trapped in a cabin in the middle of nowhere. Help me!!

I wait. Three dots appear.

How do I know this is Eva?

For crying out loud! Although I shouldn't be surprised by his response. Ryan is a policeman, after all, plus he's probably looked through my bag already and found reams of printouts confirming my story about someone pretending to be me. Another message from him pops up.

Prove that it's you.

I don't know what to say. I take a selfie and send it. It doesn't go through. I want to scream. Then I remember something he told me when we first met.

You didn't always want to be a policeman. You wanted to be a pastry chef. You told me in the pub and said you'd never told anyone before.

Ryan replies straight away.

Where are you? I'm coming to get you.

A single tear rolls down my cheek. Everything is going to be OK.

I'm in a cabin in the woods. Jacob said we're 26 miles away from Cragstone. We passed a yellow house next to a lake on the way. That's all I know.

The shower has stopped running, and I can hear Jacob whistling. I don't have much time. Ryan is typing.

Pin me your location.

Location? I just told him I don't know where I am. The bathroom door handle is turning so I push the phone into my bra, which is covered by the baggy jumper Jacob bought me, and start to chop up some chicken, adding it to the fried onions and garlic.

Jacob comes up behind me wearing nothing but a towel around his middle. He smells like minty shower gel, his hair wet and his stubble damp against my cheek.

'You don't know how happy you make me, Eva. We're going to have such a wonderful life together. It won't be long until we're on a beach in sunny Spain, you'll be pregnant and I can look after you.'

I'm glad I have my back to him and he can't see the look on my face because it would be impossible to disguise it. I don't want to be pregnant on a beach in Spain. I don't want to have his babies full stop. I just want to get out of this bloody cabin. Ryan says he's coming to get me, but he has no idea where I am. I need to get out of here right now...

'Just going to the loo,' I say, hoping the smile on my face doesn't look as frozen as it feels. 'Keep an eye on the chicken, please.'

Once inside the bathroom I lock the door and take a deep breath, but it doesn't help. Ryan has sent me another three messages asking where I am. I google how to share a location, go back to WhatsApp and send him my live location. At least that way, if I get away, Ryan can still find me. One tick appears but not the second. Why isn't it sending?

Jacob is knocking on the door.

'Are you OK in there, Eva?'

'Yes. I'm fine. Just washing my hands.'

There's a medicine cabinet. Maybe Jacob takes sleeping pills that I can crush up and put in his food. Will that work? I just need to make him drowsy enough so I can get the keys and get out of here without him following me. I open the cabinet but all I see is a box containing six aspirin, some plasters, two rolls of bandages and a small tube of antiseptic cream.

I leave the bathroom and walk straight into Jacob.

'I was getting worried,' he says, holding the tops of my arms tightly. 'Are you OK?'

I was in there less than five minutes.

I plant a kiss on his lips, and he goes back to watching his cheesy movie, laughing with forced hilarity, while I add rice to the chicken and finish the worst meal I've made in my life. I doubt Jacob will notice.

I saw there was champagne in the fridge earlier along with three different types of juice. Plus there's the cognac he bought for me. Maybe getting him drunk will do the trick.

'How about I make champagne cocktails?' I ask.

'Yes! Let's get into the holiday spirit,' he says. 'Want me to help you?'

'No! I want to surprise you.'

'There's some vodka in that cupboard too,' he says, pointing to the other side of the room. I rush to the cupboard and trip over something, stubbing my toe. I swear and Jacob looks up in alarm.

'Are you OK?'

'I'm fine.'

'Careful with that bottle. It's antifreeze. I need to sort the car out later.'

He goes back to watching his movie as I look down at the large, clear bottle at my feet full of bright orange liquid. I listened to a true crime podcast once where a woman put antifreeze in her husband's drink. I remember the story because I was shocked that it didn't kill him, it just made him drowsy. Would that work? But what if instead of making Jacob sleepy, the antifreeze makes him violently ill? I can't hurt him. I'm a better person than his mother... aren't I?

I look at the locked door, the bars at the window and the splintered pieces of laptop in the bin. It doesn't matter who I am and what I'm comfortable doing – I don't have a choice anymore. Whether Jacob is vomiting or sleeping when I get out of here makes no difference. All I need is enough time to get away and hide.

I pick up the bottle of bright orange liquid without him seeing, pour some into a smaller jug, then put the bottle back. It smells sweet, almost flowery. How much will I need to make him go to sleep? I mix orange and cranberry juice together, add vodka and champagne, then pour some of the antifreeze in. Then I make a glass for myself with just juice in it.

'Here you go,' I say, passing Jacob the drink. He places it on the table and grabs me by the waist, pulling me on to his lap.

'Movie's finished.'

'OK, well lunch is nearly done,' I say, thinking of the slop I'm about to feed him.

'I don't care about food anymore. I just want you.'

He's holding me down, lifting my jumper up. I can't let him see the phone! I push him away, scrambling to my feet.

'Drink up while it's still cold,' I say, running over to the counter and downing my own juice in one go. 'Then we can have some fun.'

'Yeah?' he says with a lascivious grin. He takes a sip of the drink. I wait. He smiles and drinks it in two gulps. 'Wow, that's strong.'

I hold my breath, waiting for something to happen.

'Another one,' he says holding out his glass.

Oh. I wasn't expecting that. I create the same mixture again, adding what's left of the antifreeze in the jug and passing it to him. He screws up his eyes as he drinks the entire cocktail like we're at a student union bar and I dared him to down it in one.

'I don't know what you put in there but it's a kicker,' he says, wiping his mouth with the back of his hand.

I give a nervous laugh and hold my hand out to him. I have an idea.

'Let's go to bed if you're not hungry,' I say, pulling him off the sofa.

His face lights up and I do my best to keep a smile fixed to my face, Bianca's voice running through my head. *Slag. Whore. Calculating bitch who manipulates everyone around her to get what she wants.* Jacob is grasping my waist roughly, digging his fingers into my hips so hard I have to bite my lips together so I don't cry out in pain.

'Oh, I'm hungry,' he says into my neck. 'Hungry for you. Whoa.' He pulls away, shaking his head lightly. 'I feel really pissed already. Do you feel drunk too?'

'Yeah, it's really gone to my head,' I lie. I don't want to have sex with him and I need to keep my phone hidden. Is Ryan on his way? How easy is it to drive twenty-six miles in this weather?

Jacob is swaying, his pretty eyes growing dark and drooping. I lead him towards the bed, where he flops down, landing like a starfish. *Perfect.*

'Do you like to play games?' I ask him.

'I love you so much,' he says, his words slurred and breath sickly sweet. My stomach knots. *It's the only way*, I tell myself. *Look what this man did to you. Look what he wants to do to you. The police will understand when they get here.*

I run into the bathroom, where I find the two rolls of bandages and start to unravel them.

'Just a little fun,' I say.

Jacob moans with delight as he lets me tie his wrists to the bedpost. I don't pull on the bandage too tightly; I don't want to hurt him.

'Kinky,' he says, a line of drool escaping the side of his mouth.

I tie his second wrist then stand up and survey my handywork.

'Kiss me,' he says. He's struggling to talk but I can see the rest of his body is still fully functioning. I'm not sure if I'm relieved or a little perturbed.

'Goodbye, Jacob,' I say, kissing him lightly on the forehead and stroking his damp hair.

'What? Wait. Where are you going?'

I don't answer. His eyes widen and his thick arms flex as he pulls at his restraints. I thought he was sleepy, but the surge of adrenaline has woken him up.

'Eva!' he shouts. He's yanking at the bandages, pulling them taut, his hands growing red with the effort. 'You put something in my drink, didn't you?'

I don't answer. I just stand there staring at him naked, spreadeagled and foaming at the mouth. Victim. Criminal. Dangerous. The man I thought I would love forever.

'You poisoned me,' he cries, his eyes struggling to focus on mine. 'You fucking bitch! You're just like my mother. All I ever did was love you... *but you're just like my mother!*'

I turn away, ignoring his pleas and insults as I put on my coat and shoes and take his keys from his trouser pocket.

As I slam the front door behind me everything falls deadly silent. As if Jacob never existed.

THIRTY-NINE

I don't realise how bad the blizzard is until I step out from beneath the porch and sink into snow so deep it covers my trainers right up to my ankles. I take a step, then another, following the direction of where I remember the path being yesterday. I'm not dressed for this weather. I go back inside the house and get Jacob's woollen hat and scarf I saw hanging by the door. I wrap it around my neck, breathing in the scent I once associated with good luck but now makes me think of Jacob and all he's done to me.

'Eva!' he calls out. 'Untie me – this isn't funny anymore.'

I push the hat over my head, covering my ears so I don't have to hear him. Five days ago, I'd have done anything to hear Jacob's voice again; now I wish he'd stayed dead.

'You won't get away with this!' he screams. He makes a gargling sound like he's trying not to vomit. 'I will find you, Eva. Wherever you go I will hunt you down!'

I slam the door shut again, this time remembering to lock it behind me. I should have tied the bandage tighter. Hopefully Jacob will pass out before he manages to untie himself, and even if he doesn't, he has no way of getting out of the house with the door locked and the bars at the window. Running through the snow is like wading through treacle, each step taking so much effort that my lungs are aching before I've even covered a few metres. The wind has picked up since yesterday, the snow hitting me in the face like a whip, each snowflake stinging like someone is throwing gravel in my face.

Jacob's car is in the driveway. I fumble with the keys in my pocket and spot a fob. I click on it and the car beeps, little yellow lights indicating that I've unlocked the doors. I rush over and get inside, shivering from fear and the sub-zero temperatures, taking a moment to gather my thoughts. It's not much warmer in here but at least without the wind I can hear myself think. I take my phone out of my pocket and check WhatsApp. The location has sent and there are three more messages from Ryan.

I'm coming.

Some of the roads are blocked off.

Get out if you can. As long as you have your phone, I will find you wherever you are.

I will find you. Ryan's words echo Jacob's, except this time it's Ryan who's going to save me. I breathe out in relief, little puffs of air filling the car like smoke. I have no idea how long it will take him to get here but he said he can find me wherever I am, so I just need to get away from the cabin and wait.

I stare at the car's dashboard. Maybe I could drive Jacob's car. It has no gear stick so it must be an automatic. I've driven an automatic before. I had four driving lessons when I was eighteen, just before leaving Cragstone. It can't be that hard.

I press the 'Start' button and the car hums into life. That's a good start. Now what? I need to turn around to access the narrow dirt track behind me. I know the pedals are stop and go, like a go-kart, but which is which? I gently press on one, then the other, but nothing happens. The gear selector has letters – P, R, N, D, S. Do I have to pick one? I choose 'S' for 'Start' and gingerly press the left pedal, but the car rolls forward a bit. So if the left pedal is the gas then the other one must be the brake. I slam on the right pedal as hard as I can and the car shoots forward, straight into the wooden wall of the outdoor toilet. I let out a piercing scream and attempt to cover my face with both arms but I'm not quick enough. All I can hear is the sound of wood splintering and glass cracking before my head crashes forward, smashing my nose against the steering wheel. I should have put my seatbelt on.

Hot, searing pain spreads from the centre of my face, my mouth filling with blood. I swallow it down and touch my swollen nose tentatively, crying out in agony.

I clamber out of the car and fall to my knees, the thick snow soaking through my jeans. I take a handful of snow and hold it up to my bloody nose and cut lip, my hands now full of pink ice. I look up and survey the damage. The car's bumper is bent, and the entire wall of the shed is smashed in half. What have I done? There's no way I can drive a car with a cracked windshield, not in this weather on a main road, and definitely not if I can't even manage to work out how to turn the car around.

I get to my feet, my arms and legs soaked through. God, it's so cold. I'll freeze to death if I attempt to walk to Cragstone in this weather. I have no idea which direction to walk in and my face is so swollen I'm struggling to see out of one eye. I'm going to have to find shelter and hide off the beaten track, but I might lose reception if I go too deep into the forest. I saw some blankets on the back seat and the bottle of water Jacob gave me yesterday is still in there, if it's not frozen solid. What if I just stay in the car, with the doors locked, and keep warm?

I wash my bloody hands in the snow and dab at my face.

The ice has stemmed the bleeding, for now. I should be OK. I get back inside and shut the car door behind me, pulling the blankets from the back seat and huddling beneath them. Every part of my body is shivering, my face tingling and throbbing. I switch the engine back on, turn up the heat and lock the car doors, then I lie down in the back to wait for rescue. I'm warm and I'm safe.

Just as I close my eyes for a moment, I hear the locks click open. I sit up with a start.

Through the blur of the snow, I see the shape of Jacob standing in the doorway of the house, pointing a second set of keys at the car. I lock the doors again but he clicks them open. *Oh God. Why didn't he pass out?* I should have made the dose higher and tied the bandages tighter. I was too careful, too kind, and now he's angry.

'I told you I was fully prepared,' Jacob shouts out into the winter wind, holding the second set of keys aloft. His voice is strong and confident, but he's gripping on to the doorframe, his head lolling back and forth. I wish I knew how long it takes for antifreeze to affect the body. Will he weaken, or has he already recovered?

Jacob is wearing his thick coat and boots. He's thought this through. Jacob doesn't do anything without a plan. He takes a step forward, supports himself against the porch post, then takes another lurching step before stumbling towards the car. I clamber over the seats and open the door furthest away from him, falling into the snow face first. I can hear him, his heavy boots, bounding towards me. My hands instantly turn numb as I pull myself up from the snow and run towards the dense trees. Ice and wind sting my eyes as I stumble blindly forward, arms stretched out before me, my bruised face screaming with pain.

'I can see you, Eva,' Jacob calls out, hot on my heels. 'Did you seriously think you'd get away?'

I weave through the trees, tripping over submerged roots

covered in snow, tangled like eels in foaming white water. The stone Jacob gave me bounces around in my pocket, banging against my thigh, but I'm running too fast to take it out. Every one of my breaths hurts like a blow to the chest, my throat torn and searing from the cold.

I can hear Jacob crashing through the undergrowth. He's close. How did he cover so much distance already? I glance behind me and see him. He's leaning on a tree trunk, spitting vomit from his mouth, it lands in the snow a bright orange-red. His thick hair is wet and plastered to his pale face, his fingers grasping the bark of the tree as if he's holding on for dear life. Our eyes lock as he wipes his mouth with the back of his hand.

'You tried to kill me,' he says quietly. We stay like that for an eternity, eyes locked together, his ghostly face shining with tears or sweat, I don't know. 'Why did you hurt me, Eva?'

Then he lurches forward, and I run. I keep running but my lungs are refusing to take in any more icy air. I glance behind me, but I can't see Jacob anymore. Where is he? Has he collapsed? I crawl into a holly bush, the leaves scratching my swollen face and bright pink hands as I bury myself as deep as I can then check my phone. The location still seems to be working. I press the call button, but it won't connect.

I type another message.

Help me! I need you!

It's nearly three o'clock and the light is beginning to dim. It will be dark soon. I adjust the scarf around my neck, but it's grown damp and is doing very little to keep me warm. I won't survive in the woods in this weather, in the dark, with such awful phone reception. *Where are you, Ryan?*

I wait. All has grown quiet; even the wind in the branches has died down. Has Jacob gone back into the house? Has he finally passed out? I'm safe under this bush, away from the elements. I'll just wait here until I hear Ryan's car pull up. I turn to watch the road, then in an instant everything turns blurry, my head hits the ground and I'm staring up at the white sky through the twisted holly branches. There's a tightening at my throat. I can't breathe. My hand flies to my neck but my numb fingers are useless as I'm pulled backwards out of the foliage by my scarf. I claw at the tight, wet wool digging into my windpipe, attempting to push my frozen fingers between the fabric and my skin, the heels of my feet failing to find purchase in the snow. Jacob is dragging me through the woods, his scarf a leash around my neck.

'Did you really think you'd get away from me?' he shouts over his shoulder. 'You're not safe out here. I was looking after you.'

He slows down, his breathing laboured, giving me enough time to scramble to my feet, but he's still got a hold of the scarf, coiling it tighter and tighter around his hand like a noose.

'Let go!' I croak, trying to twist around and push him off me.

My elbow connects with his ribs, and he cries out. He's weak and doubles over, struggling to breathe.

'You hurt me,' he whines through clenched teeth, circling his wrist and tightening the scarf around my throat further. I can't turn around. I fall to my bruised knees and so does he, wrestling me to the ground until he's looming over me. His waxy skin shines in the dimming twilight, pink saliva frothing at the corners of his mouth.

'Why did you hurt me?' He has one hand around my throat, the other pushing my face into the snow. I can feel the hard, frozen ground digging into my back, twigs scraping my scalp.

My hands are scrabbling at Jacob's back, pulling his hair, scratching his face, but it's no use. The poison may have weakened him but he's still strong, far too strong for me.

'You said you loved me. You were *meant to love me*,' he says, his bloody saliva dripping down the side of my neck. 'But you're just like my mother.'

My vision is blurring, my hands reaching out either side of me, forming mounds of snow like I'm making snow angels in my final moments.

'Only I know how to love you properly,' Jacob is saying as he tightens his hold around my windpipe. 'I love you so much, Eva. You can't leave me. I'm not going to let you go.'

My fingers close in around something. A stick? A branch? I pick it up and hit out until it strikes Jacob on the shoulder. I'm not strong enough to hurt him but it stuns him enough to make him loosen his grip on my throat. I gasp and cough, only managing to take in a small amount of air. Each breath is like a stab in the chest and everything burns: the snow against my face, my throbbing nose, my swollen throat. I lash out again with the branch, this time making contact with his face and causing him to cry out in pain. I scramble backwards and get on my feet, holding the branch out like a sword with one hand as I lean against a tree and loosen the scarf with the other.

I'm not able to speak; I'm only just about able to breathe. Jacob is staring at me, his eyes bulbous and black, his waxy skin as white as everything else surrounding us.

He lunges forward. He's so quick, I don't realise he's knocked the branch out of my hand until it lands at my feet and his hands are around my throat again, his breath hot on my lips.

'All I've ever wanted is to love you,' he says. 'Why couldn't you love me too?'

I try to prise his fingers off me but he's too strong, too determined to love me as hard as he can. He's leaning his full weight against me, his body pressing me against the tree. Something is digging into my right thigh. It's the stone he gave me. My vision blurs as I pull the smooth white stone from my coat and hit the back of his head as hard as I can. It makes a satisfying sound. I don't think I've seriously hurt him, but he lets go of me, clasping his head. I step to the side as he staggers backwards with surprise, his poisoned body languid and on the point of collapse. He hasn't noticed the roots of the trees buried beneath the snow at his feet, coiled like fighting eels; he's not looking where he's going. His eyes, like always, are only trained on me. He stumbles, arms flailing, and falls backwards with a crack. *A crack?* I blink and try to take a lungful of air and blink again until my vision clears, and Jacob comes into view. His body is a crumbled heap of limbs, like kindling left out in the cold. His head has hit a rock submerged in the snow, snow that is no longer white but pink, then red, then jet black. He's staring up at me with open eyes, his mouth a perfect O of surprise, his head surrounded by a crimson halo. And beside it all is his stone, white on white, just the bright black hearts shining wet through the snow.

Jacob is dead.

FORTY

I came to Cragstone five days ago because Jacob was dead. And now I've killed him.

I don't know how long I've been standing here. The blizzard has died down to tiny flakes blowing around like ash from a great fire. Jacob's eyes are still open, and he hasn't blinked for a long time. His hair and body sparkle with a light dusting of snow and his lips are turning blue. He's definitely dead. After days of being accused of killing him, this time I've actually done it.

I pick up the stone he gave me yesterday, now gleaming and clean from the snow, and place it back in my pocket. I'm numb all over and every breath feels like a million razor blades slicing open my throat. I can't feel my face, my right eye is so swollen I can no longer see out of it, and every inch of my body hurts. I don't know what to do. My body is screaming at me to run, but my mind is reminding me that Ryan is on his way. Ryan, *a policeman*, is on his way to save me and I'm standing over the dead body of a man who was meant to have died a month ago.

The horizon is tinged in pink and gold, making the trees shine like they're made of silver. I look around me and realise

I'm not as deep in the forest as I thought – the car is only a few metres away and there's a clearing between the trees where I can see the empty road. Ryan will be able to find me easily here... which means he'll also be able to see Jacob's body.

I have to move it, but I don't want to touch it. He looks like a waxwork dummy left out in the cold, his pale face now grey and his eyes like glass. I should have closed them while I had the chance, but it's too late now. I can't look at him. I should go back to his car and get the blanket to cover him with.

There's a rumbling in the distance. I startle and look up. My face is too swollen to see clearly. I wait for a few seconds, holding my breath, but there's nobody there.

I'll just tell Ryan the truth. Jacob's death was an accident, self-defence, and I'm clearly injured so the police will believe me. Except it *wasn't* self-defence – it was pre-meditated. I poisoned Jacob, I tied him up, I hit him over the head. Everyone in Cragstone already thinks I'm a terrible person... If I'm accused of murder, my life will be ruined forever. I need to bury him. I'll tell Ryan that Jacob took me hostage and I got away, then he must have escaped. It's the only way.

I turn back to the house, but walking is close to impossible. My entire body is shaking, my teeth chattering, my head pounding. Every step feels like I'm climbing a mountain. I can't do this. I just want to lie down. My hands are too cold to feel the keys in my pocket, my fingers fumbling as I try to open the door. I don't even know what I'm looking for. A spade? A pickaxe? Can you dig frozen earth? How do they bury people in the winter?

I get the door to the cabin open, but my hands are trembling too much to pull the keys back out of the lock. I leave them in there while I hunt around the house for something to hack at the solid earth with. There's kitchen knives. Can you cut frozen earth with a knife? I cover my face with my hands, sending shooting pains from my eye to my jaw to my throat. My injuries must be bad.

I go into the tiny bathroom and stare at my reflection in the mirror. If I could, I would gasp, but I can't because my throat can no longer make a sound. My neck is bloody and blue, ligature marks and bruises shaped like Jacob's thumbs. My lips and right eye are also red and swollen from the car accident. As for my nose, it's definitely broken.

I lean over the sink, gasping for air. I look like a monster, and I sound like one. I take the last two aspirin from the pack and crush them between my teeth before washing them down with water. Even that is excruciatingly painful. I close my one good eye and try to think. I need to deal with the body then hide outside until Ryan finds me. I need to pretend Jacob is still out there, looking for me. I need to lie to a kind man I actually like, and I definitely trust, and I need to be convincing or I'm in serious trouble.

Oh God, I can't do this.

I don't want to go to jail, but nor do I want to go back to Jacob's body. I didn't mean to hurt him. I didn't want him dead. I just want to live a normal life with no more ghosts.

I attempt to recall everything Jacob told me about this house. There's an axe outside; I know that because he used it to chop firewood. Can I dig frozen soil with an axe? Wait, he also mentioned tools in the shed next to the outdoor toilet. The shed I destroyed. What if there's a spade nearby?

I stumble back outside, past the damaged car and the splintered wood, then I stop. The sky is now a deep shade of lilac, the moon casting a white glow over everything, turning it monochrome. At the entrance to the driveway, silhouetted against the bright white snow, someone is standing, staring at me. And it's not Ryan.

I don't know what to do. Do I search for a weapon in the destroyed shed? Do I run to the body before they see it? Or do I get the hell out of here? I'm frozen to the spot, my head buzzing, my aching limbs unable to move. But it no longer matters because I'm too late – they've seen Jacob. They run over to him, falling to the ground, letting out a long wail.

Oh no. I know who that is. They swing around and point at me.

'You killed my son!'

FORTY-ONE

How did Iris find me? How did she know we were here?

I look around frantically, but I have nowhere to run. The destroyed shed is behind me, the forest behind her; my only option is the house. I spin on my heels and race back inside, slamming the door behind me, forgetting the keys are still in the lock. *Shit!* I should have taken them out.

Iris is fast. Faster than I ever give her credit for. She's inside the house before I have a chance to bar her entrance. She stops as she takes in Jacob's belongings neatly stacked in his open suitcase, clothes and shoes, his dressing gown, all the items he packed the day he died that never showed up at the scene of the accident. I can see it all in her wild eyes, the way she's calculating what happened, that he has been alive all this time... and now he's not.

'What did you do?' she screams, running towards me. 'Deep in my soul I knew he wasn't dead, and I knew you'd come back to take my boy away from me. What did you do?'

I run to the kitchen counter and grab the knife I was using to peel the onions with. What am I doing? Am I really going to kill Iris too?

'It was an accident.' My voice is nothing but a light wheeze, my windpipe too swollen to talk. She can't hear me.

'I knew I couldn't trust you!' she shouts, staying behind the sofa as I point the knife at her. 'You thought I was stupid, didn't you? That I wouldn't work out your little plan. Jacob was the same, always lying and sneaking around. Well, I'm *not* stupid. I know how to sew a tracking device into your coat. It's not hard. What's hard is being a mother to ungrateful children.'

Jacob told me she used to track him. I should have known she'd never let me get away.

'He kidnapped me,' I say. Which I think is true. I fainted, he drove me to an undisclosed place, he locked me inside. That's kidnapping, isn't it? I'm not the bad one. It was *him* – he nearly killed me. All I did was try to get away. But I have no way of explaining that to his mother and she wouldn't listen to me anyway.

'You lied!' Iris screams. 'Both of you... liars. Pretending he was dead just so you could run away together.'

'No,' I say, my body shaking so much the knife is wobbling in my hand.

She picks up a book from the coffee table and throws it at me. I duck. *What the...?* She skirts around the sofa, picks up a cushion and throws that too. It hits me in the face and hurts a lot more than it should do.

'You're going to pay for this,' she shouts.

She's by the desk now, picking up Jacob's phone and throwing it at my head. It smashes against the wall behind me. A coffee mug hurtles towards me as Iris inches closer and closer. I keep sidestepping, my back to the wall, working my way towards the front door as she nears the kitchen area. She's picking up plates now, screaming and throwing them at me like Frisbees. I need to get out of here. She picks up a carving knife, a bigger one than the one I'm holding.

'You were never family, Eva Walsh,' she screams, charging at me. 'You don't deserve to live.'

I'm close to the door now. I drop the knife I'm holding and fumble for the door handle, squeezing myself through the gap and shutting it behind me. She's there in a flash but the keys are still in the lock on the outside. I use all my strength to pull at the door and stop her from opening it on the other side as I turn the key in the lock and then throw it into the undergrowth. She's inside, and I'm outside, and now she's locked in. But, unlike her son, she has no spare keys.

'I'm going to kill you!' she screams, smashing the window with her fist. Glass shatters and falls into the snow like ice, the metal grilles at the window keeping her trapped inside. She's hanging out of the window, her arm bloody, the knife still clenched in her fist.

I back away slowly then turn around to run... and slam straight into a man's chest. I stop. I look up. It's a policeman.

Ryan Clarke is staring at Iris inside the house, screaming about killing me, taking in the smashed glass and the blood and the knife. He glances at the body on the ground, Jacob's lifeless eyes staring up at a greying sky, then he looks down at my face.

'What the hell has she done?' he says under his breath.

I try to say something, but my throat is too swollen and my lips too bloody. I slip my engagement ring off and place it in my pocket with Jacob's stone.

'Don't speak,' Ryan says, gently stroking the raised bruises at my throat. 'I heard everything. I've called for back-up.' I collapse against him, and he pulls me to his chest, resting his lips on the crown of my head. 'You're safe now, Eva,' he whispers into my hair. 'I've got you.'

FORTY-TWO
17 DAYS LATER

It took a week in hospital until I was able to breathe and speak properly again. In that time the police arrested Iris, gathered more evidence based on what Ryan told them, and spoke to witnesses including Harry and Mario. Bianca, of course, was also more than happy to confirm Iris was cruel and crazy. All of which gave me time to get my story straight.

Ryan came to visit me every day. 'You're lucky to be alive,' he said. 'You're being discharged soon.'

'I have nowhere to go,' I whispered.

'You can stay at mine. If you want.'

So that's where I've been for the last ten days, answering more questions and being fussed over by a very attentive Ryan. The bruising on my face and neck has finally faded to a dull yellow, and Ryan insists my nose is still as pretty as it always was even though they had to set it back in place. So far no one has questioned a thing I've said.

'Are you sure you're up for a beach walk?' he asks as we make our way slowly along the sand. He's been very kind, but I know I can't stay at his house forever. New year, new me and all that. I need a job and a house and a totally new life, but I'm too tired to start again. How many lives can one person live?

I grip on to Ryan's arm tightly. 'I can finally breathe properly,' I say to him in my new husky voice. 'I may as well make the most of the sea air while I still have it.'

'And you're sure you're OK staying at mine? You know, being so close to the site of the car accident.'

How do I tell him I never want to be alone again?

'I'm very happy at yours, thank you. I feel safe with you.'

Safe. He likes that word. If I've learned anything about Ryan over the last week, it's that he likes being a hero.

I take a deep breath of briny air, enjoying the privilege of being able to do so after being stuck in hospital for a week. I've always loved this little beach near Ryan's house, the only part of Cragstone that holds nothing but happy memories. Jacob and I would come here in the winter and buy hot chocolate from the café to take away. We'd hide behind the rocks where no one could see us and kiss one another with chocolatey mouths. My stomach plummets and I blink the tears from my eyes. I'm learning to separate the Jacob of back then from the one in the cabin. I've convinced myself that the man who tricked me, the one who locked me in a house in the middle of the woods and tried to kill me, wasn't the same person as the boy I once loved and buried.

'Are you warm enough?' Ryan asks me.

I nod. I've pulled the collar of my coat up, but I refuse to wear a scarf. I don't think I'll ever be able to again.

'You know you don't have to keep taking time off work,' I say to him. 'I can look after myself. I'll be out of your hair as soon as I can once the investigation is over and I'm not needed here anymore.'

'Stay as long as you want,' he says, his gaze fixed on the horizon. 'I mean it.'

We slow down and stop to face the water. It's calm today,

the sky an unusual bright blue for January and the sun glinting off the sea. I close my eyes, enjoying the warmth of the winter sun on my face that's only just beginning to look normal again.

'The toxicology report confirmed antifreeze and small traces of cyanide in Jacob's blood, just as you told us,' Ryan says, staring at three gulls chasing one another like leaves on the breeze. 'They also found the kernels in Iris's kitchen that you mentioned, and more photos of you like the ones in your backpack. It should be an open and shut case, although it will take weeks for the official medical reports to come back.'

The police tried to interview me in the hospital, but the nurses said I was too injured to speak, and they had to wait for my throat to heal.

Once I was out of the hospital and on Ryan's sofa, I told them everything they needed to know. Strangulation can also result in temporary memory loss and confusion, so I wasn't pressed too hard – any blanks I left, the police filled in.

I told them about my suspicions regarding Jacob's accident, how he never drank whisky and wasn't a reckless driver, so it didn't make sense that he would have died that way. I told them how I worked out Iris was poisoning me, that she locked me in the house and I had to smash my way out of the kitchen. None of that was a lie.

The lies came later.

Charlie sent the police her blood test results from years ago, and Harry corroborated my story about escaping Iris's house. He was more than willing to tell the police how heroic he was, how he tried to help me and let me out of the back entrance while dealing with a hysterical Iris. I told them more truths: that I'd walked to Ryan's house, but he wasn't there. I'd been right, he'd been with his family. He got back an hour after Jacob bundled me into his car, but I didn't tell anyone that part. That's when I had to get creative.

'What will happen to Iris?' I ask Ryan.

He turns to me and gives me a sad smile. 'Don't worry about that. She'll get what she deserves.'

I told the police it was all Iris. I told them she'd poisoned me so much I was feeling ill when I got to Ryan's house, so I left my heavy bag on his porch and tried to hitch a lift back to town, but I fainted. In my story it was Iris who picked me up. And when I woke up, I was tied up on a couch, locked inside a wooden cabin in the middle of nowhere. I told them I got out of my restraints and found Jacob tied to the bed with an empty glass of something orange beside him. In my story it was Iris who had been forcing him to drink antifreeze, and it was Iris who had stolen my phone, which I found locked in a drawer. I untied Jacob, he wasn't naked in my version of the story, but we were trapped in the cabin and too weak to smash our way out, so we waited for Iris to come back and ambushed her. She chased after us and attacked us both with a branch, leaving us both for dead.

When she saw me crawling away, she pulled me back by my scarf and tried to strangle me. I managed to escape and had locked her in the house when Ryan came to my rescue. Ryan witnessed enough. He saw Iris with the knife, he heard the words she was screaming, her clothes covered in her son's blood, and when the hospital tested my blood and tended to my injuries, everything I'd endured matched my story. They didn't even ask about the damaged car. I just said Jacob had told me he'd failed to escape in a car he'd found and it's a fact that I don't have a driving licence.

It didn't take long for the police to decide Iris was also behind the fake emails to Mario pretending to be my assistant, the postcards, the text message to me and the emails to Jacob. All the evidence was there in the cabin, including the extra laptop and burner phones – which, fortunately for me, were too damaged to investigate. By the time the police let her out, her fingerprints were all over the cabin.

Between my injuries, the witness statements and the

evidence they gathered, it made no difference what Iris said. As Ryan said, it was an open and shut case as far as the inexperienced Cragstone police were concerned.

'Iris's doctor has provided his report,' Ryan says. 'Dr Kumar says he's been worried about her for a long time. Apparently he'd been trying to elevate his concerns about her possible Munchausen by proxy since last year, so he's devastated it came to this. He said drugging Jacob and faking his death would have given Iris the ultimate level of attention she craved. He's willing to testify.'

I don't feel guilty about framing Iris. I know I should, but I don't. Had she left me and Jacob alone ten years ago none of this would have happened. Iris may not have struck the final blow, but she killed her boy nevertheless because she made him the madman he became.

'Did you speak to Mario?' Ryan asks me.

I nod. Mario was interviewed too, and his story matched mine: Iris screaming about me escaping her house and how much she hated me.

'Mario dropped off the last of my belongings with Orla at the hotel, including the things I left at Amanda's house,' I say to Ryan. Amanda and I have talked. She felt awful about her message once she heard what had happened, and I told her it was OK, but I doubt we'll ever be as close as we once were. I can't imagine going back to any part of my life before all this happened.

'Marios has been really kind,' Ryan says, his voice strained. 'Now you know neither of you cheated on the other, do you think you'll get back together?'

'No,' I say. 'Never.'

I lean my head on Ryan's shoulder, and he puts his arm around me.

'I like it here,' I say.

He laughs softly. 'You hate this town.'

'I mean I like it *here*,' I say, moving closer to him.

'Is that so?' He tightens his hold on me and plants a kiss on the crown of my head. 'Well, I like you here, too.'

We remain staring out at the horizon, but I can see those dimples of his appearing again and it makes something hot grow in my stomach. I catch him watching me out of the corner of my eye and I smile too.

It's so peaceful here. We're the only ones on the beach and we walk for another fifteen minutes, my arm in his, Ryan talking about his job and asking me what I want to do with my life when I get back to London. It's a short conversation because I have no idea what to do next, but I know I'm not going back to London and that frenetic life again.

We head back to his house, climbing the stairs to the little café and ice cream shop, pausing every few steps while I catch my breath.

'It's for sale,' Ryan says, slowing down to look at the menu taped to the wall of the old ice cream shop. It hasn't changed since I was a child. 'I'm thinking of buying it.'

I laugh and let go of his arm. 'Seriously?'

He turns to me, his cheeks flush from the cold and the tip of his nose pink. I've never seen him look happier, or more serious.

'Yeah,' he says. 'I told you I've always wanted to be a pastry chef and after the last few weeks I've gone off being a policeman.'

'So you're going to totally change your life, just like that?'

'Maybe. Want to join me?'

'What do you mean?'

He shrugs and looks shy all of a sudden, like he did the first time I spoke to him at the pub. I can't believe that was only a few weeks ago.

'I thought maybe you could help me run the café,' Ryan says. 'We could use your interior design skills and make the place really special. A little restaurant with proper cakes and fancy ice creams and an entire deluxe hot chocolate menu. God knows Cragstone needs a decent place to hang out. You could even curate your own range of ceramics or something, sell classy keepsakes to the tourists, whatever you want.'

He's really thought this through.

'Stay in Cragstone?'

He nods. 'Please.'

'Where would I live?'

'You can stay in my spare room as long as you want, until you've saved enough money to get your own place of course.' He gives me a sheepish smile. 'I don't know... maybe it's a silly idea.'

He turns to look at the sea again, but I gently pull his face back to look at me.

'It's a great idea,' I say. 'I'm in. All in.'

'You are?'

'Except for one thing. I don't want to stay in your spare room.'

'OK. That's fine. I can help you find—'

I don't let him finish. I reach up and kiss him softly on the lips, those beautiful full lips, and he wraps his arms around me and kisses me back. My stomach flutters in a way I haven't felt since I was a stupid teenager in love. Perhaps it was never Jacob that I missed but the way he used to make me feel. Safe. Secure. Protected. But Ryan isn't Jacob; he's better than that. Ryan is a man, a proper grown-up in charge of his own life, with no one else pulling the strings.

'You have no idea how long I've wanted to kiss you,' he says, dimples reappearing on his flushed cheeks.

'Two weeks?' I reply.

'More like two decades. I've had a crush on you since you and Bianca were in the same class together. I think that's why she was so awful to you, because I never stopped talking about how pretty and smart and cool you were.'

I groan. I'd forgotten all about his sister. 'Bianca isn't going to like this.'

Ryan kisses me again. 'As if I'd let her come between us,' he murmurs against my mouth. 'Anyway, she has her hands full with Harry now.'

I pull away and look up at his grinning face. 'No way!'

His smile widens at the expression on my face. 'Yep. They got together New Year's Eve. Apparently, they bonded over how they'd totally misunderstood you and she thinks Harry is the bravest man ever for standing up to Iris, the killer. In fact, the entire town loves you now. They'll be replacing the statue in the square with one of you if you're not careful.'

I bury my face in his chest and laugh. 'I think that's worse than everyone hating me. This town is a soap opera, and I refuse to be the main character anymore.'

'So you'll stay?' he says, swinging me around. 'We're going to do this thing, together?'

I nod and he kisses me harder, his fingers caressing the back of my neck. This is it. I know it is. Ryan is my future.

'And Charlie is moving back,' I tell him. 'For a bit. I spoke to her this morning.'

I didn't know what to do about Charlie, what to say to her, but she was the one who tracked me down in the end. She was understandably in shock about Jacob not dying the way we all thought he had, but she said she'd been mourning her brother for years and was relieved it was all over. Her mother was no longer a danger to herself or anyone else. She thanked me and it made me feel ill.

'Charlie is going to stay at her mother's house for a while, she'll go back and forth until everything settles. She and Michael have a lot to process, but it looks like I'm getting my friend back.'

'All's well that ends well?'

'Something like that.'

He starts to walk back to the house, but I stay put. He looks over his shoulder. 'Everything OK?'

'I have one more thing I need to do,' I say. 'I'll meet you back home.'

Ryan nods and smiles. I think he likes that I called his place 'home'.

'Take all the time you need,' he says, his lips brushing gently against mine.

I wait until he's out of sight before walking back down the stairs to the water's edge.

The sea is still today, as if it's been waiting for me all these years. The birds are still circling above but they too have fallen silent. It's just me and the sand and the soft lap of the waves.

I reach into my coat pocket, my hand closing in around the smooth white rock Jacob gave me. I look at it closely, at the hearts he drew and the inscription on the back. *Forever*. But Jacob was wrong... nothing is forever. Not family, not love and especially not the people we think will remain until the end. Life knocks us over, wave after wave, eroding us and shaping us, until we emerge smooth, and shiny, and brand new again.

'It all worked out beautifully, Jacob,' I say into the howling wind. 'My best friend is returning and I'm about to have a job, a home, a boyfriend and a community that no longer hates me. I'm getting it all back again.'

I lift my arm as high as I can and throw the stone, watching it plop unceremoniously into the water. I wonder how long it will stay on the seabed, Jacob's hearts staring up at the empty sky. How long will his words last? Not forever. Not as long as the stone will. He thought it was going to be the foundation to our future, but instead he gave me the means to stop one life and start another. I pull the engagement ring out of my pocket and throw that into the water too.

I can see it now, the feet of my children, mine and Ryan's children, stepping over Jacob's last gifts to me, their laughter carried on the Cragstone wind. I'm keeping this life; I'm not running away this time and I'm not ruining it. I owe it to my dead ex-boyfriend to make this version of my life work.

'Thank you, Jacob,' I whisper. 'I got everything I wanted in the end and all you had to do was die. Twice.'

A LETTER FROM NATALI

Dear reader,

Thank you so much for choosing to read *The Ex I Buried* – I had so much fun writing mean, gossipy characters, the relationships between old school friends, and the idea of being trapped in an isolated village over Christmas. I really did put poor Eva through it!

To keep up to date with all my latest releases, please sign up at the following link. Your email address will never be shared, and you can unsubscribe at any time.

www.bookouture.com/natali-simmonds

One of the themes in *The Ex I Buried* is the combination of male loneliness and tech. There have been an increasing number of disturbing stories in the press lately about people who, instead of turning to people for solace, comfort and support, are getting emotionally addicted to AI with disastrous consequences. I hope Jacob's story highlights the dangers of being isolated from those who care about us, and that we all start looking up from our screens soon before too many are lost to a virtual world.

If you enjoyed reading *The Ex I Buried* and would like to recommend it to others, I would really appreciate your review. Your comments make such a difference helping new readers discover one of my books for the first time, plus I love hearing from my readers.

You can also get in touch with me and share your thoughts through social media or my website.

Natali

www.njsimmonds.com

instagram.com/njsimmonds_author
facebook.com/NjsimmondsAuthor
x.com/NJSimmondsbooks
bsky.app/profile/natalisimmonds.bsky.social

ACKNOWLEDGEMENTS

The more books I write (this is my eleventh published novel, and fourth thriller), the harder it is to write acknowledgements as I'm starting to repeat myself. So let me begin by saying thank you to those who still listen when I talk about my books... I know it's getting boring now... and to those who buy them, read them, enjoy them and tell others about them. The only reason I'm still writing is because of you!

As always, a huge thank you to my agent, Amanda Preston, and editor, Lucy Frederick. You have both shaped me, supported me and championed me from the start. You're an absolute joy to work with and I'm so lucky I get to build worlds with you both. A big shout out to the entire team at Bookouture too: the talented designers, publicists, editors, marketing, and the incredible foreign rights team. They all work tirelessly behind the scenes and make writing thrillers a real thrill.

I read a lot of Liane Moriarty while writing *The Ex I Buried*. So thank you, Liane, for reminding me that thrillers can be filled with bitchy people and small-town gossip. I had a lot of fun with this one! And a big thank you to children's author, Rachel Delahaye, for making herself ill eating apricot kernels and sharing her ordeal on social media. You gave me the perfect solution for Iris's poison of choice (glad you're fine and happy it came in useful).

To my family – you are the best. It's too easy to take for granted the brilliant people in your life until you write books like this one and realise we are not all so lucky (I'm especially thankful that my mother-in-law, who I dedicated this book to, is absolutely nothing like Iris).

To Pete and my wonderful daughters, Isabelle and Olivia, thank you for giving me the time, the space, and the encouragement to keep going with this crazy job. And to my friends and author buddies, including Isabella May and Teuta Metra, who are always interested in what I'm writing next. And a special thank you to author Jacqueline Silvester, my Caedis Knight writing partner and bestie, who is forced to listen to all my ideas on a daily basis, whether she wants to or not (read her books... they are excellent).

But not everyone wants me to succeed. A special mention goes to my cats, Bruce and Buttercup, for reminding me that cats matter more than books by meowing in my face every five minutes while I'm deep into my edits. I wouldn't be here without you (by 'here' I mean on my hands and knees cleaning up cat sick). Cheers for keeping me grounded, guys.

And lastly, a big hug to the booksellers, librarians, reviewers, bloggers and, of course, my readers. Thank you for accompanying me on this crazy journey. Your enthusiasm and support mean everything, and I can't wait to get working on my next twisted story!

PUBLISHING TEAM

Turning a manuscript into a book requires the efforts of many people. The publishing team at Bookouture would like to acknowledge everyone who contributed to this publication.

Audio
Alba Proko
Sinead O'Connor
Melissa Tran

Commercial
Lauren Morrissette
Hannah Richmond
Imogen Allport

Cover design
The Brewster Project

Data and analysis
Mark Alder
Mohamed Bussuri

Editorial
Lucy Frederick
Hannah Wilson

Copyeditor
DeAndra Lupu

Proofreader
Deborah Blake

Marketing
Alex Crow
Melanie Price
Occy Carr
Cíara Rosney
Martyna Młynarska

Operations and distribution
Marina Valles
Stephanie Straub
Joe Morris

Production
Hannah Snetsinger
Mandy Kullar
Nadia Michael
Charlotte Hegley

Publicity
Kim Nash
Noelle Holten
Jess Readett
Sarah Hardy

Rights and contracts
Peta Nightingale
Richard King
Saidah Graham

RAISING READERS
Books Build Bright Futures

Dear Reader,

We'd love your attention for one more page to tell you about the crisis in children's reading, and what we can all do.

Studies have shown that reading for fun is the **single biggest predictor of a child's future life chances** – more than family circumstance, parents' educational background or income. It improves academic results, mental health, wealth, communication skills, ambition and happiness.

The number of children reading for fun is in rapid decline. Young people have a lot of competition for their time, and a worryingly high number do not have a single book at home.

Hachette works extensively with schools, libraries and literacy charities, but here are some ways we can all raise more readers:

- Reading to children for just 10 minutes a day makes a difference
- Don't give up if children aren't regular readers – there will be books for them!

- Visit bookshops and libraries to get recommendations
- Encourage them to listen to audiobooks
- Support school libraries
- Give books as gifts

There's a lot more information about how to encourage children to read on our websites: **www.RaisingReaders.co.uk** and **www.JoinRaisingReaders.com**.

Thank you for reading.

Made in the USA
Middletown, DE
12 October 2025